THE DEVIL COMES TO PARADISE

The place smelled, as most of these Quaker houses did, of freshly cut wood. Another scent caught his nose, however.

It grew stronger as he made his way up the stairs. There were only two rooms up there; all these houses were alike. One was Saul's bedroom, and that door was standing open. The rug was askew where Eliza had likely kicked it in her scramble to get out of the house. Tom knew the coppery smell of blood, and he knew that look on Eliza's face. Saul was dead.

He had looked fine the day before, and he wasn't *so* old. Had he just gone in his sleep? It wasn't unheard of.

Tom froze in the doorway.

Saul was in his bed under the covers. The handle of a knife stuck out of his chest, but that wasn't what had Tom's attention.

The dead man's mouth was open and full of black feathers.

RALPH COMPTON

THE TRAIL'S END

A Ralph Compton Western by
E. L. RIPLEY

BERKLEY
New York

BERKLEY
An imprint of Penguin Random House LLC
penguinrandomhouse.com

ISBN: 9780593102404

First Edition: January 2021

Printed in the United States of America
1 3 5 7 9 10 8 6 4 2

Cover art by Chris McGrath
Book design by George Towne

THE IMMORTAL COWBOY

This is respectfully dedicated to the "American Cowboy." His was the saga sparked by the turmoil that followed the Civil War, and the passing of more than a century has by no means diminished the flame.

———◆———

True, the old days and the old ways are but treasured memories, and the old trails have grown dim with the ravages of time, but the spirit of the cowboy lives on.

———◆———

In my travels—to Texas, Oklahoma, Kansas, Nebraska, Colorado, Wyoming, New Mexico, and Arizona—I always find something that reminds me of the Old West. While I am walking these plains and mountains for the first time, there is this feeling that a part of me is eternal, that I have known these old trails before. I believe it is the undying spirit of the frontier calling me, through the mind's eye, to step back into time. What is the appeal of the Old West of the American frontier?

———◆———

It has been epitomized by some as the dark and bloody period in American history. Its heroes—Crockett, Bowie, Hickok, Earp—have been reviled and criticized. Yet the Old West lives on, larger than life.

———◆———

It has become a symbol of freedom, when there was always another mountain to climb and another river to cross; when a dispute between two men was settled not with expensive lawyers, but with fists, knives, or guns. Barbaric? Maybe. But some things never change. When the cowboy rode into the pages of American history, he left behind a legacy that lives within the hearts of us all.

—*Ralph Compton*

PROLOGUE

THE SUN WAS OUT, the breeze was just a whisper, and the blue sky was big enough to get lost in.

Tom Calvert had spent more than six months in a wagon, trapped with his thoughts, most of which had to do with his mistakes. Enough was enough; he was tired of worrying about the past. He couldn't let go of what he'd done, and he certainly wouldn't pretend he hadn't done it. He couldn't forget, not with his bad leg to remind him—but he didn't want to forget. He just wanted to stop wasting time on it.

He'd never given a thought to the Idaho Territory, but he wouldn't have expected it to be quite so nice to look at. He'd likely have said the same for Wyoming, and he'd been dead wrong about that. Even laid up with a fever, he'd been able to see country there that put all the rest to shame.

Friendly Field was what this place was called, but Pretty Field might have suited it better. Bright, clean

whitewashing stood out against the green grass and the
dark earth. There were vast fields of crops, all impeccably neat.

He nudged his mare forward, drawing up alongside
the kid.

Less than a year had passed since they met, but
Asher no longer looked or acted anything like the
grubby little shrimp of a boy Tom had found on a riverboat on the Missouri. He was still small and looked
even smaller in his habitually oversized clothes. Tom
had tried more than once to convince him to see a bar-
ber, but the boy insisted on hacking off his own hair as
though he knew what he was doing. The result was that
he looked like an absolute madman, which was perhaps for the best. Past his short stature and insubstan-
tial build, the boy had good looks, so one could hope
that his ridiculous hair would keep the girls away, because even after all this time and Tom's best efforts,
Asher still didn't know what to do with them.

There was only one thing Asher was even worse at
than girls, and that was riding. His mare jostled, and
Tom reached out and caught his arm to keep him from
falling. Maybe they should've kept the wagon a little
longer.

The boy didn't even say anything, and Tom didn't
blame him. He let go and straightened up, following
Asher's gaze.

There were houses down there, but they weren't laid
out like they would have been in a real town. They
were in a sort of circle, with several generous barns and
such and a church. All of it was surrounded by potato
fields. Mountains towered in the distance under the
blue sky, and the forests ringing it all already had their
leaves back. It was fair enough to say that it was pretty

everywhere in spring, but the colors here were different. Brighter somehow.

Or perhaps it only seemed that way because Tom's fever was finally gone.

No word came to mind to describe the look on the boy's face. Asher had been searching for Friendly Field since well before he met Tom, but until not long ago they hadn't been entirely convinced the place was real. So few people had heard of it, yet it was well-known in Des Crozet, twenty miles away, where their potatoes were traded.

What *was* that look on the kid's face? Disappointment? He had to have known that even if Friendly Field was real, there couldn't be much to it. Otherwise it would have been on the maps.

Asher looked downright grim. Maybe he'd hoped there'd be someone here to play cards with, but they both knew better than that. These people were of the Religious Society of Friends. That was where the strange name for the place had come from.

Quakers. Tom didn't know the first thing about them, but he had a feeling they didn't gamble much. The boy was likely thinking the same thing.

No poker here. Just potatoes.

Tom snorted and pulled his hat down a bit, squinting in the sunlight. The kid's disappointment might not last; after all, they were here without an invitation and without a plan. For all either of them knew, they'd be back on the trail by midafternoon. And going where? There was no telling; Tom hadn't thought that far ahead.

"It isn't what you thought it would be," he said after a moment, leaning over to rub his mare's head.

Asher glanced over at him.

"It is very nice to look at," he said in that polite way he had. It wasn't haughtiness; it was just the way the boy had been raised.

Tom had a feeling he was right. Asher had hoped for something a little more robust than a few houses, a church, and a whole lot of potatoes.

"You make your bed and you sleep in it," Tom told him frankly. "We spent too long trying to find this place not to give it a chance."

Asher's brows rose, and he gave Tom a look.

"I was not thinking of leaving, Mr. Calvert."

"Well, here's hoping they're friendly." Tom snorted. "Hell, they'd better be."

They couldn't just admire the view all day; there were plenty of people to see as they cantered down the hill. And plenty more in the fields, their white shirts standing out clearly against the freshly worked earth. It wasn't clear what they were doing. Not tilling, but Tom was no farmer.

The Quakers noticed the strangers approaching. A life on the move had made Tom comfortable with being looked at this way. Everyone who played cards for a living knew him, but other folks? No.

"Hello there," a man called out, waving as he strode out to meet them. It was by no means warm, but he was in shirtsleeves and he'd clearly been working.

Tom drew up and opened his mouth, but the man went on.

"Peace be with thee," he said.

"And also with you," Asher replied, the hint of a smile on his face.

Tom raised an eyebrow. He'd expected to have to do the talking.

"Are you known here?" the man asked personally enough. So the "thee" had been just for the greeting? That suited Tom.

"No." Tom swung down from his mare and pulled his walking stick from the loop on the saddle. He limped forward and put his hand out. The man shook readily.

At least a dozen people were watching.

Asher dismounted as well.

"We've come a long way," Tom said, and it wasn't lost on him how peculiar he must come off. A well-dressed man with a bad limp who still hadn't stated his business.

But these folks looked more curious than worried.

"Alas," the man replied, giving him a sympathetic look, "we have only just planted."

Tom smiled at him.

"We aren't here for potatoes."

A BUSINESS?"

The man behind the desk looked as though Tom had just shot him. He glanced uncertainly at Sebastian, the man who had welcomed Tom and Asher to town—if "town" was the word. "Village," maybe.

Sebastian had brought him here, straight to this house, which appeared no different from any of the others, at least from the outside. It was equal parts rough and fine; though many rich touches were missing, it was still beautiful to look at. And spacious.

Tom had sat in his share of offices that belonged to men who were, at the end of the day, in charge. This man was the one who ran the place. Thaddeus Mayfair was his name. Tom was past thirty, and this man was probably twice that, and more than twice Tom's size. He was soft and genial, and he'd welcomed them into his office—or study, as he called it—with a good deal more enthusiasm than Tom would've had in his place.

"A business," Thaddeus repeated, frowning. He licked his lips and glanced at Sebastian, then shot Tom and Asher a smile. "I think we had best have Saul and Jeremiah here, Sebastian, if they can be found."

Tom and Asher had come to Friendly Field to stay, not to visit, but they had no claim, and they were not farmers. Thus, Tom had assumed that, to justify settling and making something like a living, they would have to . . . well, *do* something. As for what, that had seemed obvious until a few days ago, when the man giving Tom a haircut mentioned offhand that these people were Quakers.

It seemed safe to assume there probably wasn't much need for a saloon in Friendly Field. Unfortunately, that was probably the only business Tom would've been confident about starting up and running with a convincing impression of knowing what he was doing.

Thaddeus cleared his throat and moved his chair a little closer to the desk, folding his hands as Sebastian left the room. He was about to say something, but his eyes moved to his right, and there was a child peering through the window.

The little girl froze, and Thaddeus made a ridiculous face. She ran off.

He looked back at Tom and Asher.

"I don't know precisely how to put this," Thaddeus admitted, scratching his chin. "I do not know that I have ever fielded this query, but we are not a—or, rather, what I should say is that here we are a family. Commerce and business . . ." He moved his hands a bit vaguely.

"These things exist, but perhaps not in the way that you're accustomed to, my friends." He hesitated, frowning. "I have to say, on the rare occasion when strangers come to our door, it is because they are seeking the light within, not profit."

"'Profit' wouldn't be the right word for what we're after, sir," Tom told him frankly. "Just a living, really."

"Please, *please* do not take these words to sound unwelcoming, Mr. Smith." There hadn't even been a touch of suspicion when Tom had introduced himself with that name. "But could you not find a living anywhere? Why make your way to our humble fields?"

Tom rubbed his eyes. "Well, sir, there's a story there." He expected the older man to cringe, as Tom certainly would have had someone said that to *him*—but Thaddeus only looked intrigued.

"I am keen to hear it," he said, "but we had best wait for my good friends to arrive. I have a notion this is something we should all hear, if that suits you."

"Of course. Tell me, Mr. Mayfair, what are they like—the people who choose to join your community?" Tom asked. It *was* up to him to do the talking; the boy hadn't opened his mouth since stepping into this house, except to introduce himself. And even that, he'd done a bit stiffly. Of course he was anxious; this was all new.

"Not like you," Thaddeus replied with a smile. "And call me Thaddeus, please. We've known each other ten minutes now, and that should be enough to make us friends. No, only a few have come to us as you have. Families from other communities similar to ours and a few wayfarers, but not like you. You appear to have more means than ones such as those. I expect

those folk come here lacking an alternative, but you—
the two of you have come quite deliberately."

"I expect the boy must have heard good things about
you," Tom said, glancing at Asher, "because Friendly
Field sure stuck in his head."

"Is that true, young man?"

Asher smiled back at him. "Yes, sir. Very good things."

"Heavens, I wonder from whom. Well, we do have
rather long-standing relationships with our vendors.
Several of them are almost like family themselves. I
never thought they might be out there telling people of
us. And what about you, Tom?"

"I'll admit that I was curious to see what a place
called Friendly Field would look like. Would it be as
friendly as its name?"

"Well?" Thaddeus smiled.

"Seems nice enough to me."

There were muffled voices and the creaking of floorboards. They all looked as the door opened to admit
Sebastian with two other men. They were both leaner
than Thaddeus, but close to him in age. One wore spectacles and had a piece of cloth wrapped around his fore-
arm as a bandage. Both were eating corn bread from
cloth napkins held in their hands.

Thaddeus looked affronted.

"Did Mary's mother make that?" he asked sternly,
suddenly looking very serious.

"Of course," the bespectacled man replied, eying
Tom and Asher with interest. He glanced at Sebastian,
then swallowed and ducked his head in a sort of greeting. "Good day," he said. "Peace be with thee." The
bearded man beside him was still chewing. "Welcome."

"Thank you," Tom replied politely.

Sebastian shut the door.

"Shame on you, Jeremiah White. And you as well, Saul Matthews. It is rude to eat in front of guests that way." Thaddeus gave them a scowl. "One might also call it rude not to bring me any," he added, looking hurt.

"Oh, just finish up here and go get some yourself," Saul told him. He had a head of white hair, but he looked vigorous enough.

"I intend to," Thaddeus told him huffily. "Tom and Asher, this is Saul and Jeremiah. Our community has no need of what you might call a—a mayor or anything to that effect. Yet that might be the simplest way for you to think of the three of us. When it comes to doing things around here, we try to listen to everyone, and then the three of us quarrel about it and pray. Through the grace of God, we generally come to an agreement in time. So you understand why it's for the best that they be here."

"Seems reasonable," Tom replied.

"These two young men," Thaddeus said to the others, indicating Tom and Asher, "have come to us intending to start a business in Friendly Field. Have I understood you on that matter?"

"More or less," Tom told him, shrugging. "It might be more precise to say we're looking to make a life, and I just figured that starting a business was how I'd do it."

Saul and Jeremiah wore identical expressions of puzzlement.

"Do you come from our brothers in Northley?" Jeremiah asked, wrapping up the crumbs of his corn bread.

"No." Tom smiled. "We're heathens, I'm afraid."

Saul snorted. "Are you in a business relating to potatoes?"

"I play cards. I'm a gambler."

The silence that followed didn't surprise Tom. Even Asher looked taken aback.

"You may as well just hear us out," Tom went on. "I'm not just a gambler. Some months ago I killed a man. He attacked my character and"—he motioned toward himself—"my person. So I shot him. And I did not conduct myself well." That was a generous way of putting it, but it wasn't untrue. "And then, not long after, I made a few more enemies. And I shot them as well. I didn't come here for potatoes, and I didn't come here for any reason of my own at all. I'm hoping to make a life somewhere out of the way, because of what I just told you. The reason we landed here and not somewhere else is because the boy was keen to find you. He saved my life. More than once."

Tom let it go there. He hadn't planned to say all that or at least not in that way. There were a thousand stories he could've told that would've made these people welcome them with open arms.

He rubbed his bad leg absently and sat back in his chair.

"That's what it comes down to," he said, "who we are and what we want."

"You mean to say you are a—an outlaw," Thaddeus said, eyes a bit wide. Sebastian had stiffened, Saul looked sour, and Jeremiah's eyes had become wary.

Tom sighed, then lifted a hand and wiggled it from side to side. "Depends who you ask. That first man I spoke of—that was justified, but others might not see it that way. And to tell the truth, by now I wish I hadn't done it. The same could be said of the rest. You make enemies when you play cards and do it well, and I have not treated my enemies in a very Christian way."

Asher was looking at him as though he'd lost his mind.

"So I would understand if I wasn't welcome," Tom told them all frankly, "being a violent man. Funny enough, I never really thought of myself as one, but there's no way around it. The boy's different, though. He isn't like me. He's never hurt anyone, and finding this place meant a lot to him. I hope you won't let my mistakes color your opinion of him. He didn't know what kind of man I was when he saved me."

It was a lot of talking, at least by Tom's standards. Not every *detail* in what he said was true, but it really was the long and short of it. It was impulsive to put his cards on the table this way, but it felt good to do. This wasn't what he'd had in mind, but here he was all the same, seriously thinking about starting over. He wasn't about to try to build a life on a foundation made up entirely of lies.

"Well," Saul said, and he didn't look happy. Tom thought he might go on, but he didn't.

"What I'm coming around to is that I hope you'll still welcome the kid," Tom said, putting his hand on Asher's shoulder, "even if I'm not to your liking. I would not presume to go where I wasn't wanted."

"And if we hear you correctly, you are in fear of retribution for what you have done?" Jeremiah asked. Of the three older men, he was the one who appeared to be taking this the best. He adjusted his spectacles and glanced at Sebastian, who looked appalled.

"'Fear' isn't the word I'd use. But I wouldn't expect anyone to find me here. I don't know if anyone's looking or how hard. But to be safe, I avoid crowds."

That was the truth.

"What sort of trouble would you bring to our door?"

"Only the law," Tom told him. "If they track me here, they may come."

"And if they do?" Jeremiah pressed.

Tom sighed. "I'd like to hope that they won't. But if they do, I believe I'm finally ready to hang it up." He thumped his walking stick on the floor and gave him a dry smile. "I don't care for running ever since my leg got to be this way."

"Jeremiah," Saul said uncertainly.

"Easy, Saul. I like this gentleman's candor."

"He's a murderer. By his own admission."

"That is not true," Asher cut in. "There was nothing he did that wasn't in his own defense or mine. That is not murder."

Thaddeus appeared to consider that. "Do you mean to tell us you would go to hang without resistance if a lawman came here looking for you?"

The older man had his eyes on the pistol tucked into Tom's belt. There was a part of Tom himself that felt the way everyone else in the room looked. Even Asher was thrown by it, but Tom couldn't take any of it back now. And he didn't want to.

He didn't get to answer Thaddeus' question because Jeremiah spoke up.

"Sir, have you come here in the hopes that we will hide you from your pursuers? Because we would never turn you away," he said, as though it were obvious. In fact, it was almost startling the way he said it. "We would never turn *anyone* away. That would be . . . it would be contrary to who we are."

"We could never hide you, though," Saul pointed out quickly. "That would be inconceivable."

Tom hadn't surprised anyone else half as much as

he surprised himself. And these words rattled him further.

"I wouldn't ask you to," he told them, pulling the gun out of his belt. He leaned over with a groan, but hesitated, just holding it there.

Then he set it on the desk and never touched it again.

PART ONE

LIGHT AS A FEATHER

CHAPTER ONE

HILLS OF WHITE flowers rolled like waves, even in the gloom before dawn. They were all closed up, but still pretty and tall enough that one wouldn't so much walk through them as wade. It brought water to mind and made Tom feel light on his feet, which was no small task. He paused, leaning on his walking stick and peering at Asher, who determinedly forged a path ahead.

"Kid," he called out.

The boy paused and looked back.

"What's your hurry?" Tom asked.

"I am in no hurry, Mr. Calvert."

So Tom was just moving that slowly, eh? He pushed on.

Two weeks after arriving in Friendly Field, he still didn't know if he really meant to stay. It hadn't occurred to him that these people might welcome him, even knowing the truth about him. Or most of it, at any rate. He had made a lot of assumptions about these

Quakers, and so far just about every one of them had been wrong.

"Mr. Calvert?"

"I'm coming."

"Morning exercise is your ritual, not mine," the boy pointed out.

"I take my exercise on the road," Tom shot back. "Not in all this." The boy was leading the way for a change, and it was difficult going among the hills.

"It will be worth your while," Asher promised.

Tom wasn't so sure. The kid claimed to have found a spectacular bounty of spring mushrooms in the woods. That was all well and good, but Tom couldn't truthfully say that he gave a damn. The kid was excited about it, though. That was what mattered, but Asher might regret wearing himself out before his day even began. On the other hand, the kid had what seemed to be limitless energy. On the trail, he'd managed the bulk of the work himself to keep the wagon rolling. Tom had been deadweight with a bullet in his leg, and the boy had more or less carried them both. He was tougher than he looked.

When the sun came up, all these flowers would open, and there would be such a scent that it would make anyone heady. Tom hoped they'd be on their way back by then. He didn't know why the boy wanted to be with him when he went for these walks before dawn. Tom had a good reason for doing it: if he didn't do something with his leg, it would be stiff and painful by midafternoon. That, and the food was entirely too good in Friendly Field. If he didn't make a point to move around, he'd get soft in a hurry.

They reached the trees, and Asher stopped. He didn't look back.

"Mr. Calvert," he said.

"Yeah?" Tom caught up and leaned on his stick, squinting in the gloom. He didn't see any mushrooms.

"What possessed you to do that?" The boy was asking about the day that they arrived. He wanted to know why Tom had thrown his story out the window and told the elders of Friendly Field the truth, more or less. It would've been too easy to present themselves as victims of some misfortune or wayfarers seeking salvation.

"I'm heavy enough to drag around," he said, rubbing the walking stick absently with his thumb. "Secrets and lies just make me feel heavier."

"Secrets and lies are the game of poker," Asher pointed out.

"Not exactly, kid."

"Were you hoping they would turn you away so you could go on without me?"

"Why are you asking?" Tom had to notice the serious look on Asher's face.

"Because this life is very different from what I would picture to be to your liking."

"Different from what I would picture too," Tom told him frankly. "Turns out, I don't mind it. Do you?"

Asher just let his breath out, then took a deep one.

"What were you hoping to find here?" Tom asked, because why not? They were well enough acquainted by now for this much surely.

"This," the boy said finally.

"What?"

"What we found is what I had hoped to find," he said, appearing to wake up. He returned Tom's gaze. "It is you that I worry for. No cards, no money. What is there for you?"

"Hell, kid, do you *want* me to leave?"

Asher's eyes narrowed. "You have *shaved,* Mr. Calvert."

"Very observant."

"So there *is* something of interest to you."

It wasn't a particularly astute observation; in fact, for the boy to be making it just now—he really wasn't paying much attention. But that stood to reason; they had found this place, and everything had changed. Things weren't the way they'd been on the trail. The wagon made for a small world, but this was a community. It wasn't just Tom and Asher anymore, so the boy could have his own life.

But he still wanted to get up early and drag Tom off to find mushrooms.

"Do you even like mushrooms?"

"No, I dislike them," Asher replied, but he forged on. "There are those who enjoy them, though."

"And you're sure they aren't the poisonous kind?"

The boy halted. "Poisonous kind?"

"For God's sake, kid. Your people taught you to talk pretty, but not that?"

This was turning into a long hike; ordinarily Tom liked to do a mile each way. They had to be close to twice that now, well beyond the potato fields—but there was no danger of straying onto someone's property. The Quakers were all alone out here; that was what made Tom optimistic that no one would come looking for him.

"Hold up a minute, kid."

"Another rest?"

"No." Tom looked over his shoulder as though there was even the slight possibility anyone might have followed. They were plenty far from the settlement. He unbuttoned his coat and reached into the pocket of his waistcoat, taking out his derringer.

Asher's brows rose. "I noticed that you did not volunteer that item."

Tom didn't think of the little gun as a weapon; he never had. It was almost too pretty to shoot, with its gold inlay and pearl handles. He'd won it in a poker game from a very pretty woman who he remembered fondly. It was just a trinket for luck.

That was, until a while ago when he suddenly found himself with nothing else but a club that he was in no state to use. He'd never bothered buying bullets for a keepsake. That day he'd needed them.

He had bullets for it now. They were far enough from the houses that the report of such tiny cartridges wouldn't be heard.

"Who do you mean to shoot?" Asher asked, intrigued.

"Nobody, kid. I just wonder if I could hit anything with it if I wanted to." The barrel of the gun wasn't even as long as his little finger. All the same, he hefted it in his palm, then lifted it and took aim at a tree some seven or eight yards off.

Asher covered his ears, but he didn't have to. The little pop of the pistol would have been a good deal quieter than the constant hammering of nails and timber in Friendly Field during daylight. There was always a new barn, a new window, a new door being put on someone's house. Always. Tom had nearly gotten to where he didn't notice anymore.

After a moment the boy looked at him uncertainly.

"Why don't you fire?"

Tom took his finger off the trigger and lowered the gun, then shook his head.

"Sorry, kid. It's a habit. I figured I'd be past it by now."

Asher peered at him, and there was a shrewdness there that Tom wasn't accustomed to seeing on him. "Your habit is to be prepared."

"That's right."

"There's no harm in that."

Tom glanced at his bad leg and wondered if that was true.

"No sense arguing," he told the boy. And after a moment he held out the gun. "Why don't you take it?"

"There was a time, Mr. Calvert, when you wouldn't hand me a pistol no matter how incessantly I asked it of you. I did not ask for this one," he pointed out.

"I don't want it anymore."

Asher hesitated. "Why should I want it?"

"I'm lame, kid. Not blind." Whatever he said, the boy did covet the gun. Tom wasn't wrong about that.

Asher appeared to consider it; then he took a step back. "I think not, Mr. Calvert. I think neither of us has any need of it here."

That was very likely true. Tom considered the gun for a moment, then tucked it back into his pocket with his watch. He took up his stick and they pressed on.

For a moment he'd considered just dropping the little gun in the loam, but that would've been a shame. It had value, and now that it was unlikely he would ever have another taste of his old life, the memories meant more to him than the pearl or the gold. That was what he might've said if asked, but it wouldn't have been true. The truth was that he'd carried a gun for a long time, and he'd have felt naked without one. It didn't matter that the little toy probably couldn't protect him from a squirrel. It was just the principle of the thing.

But it was because of his trigger finger that he was struck by a gut-churning wave of panic whenever it even *appeared* that someone might be riding toward Friendly Field. The place wasn't even a village; it was just one large farm. No one would look for him there. Even if he'd told the Quakers his real name, he'd *still* have been safe.

He knew that. But what he knew just couldn't seem to make a dent in what he felt. He remembered the worst of the pain and the fever from his leg, and he'd gladly have traded his fear and unease for that agony.

Maybe it would get better in time.

He paused.

"Kid," he said, pointing with his walking stick. Asher looked back. The trees were thicker here, and there would be little light even at noon. "Is this the sort you saw?" He indicated a mushroom at the foot of a crooked tree.

"It is."

"Well, did you bring a sack or something?"

"What?"

This boy. Well, it was all right in this case.

"If you're going to gather something, hadn't you better bring a sack?" Tom asked, stifling a yawn.

"Yes, Mr. Calvert. I apologize."

"Well, you'd just as soon not gather ones like this."

"Why not?"

Tom leaned over and plucked the mushroom, holding it up. "One of these won't kill you, but it'll make you sicker than hell."

Asher was stunned.

"You said you found more? We'd better find them and get rid of them in case someone else as ignorant as you stumbles on them," Tom said tiredly, crushing the mushroom in his hand and throwing it aside. "I'm fairly sure you could die if you ate too many of them."

Asher wasn't listening.

"Kid? You all right?"

Asher looked around worriedly. He didn't reply. He just kept searching with his eyes, putting his hand on the trunk of a tree and leaning to look behind it.

"I believe this is the place," he said uncertainly.

Tom took a look for himself. "What were you doing up here anyway?" he asked, though he already knew the answer.

One might think that after months in a wagon with Tom, the boy would *want* other people around. The Quakers were about the best folks Tom had ever met, but their friendly way of doing things was sometimes too much. It was nothing he couldn't handle, but the boy was being stifled.

"This is the place," Asher declared, annoyed. "I am certain of it."

There were no signs of mushrooms, apart from the one Tom had picked. It was difficult to see in the gloom, but the mushroom was pale. More like it would stand out clearly.

"Something probably came along and ate them."

"There were so many," Asher said, giving him a look. "But I suppose you are right." He was still suspicious. He moved through the shadows, searching irritably. Was he bothered that they'd made the trip for nothing? They didn't *want* these mushrooms; they were poison.

"There were so many," the kid repeated.

"Come on back." They'd already spent longer on this stroll than intended.

"We will be forgiven for tardiness," Asher replied, distracted.

Tom wasn't worried about God, but he believed in good manners. He always had.

"Kid, these folks are good to us. Let's return the favor."

Asher didn't reply. Tom straightened up and limped after him, finding the boy standing with his back to him, holding something. Tom took a look for himself, but he couldn't be sure what he was seeing. Asher looked up, then offered the object to him.

Tom took it and frowned.

It was a couple of sticks and some black feathers. And something else: a tiny skull. And it was all tied together with thread. The sticks formed a sort of cross, and the feathers had been arranged to fan out behind the skull, which must have come from a bird.

The thread was tied *very* neatly. Someone had made this with care.

And Tom didn't have the faintest idea what it was supposed to be.

CHAPTER TWO

⌒

RATHER THAN STIFF and sore, Tom's leg was just sore from the morning's exercise. He didn't mind that particularly, and the ache was less severe in a warm spring than it would be in a cold winter. It was hot enough now to have all the windows open in the sewing room. Nothing could push all the worry away, but the sunlight and the breeze made a gallant effort.

Tom did as well.

Mrs. Heller whispered to Mary Black, and in the hush of the morning, there was no secrecy to be had at all. Some of the men were doing work on the roof of the Pilkin house just a hundred feet away, but when the hammers stopped, the whole place was as quiet as a grave.

Mary bore Mrs. Heller's foolishness stoically. Tom had noticed her change her seat on several days in the hopes of having a new neighbor, but to no avail. Mrs. Heller followed her, and the other ladies made no effort to rescue the widow. One nice thing to come of it was that Mary's poker face was getting better every day; when Tom first arrived, she had blushed when Mrs. Heller said these things. Now her face hardly changed at all.

Mrs. White sat closest to Tom, and she was visibly entertained. Tom wouldn't say it, but because she was the wife of one the town's leaders, and also the oldest in the room, it should've been her place to do *something*. It was also her house. This was a tedious way to spend the day in the best of times, but having to get through it with Mrs. Heller in your ear? That bordered on inhumane.

Mrs. Young was too shy to interfere, and Mrs. Pilkin clearly didn't consider it her place. She was like Tom: an import to this community, though she hadn't shown up uninvited; she'd merely married into the Friendly Field family.

Tom had made a business of watching people, and it hadn't been difficult to figure out the odd little hierarchy in this room. The broader state of things, he wasn't so sure about, but he had a good feel for the five women he spent his days with.

Mrs. White always watched him from the corner of her eye, but not out of suspicion. She'd been the one to teach him to handle a needle and thread, so she considered it a point of pride that his work not be shoddy. At least, she believed she'd taught him.

For reasons that weren't clear to Tom, *Asher* was handy with a needle, and he'd been the one to impart the finer points—but then Mrs. White had been affronted, and now Tom had to be careful to at least appear as though he went about things her way.

He'd spent so much time handling cards that fine

work with his fingers should have come easily to him, but it wasn't that simple. And they didn't have a thimble large enough for him, so he was obliged to be very careful.

It hadn't been his choice to spend his time this way, but he wouldn't have been able to do a useful amount of tilling in the fields with his bad leg. He had no other skills; sewing seams was something nearly anyone could learn to do. Thaddeus had proposed it rather hesitantly, as though he expected Tom to take offense at the notion or refuse. That wasn't unreasonable; Tom expected a lot of men would've been appalled.

"Mrs. Heller, do you know where to gather mushrooms nearby?" he asked curiously, keeping his eyes on his work.

She looked up. "Oh—mushrooms? They are found in among the trees to the east."

"They have little flavor," Mrs. White noted.

"Are mushrooms to your liking?" Mary asked, seizing the moment.

"I like them as much as the next fellow, I guess. I ask because I understand they grow here plentifully."

"Who told you that?" Mrs. White asked, frowning. "I have seen them, sure enough, but no more than a few here and there."

"It has been some years since you were in the wood a great deal," Mrs. Heller pointed out. It was not a diplomatic thing to say, but Tom wasn't sure she knew what diplomacy was.

"It's not important," Tom said, curtailing anything that might have come of the exchange. "It's because of the boy. He likes to wander in the mornings, and he found some up in the hills to the northeast, but they're no good for eating."

"He does not wander to the pond behind the Wilson house, does he?" Mary asked lightly. That was where the ladies bathed.

"Not to my knowledge. He was proper about that courtesy on the trail, and I expect he will be here as well."

"He is so well-mannered," Mrs. Pilkin remarked, and her expression was uncertain, as though she worried even such a harmless thing might draw a rebuke. There were no rebukes to be had here; if there were, Mrs. Heller would've drowned in them long ago.

"He certainly is. That's always impressed me about him," Tom told her. "Does anyone live in those hills?" He asked the question bluntly.

"Heavens," Mrs. Heller replied, looking taken aback, "why would they?"

"Rough country," Mrs. White said to Tom. "Hilly and rocky. No soil worth having, as I understand it."

Nothing to farm, and nowhere to graze, so there would be better game elsewhere. Trappers would be unlikely to waste their time, and there was no talk of prospecting. That left relatively few reasons that anyone might be up there. Even the timber was poor.

And there *was* no one up there. Tom already suspected that; the thread that had been used to make that strange thing up in the hills was the same as the thread in his hands now. He just wanted to be sure.

There was a tap at the door, and Phillip Lester let himself in, ducking his head.

"Ladies," he greeted them, "and Mr. Smith, peace be with thee."

"Same to you," Tom replied.

Phillip had something in his hands, which he brought directly to Tom.

"This is the best Sebastian was able to do," he said, producing something small and copper.

"I'll be damned," Tom said, and Mrs. Heller let out a little gasp while Mrs. Young's eyes widened.

"I apologize," Tom said quickly, taking the crude thimble. "Thank you, Phillip. And I'll thank Sebastian as well. This will save me a share of grief and a pint of blood."

"I hope it will. And here is some tea from Mrs. Lester; you will find it stronger than Mr. Mayfair's leaves."

Coffee wasn't a vice to these people; they simply didn't drink it. Tom fully intended to lay his hands on some at his first opportunity, but until then he had no choice but to drink this god-awful tea.

"That is mighty thoughtful," he said. At first, this had been an uncomfortable ritual, but he was used to it now. These people just gave one another things. They didn't ask or expect anything in return. "And the kid? Is he doing his job out there?"

"Gabriel tells me he has never seen a harder worker."

"That sounds about right."

Phillip put his hand out, and Tom shook it.

T HE DAY'S WORK wasn't over until the sun set. Tom went stiffly out onto Mrs. White's porch, returning Jeremiah's wave as he passed—but the older man changed course. He nodded to Mrs. Pilkin as she descended, moving past her to join Tom. He took off his hat as he stepped into the shade.

"Tom," he greeted him. "Taciturn" seemed too mild for the man, but Tom liked him. Jeremiah was the only one who really showed any measure of distrust of Tom and Asher. He didn't act on it; he extended them the same courtesy that everyone else did.

But he seemed to have a little more sense than the rest.

"Sir." Tom held his own hat and squinted at the sunset; it was another pretty one.

Jeremiah drew up beside him, and he let Mrs. Pilkin get a few steps away, then glanced at the door. They were alone, but he spoke quietly.

"I just wanted to tell you that I'm glad things are going well. You're a gentleman, Tom. And the boy's got more wits than all my sons combined."

This was the other thing these people would do: they would say these kind things. And they'd do it without a single thought for how uncomfortable Tom would find it.

"You have a good life here. I'm grateful to be a part of it."

"It's not an easy life. We have to work for it."

"I don't so much mind that."

"Some men do," Jeremiah noted.

And anyone would have expected a man who made his living with cards to be one of them. That was what Tom would've thought in Jeremiah's place, but he wasn't the same man anymore. He didn't even miss the cards most days. Or the money. He certainly didn't miss his gun.

His friends, he still missed. And he suspected he always would. But it wasn't his decision to stay in Friendly Field that kept them from him. He had done that with his trigger finger. He couldn't go back, and that was no one's fault but his own.

Jeremiah put on his spectacles, then laid a hand on Tom's shoulder for a moment.

"I was wrong about you, and I am glad to admit it."

"You weren't wrong. You'd have been wrong to let a stranger like me by without a second glance."

Jeremiah just nodded and went on his way.

Mary Black emerged from the house, tying on her bonnet. She saw Tom waiting and broke into a smile. It came so easily to her when she was anywhere but the sewing room.

She was no beauty. Not even close. Her skin was much too pale, and her nose was more than a little too strong. Her bony frame made her nearly as tall as Tom, and he wouldn't have thought it was possible, but her smile was too big and too toothy. She was close to his age, and her dark hair always looked a little wild. She had been a widow for two years.

The light this time of day had a way of making everyone and everything beautiful, but it wasn't the light that made him want to stare at her.

"Good evening, sir."

"Ma'am."

"Would you do us the honor of joining us for dinner?"

She knew damn well that he would, and this was only a formality. It was a standing invitation, and Tom wasn't about to miss it.

"We're obliged to you, ma'am. On the trail, the kid did most of the cooking. After all day in the fields, he's beat."

"He *is* a small young man," she remarked, looking sympathetic.

"And it looks like hard work."

"Are you relieved to perform your day's labor with the ladies?"

Tom leaned on his stick, frowning. "I believe I would rather work outdoors," he said finally, "though my leg would frustrate me out there in the rows. You see how they all move along while they sling the dirt."

She nodded, still smiling. She was thinking of what Asher had said at dinner some nights ago: that it was unjust that the women had to work the same day as the men, only to still be the ones to prepare the evening meal.

Mary had just worn this look of saintly patience on her face while the boy spoke.

"Would you like help with your cooking?" Tom asked.

"That is very generous, sir. As you know, precious little cooking falls to me."

"True enough. Me and the kid might be a few minutes late. We need a word with Thaddeus."

He'd had all day to decide what to do with the thing the boy had found, but he hadn't needed all that time. He had to tell the elders; maybe they would know what it was.

Mary would've made a terrific poker player; her control of her face was all but perfect—but the curiosity was there in her eyes.

It was a pity these Quakers didn't gamble.

CHAPTER THREE

THADDEUS ANSWERED HIS door in the twilight, looking curious. The paunchy man was dressed and presentable; he'd no doubt planned to step out. He lived alone in his house, which was rather large, and always ate his evening meals with other families, different ones in turn.

"Peace be with thee."

"Yeah. Can we have a moment of your time?" Tom asked.

"Of course. I'm afraid I don't have any tea ready."

"That's all right. We don't mean to keep you long."

Thaddeus saw Tom's intent. "Oh, inside? Very well." He stepped aside for them, and the lamp in the foyer was out. He really had been just moments from leaving.

Tom got straight to the point. "Me and the kid were out that way this morning." He pointed northeast. "Up in the hills."

"I was there yesterday," Asher cut in. "I found a great deal of mushrooms, and I meant to harvest them."

"We didn't find any mushrooms today, though," Tom went on. "Just this." He took out the feathered object.

Thaddeus' frown deepened, and his brow furrowed. He took the object hesitantly, turning it over in his hands.

"I was kind of hoping it might be meant to be a sort of doll," Tom said halfheartedly, scratching his head. "But I don't think it is."

"Strange thing."

"What do you make of it?"

Thaddeus shook his head. "It was up that way, you said?"

"Just short of that rock cliff." Tom hesitated. "I think it's an odd thing to find in the woods. Someone put that together, and they were particular about it—it looks wild, but those knots are tidy."

"I see that." Thaddeus shook his head and placed the object on the sideboard. "I'll speak with Saul and Jeremiah about this."

"I'm not looking for trouble. I just thought you should know."

"Of course. Of course."

Thaddeus didn't appear concerned, and that suited Tom. They left the house and parted ways in the street, though it wasn't really a street, this open space surrounded by all the houses. Thaddeus was heading to Saul's home or perhaps the Heller house.

"You coming to Mary's?" Tom asked the boy.

"Not this evening, Mr. Calvert. I've received an invitation from the Bockners."

"Is he that tall, thin fellow with yellow hair? Pretty wife, sort of plump? Lots of kids?"

"Yes."

Tom had been introduced to that family, but he had no dealings with them. He had no doubt that they were friendly, but he was also fairly sure they wanted Asher for one of their three daughters. Those daughters were in Tom's opinion too young to marry, but Asher's gentle manners and hard work placed him in high demand for these courtship exercises disguised as meals.

On the trail, Tom had done his best to guide the boy in these things, but he'd failed. Now the kid was on his own, though he seemed no more interested in Quaker girls than in Norwegian ones.

"What's wrong, kid?"

The boy was tense, though he was trying not to show it. "That thing. It looks like something to do with witchcraft."

Tom raised an eyebrow and put his hat back on. "What do you know about that?"

"Only what I was told by my aunt." The boy folded his arms, scowling. "And she was no authority."

"Let the Quakers worry about it. It's not our problem."

"I did not tell you the truth, Mr. Calvert. I was not looking for mushrooms. Yesterday, when I went up that way, I went because I saw someone, and I wanted to know who it was. That was how I found the mushrooms."

"Who was it?"

"That, I do not know. I lost them in the dark."

"Made you suspicious?"

The boy nodded, and Tom sighed.

"Just be easy, kid. Anyone else is as free as you are to take a stroll up there. It's nothing to worry about."

Asher nodded, and they shook hands. With that, Tom limped off one way, and Asher went the other.

Mary's door was open, but Tom knocked all the same.

Mrs. Washburn, Mary's mother, greeted him dryly, as she always did. "Back again?"

"Yes, ma'am."

"Peace be with thee, then," she grumbled. "Mary's almost got dinner ready." This was a lie, but Tom was glad to hear it. If Mrs. Black wanted him to believe the blatant falsehood that her daughter could cook, it meant she was coming around to the idea of him as her son-in-law.

He helped with the settings and fixed a high shelf that was going crooked, and then it was time to eat. Mrs. Washburn lit the candles, and Mary brought out the food. Neither made any inquiry about Asher.

"I trust you received Mrs. Heller's generous compliments today," Mary said lightly as they ate.

"She flatters me," Tom replied. That was what Mrs. Heller would do when she sat next to Mary: remark on Tom's looks and what exotic things he must have learned abroad in the country. What an eligible fellow that made him, even if he was a cripple.

Tom took no offense, and he didn't think of himself as a cripple. He could get around all right, even if he couldn't run or dance anymore. At first, he thought Mrs. Heller said those things for fun, to make Mary blush. She didn't, though.

She just said what was on her mind, often loud enough for others to hear it. She had no sense to speak of. There was no blaming her for that.

Mary had sense, though.

"You've got no lawman," Tom remarked. He couldn't get that thing from the woods out of his mind, and no matter how he looked at it, it seemed like trouble. If there *was* trouble, what would these people do about it?

"Your pardon?"

He cleared his throat. "You have no mayor. No preacher." The Quakers held regular services, but there was no particular man to give the sermons. The people of Friendly Field would do it in turn. The day might even come when Tom was called upon, if he stayed long enough.

"Thaddeus, Saul, and Jeremiah—they're your mayor more or less. Are they also your sheriff for when someone gets out of line?"

"I take your meaning, but, to be truthful, we rarely have a need," Mary told him.

Tom could believe that, but only to a point. They had a good life here. Not easy but sheltered in many ways and stable. Potatoes weren't a glamorous business, but these people had all that they needed and more. Good, organized farming could make for a handsome business if the weather and the seasons played along. And with that in mind and their shared values, he could see how it might have been enough to keep some of the common problems away.

But the townspeople weren't *perfect.* How did they handle things when one of their own slipped up?

"When you do have the need, though." Tom wiped his mouth with his napkin and looked across the table at her. "When someone does something they shouldn't do."

"Jeremiah and the others talk to them." Mary didn't seem bothered by the question. "I suppose if someone *really* could not abide by our ways, they would have to go."

"It's never come to that?"

"No. Well . . ." Mary frowned and glanced at her mother, who for once had her eyes on her plate. Mrs. Washburn was ignoring her.

"Was I wrong to ask?"

"No," Mary said to Tom, shaking her head. "No. We are not *utterly* apart from everyone else. We know about the trouble they have in other places. There's only the one time I remember that we had that here."

"What happened?"

Mary looked pained. And Mrs. Washburn had her poker face on.

"The . . . guilty party was hanged," Mary said after a moment, and with a look of surprise, as though she'd genuinely forgotten until just now. "It's been a long time. More than ten years. A good deal more. I've stopped thinking about it." She swallowed, though. The memories were still there, and she didn't like them.

"I apologize," Tom said quickly. "That's not what we should talk about during a meal."

"Agreed," Mrs. Washburn said mildly.

THE COOKING IN the Black household really was something to take note of, and Tom looked forward to it every day. It wasn't free, however. It was becoming something of a ritual to have dinner, then retire to a game of cards.

Mary had no interest in cards, but her mother loved them. Not poker—they couldn't have any stakes, because that would make it gambling, which was apparently sinful. These people didn't play poker, but they did play other games, and Mrs. Washburn was pretty good. Good enough that if she played with the other

Quakers, it wouldn't be much of a game. She had hoped for a worthy opponent in Tom, the professional gambler who'd played in all the big cities in the East and the South.

What she'd gotten was a man whom she couldn't beat at anything. At first she'd found that frustrating, but it upset her even more if Tom lost to her on purpose. She'd mellowed as the days had gone by, and Tom suspected that Mary's fondness for him played a role in that.

Now Mrs. Washburn worried him more than the thing from the forest did. He didn't like the way she'd stiffened up when Mary mentioned the hanging. Of course she would find that sort of thing objectionable, but there had to be something else. He'd spent countless hours watching for tells, and he knew when the way someone acted didn't line up with the situation. That incongruity was always a sign of danger. And the notion of Quakers hanging someone in the first place— that wasn't right, was it?

The town had been around for a while, and the inhabitants couldn't be the saints they pretended to be. Tom didn't know it because he'd seen anything untoward; he knew it because he knew people. To keep everything running smoothly, *someone* had to have a way of solving problems. Whatever that was, maybe these folks weren't proud of it.

That was fine. Tom was the last man who would judge someone for doing something ugly, particularly something ugly that needed doing. He'd been there himself, more than once.

No, it wasn't alarm so much as old-fashioned curiosity. Imagine making that inconvenient trek up into some rocky woods, tying together some sticks, feathers, and bird bones, and leaving them out there.

That didn't make sense. Someone had dropped it by mistake, he was sure—but that still didn't answer the question of what it *was*.

"Mr. Smith?"

That woke him up.

"Is our little game boring you?" Mrs. Washburn asked dryly, seeing that he was distracted.

"You know it isn't," Tom told her, drawing a card. He hoped the kid was doing a better job than he was of keeping his thoughts hidden. They drew enough attention here as it was; nothing good would come of drawing more.

Mrs. Washburn won the game. Tom hadn't let her do it, at least not knowingly.

"I guess I would be foolish not to end on that note," she said, giving Tom her usual scowl.

He got up to help her to her feet, feeling a twinge of guilt. She probably didn't want to quit just yet, and she thought she was doing him a favor.

But Tom wasn't going to protest. It was the perfect opportunity to stay and talk a little while with Mary alone or as close to alone as they could be. The sense of propriety here, at least in regard to unwed men and women, wasn't entirely to Tom's liking.

On the other hand, it did make things interesting.

Mrs. Washburn went up the stairs on her own, and Tom turned to Mary. He meant to apologize for his morbid conversation and distraction, but she cut him off.

"What's the matter, Mr. Smith?"

He opened his mouth to lie, but stopped that before it could get out. She was inches away from him, and he liked the sight of her in any light—but lamplight was best. He sighed.

"I like it here," he admitted finally.

Her smile had been a bit hesitant, but now it grew to its usual size, which was really something. "Do you?"

He leaned on his walking stick and smiled back at her. "I do. But I'm a busybody, and I worry. There's something wrong with me, Mrs. Black."

"What do you mean?"

He searched for the right words. "I always want things my way. I think that's why I did what I did. Living on the road. It was just me, and I could always make sure that things were just the way I liked them."

She frowned. "I don't understand."

"It's different here." He snorted, gesturing vaguely. "This place. When it's just me, I run the show. I don't run things here. I can't."

"Put the burden down," she said immediately. "It's one less worry. We all look after one another, Mr. Smith. If I fall, you're there to catch me. The same for you. Don't you listen on Sundays?"

"I've only been here for two Sundays," he pointed out, and she grinned.

"I am sure it will be easier in time."

"It's difficult now, though. You have no idea how hard I worked over the years to be prepared."

"Prepared for what? What do you mean?"

"Well," he said, meeting her eyes very directly, "for trouble. I worked hard at shooting a pistol, for example."

"Oh." Her smile shrank a bit.

"When you play cards, you make enemies. If you want to play cards for a long time and live to tell of it, you have to be ready. So I always made sure I was." He took his coat and hat from the rack. "That's what it is, I think. That's what bothers me. I worry that you all aren't ready for trouble. And it makes me itch."

Mary's grin returned. "You're forgetting something, Mr. Smith."

"Oh?"

She leaned in a little closer. There was no perfume in Friendly Field, but Tom didn't mind that. He just gripped his walking stick. It wasn't easy to have her this close and just stand there. It was unnatural.

"The Lord," she said, and he couldn't tell if she was being ironic. "He will see to things."

Tom glanced toward the stairs, though there was no danger of Mrs. Washburn spying on them—but Mary saw him and read his mind. She stepped back, hardly out of reach, but he couldn't fail to take her meaning.

Other people weren't supposed to be able to read him that way, but the rules didn't apply to Mary. For God's sake, did these Quakers think there was any harm in a damn kiss? Fine.

She showed him out, and he pulled on his coat as she closed the door. Tom put on his hat, then stepped down into the night. There were still plenty of lit windows; it wasn't *so* late yet. Yes, he might have talked another hour with Mary, and he'd have liked to.

But he didn't trust himself, and apparently neither did she.

Shaking his head, he started the walk back to the house he shared with Asher. There was a light on; the boy was already home. The house had been only half finished when they arrived, and it had been intended for a Quaker family who meant to come here but had been delayed in Boston.

What kind of people would do that: just give a house to a man and a boy who turned up unannounced with nothing to offer in exchange?

Well, Tom had money, but the Quakers weren't interested in that. All they wanted was for the two of them to put in a full day of work, sit for service, and mind their language. And Asher never swore, so that last rule was just for Tom. And they wanted at least Asher to marry one of their girls—they definitely wanted that.

Still, it wasn't unreasonable.

Tom paused, gazing toward Thaddeus' house. The windows were lit there, and he could see two—no, three silhouettes. Saul and Jeremiah were inside. And someone else, but Tom couldn't be sure who. He wanted to knock on the door; it didn't appear to be the calmest conversation, and he wanted to know what was being said.

But it wasn't his place. It was easy to admit he was a busybody. It would be harder to change it, but he had to start somewhere.

He had to.

CHAPTER FOUR

THE QUAKERS WERE nothing if not orderly. The rows in the fields were perfect; they were as clean and straight as if someone had parted them with a comb. Tom had never known that potatoes were so much work; every day they were out there. As the plants grew, the men kept covering them with soil so they wouldn't be exposed to the sun. It had to be every bit as tedious as sewing pillowcases and a good deal more difficult.

But it wasn't the lovingly minded fields that made the valley beautiful; it was the sun and the way it caught on the dew. That, and it was easier to appreciate beauty when he wasn't completely out of breath.

The temptation to go up into the hills again had been strong, but to what end? Was it the dullness of days of sewing that made him so much more susceptible to his curiosity now? Or something else? He didn't know, and that bothered him.

He turned, leaning on his stick and gazing back toward

the houses. One thing that still took him aback about Quakers was their church. It wasn't that the church had no regular preacher; it was that the church itself was so humble. It was big enough that everyone could fit inside without undo discomfort, but it was still dwarfed by the barns. These folks spent so much time thinking about God that Tom would have thought they'd have a fancy church. The truth was, they didn't have a fancy anything. Not even the elders—and those three were the ones holding all the money. A part of him had expected to find their homes full of fine things. He had just *assumed* that they were enriching themselves with the work of the townsfolk.

That didn't appear to be true, though. He spent his days in Jeremiah's house, and he had been in Thaddeus'. Both were more or less the same as Mary Black's home and the one that Tom now shared with Asher.

There was a fair amount of money coming in from these potatoes. What were they doing with it, apart from making sure everyone had what they needed? Or was that all they did? Was the rest really just stacking up somewhere?

It was none of Tom's business, and there he was, wondering about these things again as though *he* were the one running Friendly Field.

He turned back to the east to see that there was someone on the road. A stagecoach, still far off, but not so far that Tom could hope to limp back to shelter before it passed him on its way to town, because there was nowhere else it could be going. His own clothes weren't so different from what the Quakers wore, just finer. He pulled off his coat and tie, tossing them out of sight. In his shirtsleeves he could have been anyone. As the stagecoach approached, he stood to one side and leaned on his walking stick, and as it passed, he tipped his hat and in doing so hid his face from the driver and anyone who might have been inside.

They rattled on.

Whoever it was in there, they'd traveled through the night, so they were in a hurry. It was the first stage he'd seen since coming to Friendly Field. Relief hit Tom hard; it wasn't a posse of lawmen, after all. Curiosity took relief's place in a heartbeat, but he caught it and didn't let it go. It wasn't lost on him that he had a tendency to think he knew everything. Mary was the one who really had the answer, though: he had to learn to mind his business.

T HE STAGE WAS already gone by the time he returned to town. It was time to get to the sewing room; most of the men were already making their way out to the fields. He even saw the kid walking alongside another young man, a much taller and broader one Tom hadn't met.

Jeremiah was over by the church, letting himself in. Why? There would be no service today. Tom hobbled after him.

The church was quiet and just big enough that even small sounds carried. There were pews, and that was all. There wasn't even a lectern for the lucky parishioner who had to give the sermons or homilies or whatever the Quakers called their little chats. Tom still had some adjusting to do.

"Morning," he said, and Jeremiah looked over his shoulder.

"Peace be with thee."

"Same to you. Is everything all right?" Tom *wanted*

to ask what he was doing in here. He wanted to ask what the elders had been arguing about last night too, but that was none of his business.

The white-haired man hesitated only for a moment; then he put his hand on a pew and leaned. "I think you know it isn't."

"That thing mean something to you? The thing with the feathers?"

Jeremiah shook his head. "No. Thaddeus thinks it's something to do with witchcraft."

"And Saul?"

"He's like me. Not sure what to think." He looked over at Tom. "What were you doing looking for mushrooms, Tom?"

"We weren't. Not really. The kid went up there in the first place because he thought he saw someone."

Jeremiah was openly baffled.

Tom was prying instead of doing what he should have been: making for the sewing room. He didn't stop, though.

"You hold with this witchcraft foolishness?"

Jeremiah just looked helpless. He spread his hands and shook his head. Tom had a feeling the other man didn't believe in witchcraft any more than he did.

"Well," Jeremiah murmured, scratching his beard, "I suppose we did come across it. Some years ago."

"It's not real," Tom told him bluntly. He regretted it immediately, but Jeremiah was too distracted to be affronted. "Has it got you that worried? One little doll?"

It wasn't really the doll, of course. It was that none of them had an explanation for it. These other fellows might not be as bad as Tom when it came to needing a hold on things, but they couldn't possibly like what they couldn't explain.

"What? Oh. No, it's— Well, keep it to yourself." Jeremiah glanced at the door. "The object you found is gone."

"What?"

"Someone must have taken it from the house last night while we were talking. Thaddeus meant to show it to us." He sighed. "He couldn't find it."

"Well, we already knew that whoever made it was, you know"—Tom swirled his finger in the air—"one of us."

"How's that?"

"The thread. It's the same thread I sew with. There's some in every house. There's not one woman in Friendly Field without it."

Jeremiah's brows rose; then his eyes narrowed.

"I'm glad you're here," he muttered. "Thaddeus didn't mention that. He probably didn't notice."

"No fault of his. He's not the suspicious sort."

"A little suspicion isn't always a bad thing."

"I agree."

IF HIS CONVERSATION with Jeremiah hadn't been strange enough, the sewing room was. The windows were open and the rising sun was shining. There was a breeze, but still plenty of warmth already. It was as pleasant a day as anyone could hope for, but Tom felt as though he'd just walked into a funeral.

He took his place in the chair next to Mrs. White and picked up his work.

"Good morning, ladies."

"Good morning, Mr. Smith. Peace be with thee." Usually it was a chorus; today it was just Mary and something like a mutter from Mrs. Pilkin.

Tom put on his new thimble, and he considerately waited a full minute before poking his nose in.

"Looks like you all know who was in that stagecoach."

This miserable hush *had* to be something to do with that. Tom was certain the ladies did not know about the witchcraft business. The stagecoach, though—it was unlikely that anyone had missed *that*.

Mrs. Pilkin and Mrs. Young kept their eyes down, but a look passed between Mary and Mrs. White. Mary started to speak, but Mrs. White was faster on the draw.

"A Miss Adams, I understand," she told Tom. Her way of speaking was always gentle and proper, but here it was a little much. Was that irony underneath? It was difficult to be sure.

The women in the room weren't afraid or worried; they were merely uncomfortable.

"Adams," Tom repeated, watching them closely. "Is she alone?"

"She is," Mrs. Heller said, but her eyes were still on her work. She was embroidering a kerchief, something she did beautifully and generally quickly. Today her needle was even slower than Tom's. If she was exercising discretion, then the business at hand was serious indeed.

Mrs. Young pushed a lock of golden hair aside, and Tom knew that look well. She was trying to see this in a charitable light.

"Is Miss Adams not known to us?" he pressed.

"She is not. She was invited here from some distance away, I understand," Mary told him, and her eyes said more than her words did. She wanted him to drop it, but he had no plans to let them off so easily.

"Will she be joining us? Or the other ladies, perhaps?" The womenfolk did far more than just sewing. There were plenty of chores in Friendly Field.

That did it; Mrs. White snorted. She didn't mean to, but she couldn't help herself.

"No," she replied. "No, I think not. In any case, Tom, we will be as welcoming to Miss Adams as we would to anyone else. You as well."

"Of course."

The topic was closed, then. There were limits to how far he could push. He was glad that Mary was there to remind him where the boundaries were, even if he didn't always take her advice. He wasn't terribly interested in this Miss Adams in any case.

"You know," he said, going back to his work, "in all my travels, and they have been considerable, there's one thing I've never seen. And that is a witch."

If he'd irked them with questions about this Miss Adams, now he'd done the same again. They all looked up in surprise.

"Really, Mr. Smith, this sort of talk is hardly," Mrs. White began, giving him a frown, "well, Christian."

"It's a theological matter, isn't it? Though I've never met any of them myself, I have heard things. Actually, in New Orleans, I spoke to this man who—"

She cut him off. "Mr. Smith, no one begrudges you your past, but perhaps not *all* your exploits need be shared here. Your candor does you credit, but I think we had best let things of that nature lie. They don't have a place in Friendly Field."

Mrs. White had meant to end there, but Tom held her gaze, looking expectant. Flustered, she did what people tended to do and went on, though she didn't really want or need to.

"We *have* had difficulties with such business. But that was a long time ago, and I would not expect to ever have that sort of trouble again." She hesitated. "We should not speak of the devil, or he may hear us and come to listen. And if he's to hear us, he might as well hear us talk of something he won't care for. Lunch today, for example. Alyssa is in charge of the cake, and I believe you'll find it heavenly."

FRANKLY, TOM WAS surprised that he'd been able to go a full two weeks in Friendly Field without getting so much as a hint of a secret.

"The stagecoach?" Asher frowned, wiping his brow. The sun was all but down, and the boy frowned up at Tom in the twilight. "It was hardly mentioned, but you understand there is not *so* much time for conversation in the fields."

There was a hint of annoyance there, and it was one of the rare times that Asher looked like someone his age ought to look. He put his back into it out there each day, and that would wear anyone down. All the while, Tom sat in a parlor with a needle.

"It's all right to complain a little," Tom told him.

The boy sighed, but his heart wasn't in it. "Mr. Calvert, why not ask the Widow Black about the stagecoach?"

"Oh, I aim to. Seems there's been talk of witchcraft here before."

That got the boy's attention. "Oh?"

"They wouldn't give me details. I guess it isn't a subject they much care for."

Asher smiled, but he was tired. "I would wager you are correct."

"Thaddeus and the others don't know what to make of it."

"Surely they are not afraid of a simple trinket."

"That's the thing, kid. There's nothing simple about it."

"I am hungry. *That* is a simple matter," the boy said bluntly.

"Me too, but forget it. We'll eat when we get back. I already refused our invitation."

The boy looked stricken. "You *what*?" His voice came out a bit high and shrill. Would it *ever* change?

Tom knew how fierce the kid got when he was hungry, but he didn't care. He'd already told Jeremiah where they were going, and he had his lamp ready.

Tom clapped Asher on the shoulder. "Maybe we'll find your mushrooms this time."

"But I cannot eat them," the boy moaned.

The trek was as difficult at the end of the day as it had been at the beginning. The stars came out, but Tom and Asher kept climbing.

"Which way, kid?"

"There, I suppose" was the miserable reply.

Tom was sympathetic, but Asher had started all this, and Tom couldn't very well come alone. If he slipped and hurt himself, he might not make it back.

The going was hard enough to leave him short of breath and sweating, but not so arduous that he didn't feel the night's chill. Shivering, Tom hauled himself up the slope, and Asher doggedly led the way.

"Are you afraid of a witch, Mr. Calvert?"

"I am," Tom replied without hesitation. "It's not like you think, though." He put his hand out, and Asher reached back to help him past a tangle of roots. "I don't believe in the devil. But there are folks who do and likely folks who believe in witchcraft. I'm afraid of people who don't think clearly. You never know what they'll do. You can work with a reasonable man, but the sort that would—well, that would make that thing you found, he's the one you have to watch for. He'll do things, and you won't see them coming because they don't make sense."

"I think I take your meaning."

"I'm afraid of what I don't see coming," Tom said, "because that's what gets you."

"I think that's very well said, Mr. Calvert."

It was. Tom never would have thought that it would feel good to say these things; it just wasn't done for a man to go around talking of the things that frightened him. But Mary didn't seem to disdain him for it, and neither did the kid. It was sensible to worry about the unknown, at least a little.

Particularly now.

He doused the lamp and clapped his hand over the boy's mouth before he could go on.

"Easy, kid." He kept the words to a whisper; the boy had gone rigid. "There's someone here."

CHAPTER FIVE

⌒

Tom hadn't come up here hoping to find *people*.

What he wanted had been some sign, something to help him make sense of things. After all, it was just some feathers and a bird's skull. It wasn't harming anyone, and if the kid hadn't stumbled over it, no one ever would've known it was up here.

Jeremiah had given Tom his blessing to come up to nose around. Tom had seized on that, as he did when he heard things that suited him. He'd allowed himself to overlook the detail that just because one of the town elders approved didn't mean it was actually a good idea. His curiosity was to blame. He just couldn't leave a loose thread hanging.

The right thing to do would've been to just let it lie. It wasn't his first regret, and he just had to hope it wouldn't be his last.

He gently pressed Asher against the tree and held him there with his hand on his shoulder so he wouldn't move.

There wasn't much moonlight getting through the leaves, and there were still green stars in his eyes from his lamp, but none of that posed a problem for his ears.

Someone was over there, not even twenty feet away. Whoever they were, they knew how to move in the brush, because they'd gotten awfully close. The noise of the crickets had nearly covered it.

Tom was more or less in the open, and he'd have liked to find a tree of his own to hide behind, but everyone present would hear any move he made.

So he kept still, and the night thickened around him and his ears.

It was one thing to stare a man down over a card game, or even with a gun in hand—but Tom couldn't take the measure of someone he couldn't see.

He was out there, though. The kid was getting squirrelly; even if he understood why they had to wait, he wouldn't have liked it. The boy was patient for someone his age, but that wasn't saying much.

There was one way to take the upper hand: Tom could try to scare them, but it wouldn't be convincing. His silence up to this point had signaled caution; the man out there would know that Tom wasn't as confident as he wanted to sound. That, and the lamp. They might have gotten a look at Tom and Asher and seen for themselves that they weren't threatening.

This other party had no light at all. There were only so many possible reasons for that, and Tom didn't like any of them.

The minutes stretched, and only the breeze and the crickets disturbed the dark blanket of the evening. Nothing stirred.

Had he been wrong? It would be a good joke if he was out here pretending to be a statue because of a rabbit.

Tom started to let his breath out.

"Well," said a man in the dark much closer than Tom had realized, "I can't tell if there's one or two of them." He sounded irked.

A second voice spoke up. "It's two." This one was a little farther off to the right.

Swearing silently, Tom pivoted and put his back to another tree. "One and a half, more like," he said.

"And who are you?" the first man asked.

"My name's Tom. This is my nephew."

There was a little pause, which told Tom something. This fellow wasn't sure what to make of Tom's confident and articulate way of speaking.

"I ain't looking for you and your nephew."

"Who *are* you looking for?" Tom replied easily.

"A girl."

"What's her name?"

"I don't know her name."

"What's she look like?"

"I ain't seen her face," the man replied. "But I seen the rest, and I liked that well enough."

"If you aren't looking for us, you might as well come on out. I won't shoot you," Tom said tiredly. He emerged from behind the tree, squinting in the gloom. Two figures materialized, one to his left and one to his right.

"How about your nephew keeps his hands where I can see them?" the man on the left asked. There was a funny scarf around his neck, and it was bunched up, making his silhouette look unnatural. The other one stood a full head higher than Tom.

Asher complied. Tom was close enough to see the boy's face, even in the dark. It was stony.

"You all got no manners at all," Tom scolded. Scarf

had a hand on his gun, and the tall one had a rifle in his hands. "I didn't pull on *you*."

"Ain't no harm in being cautious, folks creeping around in the dark," Scarf replied, shrugging.

"Creeping?" Tom spread his hands. "We have a damn lamp, which I'm going to light again presently, and you were the ones creeping in the dark. My nephew and I were not creeping. Creeping is what dubious characters would do."

Clearly taken aback, Scarf didn't have a reply for that.

"Dubious characters," the tall one echoed.

Tom struck a match and lit the lamp, holding it up. The two men didn't shy from the light; they were dressed for travel and grubby, but not too filthy. Scarf looked as though he'd taken some punches in his day, but he was only as old as Tom. The tall one was younger and in a little better repair. Their clothes weren't exactly ragged, but these two weren't bankers.

"Nothing dubious about strolling in the moonlight," Scarf said.

"Looking for girls in the middle of the night?" Tom accused. "In the woods?"

"It was night last time I seen her too."

"And when was that?"

"That ain't none of your business!"

"The hell it isn't," Tom shot back. "I'm up here looking for a girl too, and I'll wager it's the same one."

"What's her name, then?" Scarf asked.

"That's what *I* want to know."

"Mister, you don't make any damn sense."

"I'm not the one out here with no light."

"Would you let that go, please?" the tall one asked.

"I will not," Tom replied. "Makes me think you're up to no good."

Scarf snorted. "Up to no good," he repeated. "You haven't told me your name yet. How're we to know you ain't the one up to no good?"

"I told you my name's Tom. You just weren't listening. What's your name?"

"My name's Tom too."

"So's mine," the tall one snickered.

"Now, you come from down there, don't you?" Scarf pointed, and Tom turned to look. They were fairly high up, and there was the slightest glow from Friendly Field. It wasn't a proper town, but there were just enough lit windows to be visible in the distance.

"I do."

"What sort of place is it?"

"The village? Haven't you ever visited?"

"We have not. In fact, we never knew it was even there. Quiet place, ain't it?"

"It is," Tom admitted. "Even when they're singing hymns they got no music. No musical instruments, not a one."

"Not even a piano for company?" Scarf sounded taken aback.

"There *is* no company," Tom told him frankly. "Don't you know? They're Quakers. Most fun they ever have is picking potatoes."

"Quakers." The tall one made a face.

"That's how I feel," Tom said truthfully.

"Ain't you one of them?"

"No, I'm not one of them. I don't plan to stay. The deputy's all right, but the sheriff's a real son of a bitch. Truth is, it's not my kind of place," Tom lied.

"God-fearing people, aren't they? Quakers?" Scarf said, glancing at the tall one. "Don't much like guns, do they?"

"That is what I heard," the tall one replied, leaning his rifle over his shoulder and scratching his unruly beard.

"I heard that too," Tom said, and shot him. Even the tiny shot from the derringer was loud in the stillness.

He flung the lamp at Scarf, who recoiled and raised an arm to protect his head; the lamp burst, and flames spread across his jacket. Tom took aim and fired. Scarf jerked and stumbled out of sight behind a tree, falling to the ground and rolling to put out the flames.

Tom limped forward and fell to his knees beside the tall one, who was flat on his back, blood spurting from his throat, eyes wide in shock. Asher stood frozen as Tom felt in the loam for the rifle. He found it and snatched it up, sending leaves flying.

Curses and groans carried clearly; the shots had momentarily silenced the crickets.

Tom worked the lever and lurched to his feet, but he couldn't even raise the rifle before Scarf was up and running—shambling, really—and gone among the trees. Tom squinted and tried to follow, but it was too dark, and the woods were too thick.

Heart thudding, he lowered the rifle and let out his breath.

Behind him, the tall one gave one last, rattling gasp.

Asher tore past him, intending to go after the wounded man, but Tom caught him by his coat and jerked him back, holding him fast.

"No, kid." His throat was dry. "Don't try it."

CHAPTER SIX

ASHER HAD FIGURED out a moment too late that they couldn't let either of these men go.

Tom wished he could've let the kid chase that man down, but it was too easy to picture Scarf out there, hearing the boy crashing after him, hiding behind a tree with a knife. Asher would get himself killed; Tom wouldn't risk it.

He looked down at the dead man at his feet, and Asher touched his arm.

"Mr. Calvert?"

"Hmm?"

"You think they would have killed us?"

Tom peered at the dark trees for a moment before answering.

"I don't know," he replied, shaking his head. He cradled the rifle in his arms and stood up, nodding at the corpse. "But that's Ben Garner out of Utah. I wasn't sure at first, but it's him all right." He looked up from the body and squinted into the trees.

Asher's eyes widened. "Your acquaintance?"

"No, kid. He's—he's a wanted man, or he was. He robbed a train with John Porter and Harry Peckner if my memory serves. And there was something in El Paso. More posters for him than for . . ." Tom trailed off there, rubbing his chin.

"An outlaw."

"Not just one," Tom told the boy, though he wasn't really paying attention. "Look at him. He's fed. Groomed, at least a little. He's bathed in the past few days. He's not on the run, Asher."

"I do not understand."

"*That's* why nobody's caught up to the Porter gang. They're camped out here." He looked east. "In these hills somewhere. There'll be more of them. I don't know how many."

Scarf was gone; Tom didn't know what his name was, but there was no doubt in his mind that he was part of the gang. The question was, how badly was he wounded? Was it mortally? His first shot had been good, but Tom had all the time in the world to stand there and plan it while he jawed with the outlaws. The *second* shot, the one meant for Scarf—that had been another matter, and the derringer just wasn't meant for this. With his own gun, they'd have been sure, clean kills.

And that was what he'd needed.

Tom had *tried* to find the right thing to say, something that might make those two lose interest or turn back, but there had been nothing. What could he have said? Telling them it was an ordinary camp or town down there wouldn't have worked. They wouldn't have been able to resist the temptation.

The truth was even worse. Nothing would've stopped those men from wanting a closer look at Friendly Field.

"There are outlaws here?" The boy was still a step behind. He'd figured out that Tom hadn't wanted Scarf to escape, but he didn't see why.

"Yes. And I didn't want them to know about *them*," Tom said, frustrated. He pointed toward Friendly Field. "They take what they want. They don't ask. They're hiding from the law, hiding from people, but they won't be afraid of some Quakers. They wouldn't be able to stay away."

"But there is nothing to take," Asher protested shrilly, and Tom didn't blame him. He was shocked; it had happened suddenly, and the boy hadn't seen it coming.

"You heard him, kid. They're hiding in the woods. What do they *not* have?"

The look on the boy's face spared him the trouble of saying he didn't know. Asher still had some growing up to do.

"It's not comfortable to camp for a long time, kid. You know that." Tom pointed at Friendly Field again. "Decent food, women. They want what they want, they're going to come looking for it, and they're going to realize a crowd of Quakers isn't likely to put up much of a fight."

The boy's face hardened. "I see," he said. "We should go after him."

Tom sighed, and his jaw hurt from the way he'd clenched it. "I wish we could."

The little gun had fooled Scarf with its pitiful bullets, because it had killed Ben Garner easily enough. Tom tried to swallow the queasiness that came of thinking about where Scarf might be by now, scrambling through the woods. There was no estimating the odds of him making it back to his people, not when they couldn't know how badly he was hurt or how far off those people were.

Even if the Porter gang was composed of nothing but perfect gentlemen, they'd still rob the Quakers blind for food and supplies. They might even move in if they were getting tired of sleeping in the woods.

"Did you hit him?" Asher asked from the dark.

"I think so."

"What will we do?"

Tom didn't have an answer.

Throwing the lamp had been a mistake; now they had nothing to light their way back. As his eyes adjusted, he knelt beside the body of Ben Garner.

It was hard to guess exactly what the Porter gang would do now. If Scarf made it back, would they come out this way to settle up? It was possible, but not certain. If Porter had any sense, he'd relocate, even though Tom had been careful not to give any indication that he recognized them, which would've gotten them gunned down on the spot. Of course, Tom was fairly sure they'd intended to do that regardless. They didn't want anyone knowing they were out here, and they wouldn't be inclined to take chances.

But Porter might not realize that he'd been found out. Would he care enough about Ben Garner to want retribution?

And if Scarf never made it back, what then? Would the others come looking for these two? If they did, it was best that they not be found. Two men disappearing would shake up anyone leading a gang, and it might incline them to move on to somewhere else. Ultimately, that was what Tom wanted.

He couldn't control what would happen with Scarf. He might make it back; he might not. If he didn't, his body could be found or not. There was nothing more frustrating than uncertainty. Tom liked things *his* way, and his way was certain.

With effort, he controlled his temper. A Quaker for two weeks and he'd already shot someone.

"God*damn* it. We'll have to do something with him," he told Asher, indicating the body. "Do you recall the crevice back that way?" He jerked his chin down the slope. "The one you nearly fell in? We'll throw him down there."

The boy swallowed, but gave no other sign of squeamishness. "It will look as though he fell."

"As long as the other one never tells his story, that'll be as good a notion as any if he's found."

They got to it. It would've been difficult even in daylight; Tom wasn't as strong as he'd once been, but Asher was a good deal stronger than he'd been when they met. The trail had toughened him up, and now working in the fields would be sure to put some muscle on him.

Careful not to fall in themselves, they fumbled through the dark, back to the rocky opening. Tom searched the dead man before they threw him in, but he had nothing of value apart from a few loose shells for his rifle.

In the forest, it was dark, but in the crevice, it was black. The tall man vanished with relatively little fuss, just a bit of muffled thumping as he toppled down.

"You all right, kid?"

"Yes, Mr. Calvert. I am well."

Tom knew better than to take him at his word, but it would've been strange if the kid *hadn't* shown some nerves at this business. He'd seen worse, but that didn't make it easy. The boy liked to act tough, but at the end of the day, he wasn't as cold as Tom, and that was not a bad thing.

At the edge of the woods, Tom took Ben Garner's rifle, wrapped it in his coat, and hid it in the loam at the foot of a tree. It was getting late, and there weren't too many windows still glowing in Friendly Field.

They'd been settled just long enough to know which houses belonged to whom, even at night. The Black house was dark and silent. Tom didn't know which would've been worse: if he'd just gone to dinner as he'd wanted to or if he hadn't. It wasn't a matter of *if* those men would've found Friendly Field. They'd already noticed it when they ran into Tom and Asher.

There was a queasiness in Tom's belly that wanted to bring to mind other times he'd pulled the trigger, but Tom didn't let it have its way. Lying in the back of that wagon in a fever—he'd spent enough days and nights there doubting himself for a lifetime. There wouldn't be any more of that. There was no saying if what he'd done had been right, but there was also no changing it now.

He and the boy made their way across the field and back to the houses. There, between their own place and the Taylor house, Tom turned on Asher.

"Go on to bed," he told the boy. "But eat something first, even if you got no appetite."

"Where are you going?"

"We can't just hope for the best, kid. If the Porter gang comes here, we'll have a problem."

"What can be done?"

Tom sighed. "These people can't protect themselves. They need someone who can."

"You?"

It was all Tom could do not to laugh. "No. No, kid. Maybe twenty of me, but no—these are wanted men. Real outlaws, not like me. We need the law."

Asher cocked his head. "Mr. Calvert, your reason for being in this place is that the law is *not* here."

"Well, we need them now. These people need them. They have to be protected." Tom shrugged. "Trust me, it isn't my first choice."

"Mr. Calvert, *these people* told you directly that they would not hide you."

Tom frowned. "Kid, I'm surprised at you. You want me to just throw them to the wolves?"

"What do you owe them? You could be hanged," the boy hissed.

"For all I know, what I did could bring all hell on this town." Tom eased off his walking stick and tested his bad leg. "I have to try to do right by them."

"How can you bring them *here*, though? If you bring them to seek wanted men, *you* are a wanted man!" He was raising his voice.

"Easy, kid. We don't know that I'm wanted, and if I am, we don't know who *knows* that I'm wanted. Besides, I had a beard when I shot the Fulton brothers. I play cards. I know my chances, and there's a good chance no one looks at me twice, not with a pack like the Porter boys out there. There's got to be twenty thousand in bounties camped in those hills."

Asher shook his head in disgust. "It is a foolish risk."

Tom was taken aback, but he wasn't inclined to argue. "It's my decision," he said simply. "And I plan to make the right one for once."

"Shooting them *was* right," the boy said, shaking a finger at him. "They were bad men, Mr. Calvert. You knew it when you saw them, and you would not be wrong about that."

That was what he said, but he was distracted. Someone was leaving Saul Matthews' house: it was Eliza, the daughter of Frederick and Henrietta Vogel. Saul's wife had passed years ago, and Eliza kept his house tidy. She did the same for another widower, but Tom couldn't remember his name. This was the normal time for her work to be done.

He turned back to Asher. "If you trusted me then, trust me now."

"You take it too far," Asher accused. "As you did when we arrived, telling them everything. There was no need to unburden yourself."

"I *like* unburdening myself. And when you get to have burdens like mine, you will too. Go on." He gestured.

Asher, eyes rebellious, clearly wanted to say more. He didn't, though.

Tom didn't watch him go; he just limped off toward Jeremiah's house. Saul was still up—his lights were on, but Saul wasn't the man to speak to.

"Tom," said a voice in the night.

He turned and looked back to see Phillip Lester leaning against the side of the house. He'd been out of sight from where Tom and the boy had argued, but barely ten paces away.

There wasn't even the slightest chance that he hadn't heard.

Panic struck, but just for a moment. Tom swallowed and pointed a finger at him. "You didn't hear anything that I'm not about to tell Jeremiah. Come on with me."

"He is asleep," Phillip said, as though Tom might care.

"Then I'll wake him up."

Phillip looked surprised by that, but poor manners were the least of anyone's worries at the moment. Besides, if Phillip really had heard, then it would confirm for him what he should've already known: that, crippled or not, Tom wasn't someone to be trifled with. And Tom wasn't worried about being trifled with by Quakers in any case.

Though if there was *one* who might actually be a threat, it was Phillip. The man was all muscle, and he had some sense. He might have been pious, but he seemed like the type to do what he had to—that was why he wasn't in a panic over what he'd heard. It was a good thing he was here; it meant there was at least one man in Friendly Field who might keep his head if there was trouble.

The surprise faded, replaced by an impassive look, but Phillip came out of the shadows and followed Tom to Jeremiah's house. There, he pounded on the door.

It didn't take Jeremiah long to answer, a candle in his hand.

"May we talk?" Tom asked.

Jeremiah saw the look on his face and Phillip's and beckoned them in. His house was even humbler than Thaddeus', but just as tidy. He shambled into the parlor and knelt in front of the hearth.

"I can do that," Phillip said, taking his place. Jeremiah let him and sat in a chair, smoothing his nightgown.

"Peace be with thee," he said, a little grumpily. "If you'd keep it down, Mrs. White is sleeping. And what is that smell?" he asked.

It was gunpowder, but Tom didn't feel a need to go into that. He took a seat and leaned forward.

"Sir, the boy and I were in the woods this evening. As we talked about."

Jeremiah nodded, squinting at him. Phillip struck a match and lit the kindling. The fire started to grow. Tom wasn't cold, but he was a good deal younger than Jeremiah.

"What did you find?"

"No witches, but there were two outlaws. One of them was Ben Garner. I'd never met him, but I'd seen his posters. The other one I can't be sure about, but it's fairly well-known that they're both with the Porter gang."

"It is not well-known here," Jeremiah said pointedly. "What is the—the Porter gang?"

"Porter and Peckner. They did a robbery in El Paso that impressed enough folks that their gang got a lot bigger. Then they did an even bigger one there again, but I gather it was a little much. It's bad enough that the Army wants them, or it did a year ago. I don't know about now. I suppose they went quiet. They've been hiding."

"Near us? These criminals?"

"That's what I gather," Tom told him frankly. "And they know you're here."

For the first time since getting him out of bed, there was worry on Jeremiah's face. "And?" he grunted.

"And they're not likely to leave you alone."

"How could you know this?"

"I heard their intent from their own mouths," Tom told him, knowing the older man's thoughts.

Jeremiah didn't care much for the notion of disreputable neighbors, and men had a way of being skeptical about things they preferred not to face. Thaddeus and Saul would outright deny anything that Tom might say;

there would be no convincing them that they were in danger.

Jeremiah was different. "Did you?"

"Yes, we conversed. Their intentions aren't honorable, sir. I won't offend your delicate ears with the particulars, but I assure you these men who've been living a rough life would take an interest in Friendly Field. I'm not a fortune-teller. It might be your food they want, or your money if you've got any. Or your daughters. Or all of it. But like as not, they will turn up here, maybe in numbers."

Jeremiah listened to all that with nary a flicker. "Are they responsible for that token you found?" he asked finally.

"I doubt it." Tom glanced at Phillip. "Like I said before, I think that business lives a little closer by."

Jeremiah grimaced and rubbed his eyes, then glanced at the fire. "I'm to take your word for all of this?"

"The boy was there."

"The word of two outsiders."

"How little faith you have," Tom said dryly, but he threw up a hand as Jeremiah's brows rose. "I'm joking, though I guess this isn't the time for it. What reason could I have to lie to you? I brought back the man's rifle, if you need proof. There's no profit in this for me."

"I'm still waiting to hear your proposal. You have one, don't you?" Jeremiah wasn't stupid.

Tom sighed. "I do."

"Then get it out."

"Someone should ride to Des Crozet to send word that the Porter gang's been found. That'll bring people here to go after them. They're only a danger to us if they're here, but if the law comes, they'll run." Tom shrugged. "That's what I propose."

In the light of day, Jeremiah was too well-mannered to be openly suspicious. It was dark now, and he stared hard at Tom before turning his gaze on Phillip. "What do you make of it?"

The strong man didn't hesitate for long. "I don't see how it would wrong us," he said. "Or how he might profit from someone going to do this thing. I believe him when he says these men are out there. I heard him speaking to the boy; they didn't know I was listening. Near as I can tell, he seems truthful."

"You want to see these men hang," Jeremiah accused.

"That isn't against your teachings, is it? *You* aren't the ones who have to ride out after them," Tom pointed out.

"It is not our way to see *anyone* killed," the older man hissed.

"Hell, didn't I hear that you all hanged someone yourselves once?" It was Tom's way to fire back. He always did it, even when it wasn't a good idea.

Jeremiah stiffened. He was an easygoing man, a man who lived in the same world that Tom did, but he was still a Quaker.

"That was another matter," he said tightly.

"And I have no plans to start a quarrel over it," Tom said, keeping his bearing and staying on the offensive. "Because I frankly think it unlikely that anyone will hang. Like I said, I expect the gang to run at the first sight of a badge."

"It does not appear to serve his interests," Phillip admitted, moving closer to the fire. He'd probably never played poker, but he had his poker face on regardless. He wouldn't want to appear too quick to take Tom's side, but was that what he was doing? Taking Tom's side? It was hard to be sure.

"If we are obliged to surrender any wanted men to the law, then are we not obliged to surrender you as well?" Jeremiah asked.

There was nothing in those words but plain stubbornness. Tom had seen this before: it was fear. Jeremiah had no problem with Tom; his problem was that he didn't like what was happening, and he didn't know what else to do but push back any way he could.

Fear of change wasn't exactly unheard of among men Jeremiah's age, but Tom still had no patience for it.

"There is a difference between me and those men," he snapped. "Don't turn them in because they're wanted. Turn them in because if you don't, there's a good chance they will make some hard times for your people. I *am* trying to serve my own interest. I like you, Jeremiah. I like your people. I like living here. But I can't live here if there's no here to live in. These men are like the locusts in your Bible."

"You seem very sure of yourself."

"If I don't have my judgment, what does that leave?" Tom answered at once.

Jeremiah had nothing to say to that.

"I don't object to carrying word to Des Crozet," Phillip volunteered. That was what he said, but his face was still neutral.

After several seconds of holding Tom's gaze, Jeremiah gave it up.

There was silence. The older man clearly wanted to think it through, but there was no scenario where this was some manner of grift from Tom. Tom would not be enriched by what he was proposing, nor would Friendly Field be harmed.

It was just strange and sudden, and Jeremiah was old enough that he didn't care for either of those things, particularly so soon after the strange object had been found in the woods. Tom was acutely aware that all the strangeness lately was coming to these people through him, and he was sorry about that, but being sorry had never changed anything before, so there was no reason to think it would start now.

The other thing that Jeremiah probably didn't like was that he was having this conversation alone, without Saul and Thaddeus present. But he knew as well as Tom did how helpful those two would be if there was ever any real trouble.

"Be discreet," the older man said finally. "And hurry."

Phillip ducked his head and turned to go. Tom followed without a word, and in a moment, they were on the porch. Phillip went down the stairs and paused to gaze up at the night sky.

"You did not tell him everything," he said as Tom drew up alongside him.

Tom *had* left out the part about shooting the two men.

"I'm beat. You want to tell him what you heard me say, be my guest. I shot them, and I'd do it again. I wish there'd been another way. One that I really thought might have worked."

CHAPTER SEVEN

T OM WOKE IN his bed.

His bed. How strange that sounded in his mind. When had he last been able to say that? He'd never owned a house and never stayed in the same city for more than a few weeks at a time, let alone the same bed.

Summer was coming, but there would be a while more of this morning chill before it got here. He'd made a habit of rising as soon as he woke; it was always easier to face the day that way.

Not this morning. He saw Ben Garner and that other man, the one in the scarf. He'd made decisions the night before, and he'd resolved not to worry over them. That resolution hadn't held: here he was, lying in bed, trying to figure where he'd gone wrong.

He hadn't gone wrong. If he hadn't struck first, he and the kid would've been killed. And sending for help was all they could do; the Quakers couldn't protect themselves, and even at his best, Tom was only one man.

The sun was coming up out there, and normally Tom would've been on his way back from his walk by now, but it had been a late night. He dragged himself out of bed and paused to knock on the kid's door. The usual rustling came from the other side. Sleep had been Asher's vice as long as Tom had known him, and if it was his worst vice, so be it. The kid would get himself up and be out in the fields working with the others; Tom wouldn't have to pretend to be his pa and coax him out of bed.

At the front door, he considered his walking stick, then leaned it against the wall and made his way out without it.

He left the house and made for the pond where the men bathed, got cleaned up, and limped back. Everyone was already out and moving in the pale light. He got biscuits from Mrs. Rollins and took some back to the house for the boy, then ventured back out. A man named Germaine waved to him and jogged over.

"Peace be with thee."

"Good morning," Tom replied.

"Have you seen Phillip, Tom?"

"He's gone on an errand to Des Crozet. I'd expect him back soon." Tom considered the fields, and the trees and hills beyond. His whole time on the trail, he'd been looking over his shoulder. He still was.

Now he'd be looking over that way as well.

It was typical of him to be the last to arrive in the sewing room, and today was no exception. The feeling in Mrs. White's house was better than it had been yesterday, but Tom was most worried about her. She knew that Tom had been the one to rouse her husband last night. She might have heard everything that was said, or Jeremiah might have told her nothing. Or she might have gone back to sleep and he might not have said anything.

Tom didn't know. He took his seat beside her and picked up his work, but paused when he put on the thimble that Phillip had brought him. Phillip wasn't in any danger; the gang was to the northeast, and the road to Des Crozet was just about due south.

He'd be all right, but Tom still didn't like it. He should've been the one to ride for help, but that would've been too much. If the law came to Friendly Field, he'd stand a good chance of going unnoticed. If he went looking for the law—well, that wasn't a good idea. Tom wasn't afraid to die, not the way he had been a year ago, but he still wasn't about to put the noose around his own neck.

"Good morning," he greeted the women.

"Peace be with thee," they all dutifully replied.

Mary didn't look cross with him for his rudeness the night before, when he'd gone off into the woods with the boy instead of coming to dinner. He'd have liked to give her some explanation for what he was doing, but he didn't want to lie to her. And he didn't want to tell her the truth, either. It wasn't fair to her; what was she supposed to think? She wasn't one of these women prone to unreasonable worry and trepidation, but still . . . His absence from her table last night probably bothered her, and he didn't care for that.

She sat as she always did, with a straight back and a little smile that made her appear as though she knew everything, and that nothing could possibly bother her. It was that bearing that had drawn his eye in the first place; it reminded him of Miss Ayako, a cardplayer from overseas who had taught Tom a pair of important lessons. First, that he wasn't as good as he thought he was. Second, that he *couldn't* have everything he wanted, even if he put his mind to it.

"Are you well, Mr. Smith? You appear fatigued," Mrs. White remarked.

She'd heard everything. Did *all* of these Quakers have poker faces? It was starting to look that way.

"I'll manage," he told her easily, leaning over to take a peek out the window. A slim figure in a lovely dress was sweeping Thaddeus' porch. Tom couldn't see her face, but that dress was certainly new to Friendly Field. "Is that Thaddeus' new housekeeper?" he asked. According to the kid, that was Miss Adams' position.

"It is," Mrs. White replied. Her poker face could hold, but the room itself gave it away.

It seemed the pretense of the young woman being a housekeeper wasn't doing much good. Well, the ladies might not approve, but Tom wasn't bothered. There were real problems to worry about, and propriety wasn't one of them. Thaddeus was an aging widower, and Tom was no puritan. Why *shouldn't* he pay some girl to take some of the chill out of his evenings?

Tom watched a little longer, and the housekeeper looked south. Tom leaned over farther. It was about time for Phillip to be coming back. Yes, Sebastian was out there as well, and he was waving. It had to be Phillip.

Tom set aside his work.

"Ladies, I apologize. I'll be back shortly." He left the house and hurried down to the grass, limping out as quickly as he could. Phillip spotted him and changed course, swinging down from the back of his mare.

The girl on Thaddeus' porch was watching, but Tom didn't pay her any mind.

"Well?" he asked quietly.

"I was able to relay the message," Phillip reported. He looked fine; it hadn't been a particularly demanding task. So what was this worry in his eyes?

"What's the matter?"

"The sheriff and his deputies were concerned of the danger in pursuing these men."

Tom shrugged. "Dangerous, sure enough. But there'll be bounties aplenty to make it worth their while."

"Seems not. They plan to wire Boise and see what they think." Phillip folded his arms, searching Tom's face. "I imagine you will have your intended result."

He was right: word would get around, and *someone* would come. Maybe even the Army if there weren't any lawmen brave enough try their luck. The trouble was that it would take time. Tom wasn't *surprised* that help wasn't immediate from Des Crozet; there was a sheriff there, and a few deputies—he'd hoped they might round up a few men from town and that would be enough, but would it? Maybe not.

Tom didn't know how big the Porter gang really was. They'd done big jobs; it must have taken quite a few hands to accomplish. The notion of chasing after a dozen outlaws on this terrain wasn't very appetizing, and going after that number of *competent* ones didn't appeal to Tom at all.

It wasn't good news, but there was no changing it.

"Good. We'll be all right," Tom told Phillip, and they shook hands.

The door of Saul Matthews' house banged open, and they both turned at the sudden noise. Eliza spilled out onto the porch, face pale and streaked with tears. Phillip and Tom both had the same notion, but Phillip was faster. He took off running, and Tom did the best he could without his stick.

The girl caught herself on the railing and stayed there, knuckles as white as her face. Phillip bounded onto the porch and to her side.

"What's the matter?" he demanded, but the girl didn't have a reply for him. She stood, fingers locked on that railing, eyes fixed on the ground. Tom went to the door and peered in. Where was Saul? Tom would've expected him to be eating breakfast by now at least. He occupied his days caring for the animals; it wasn't heavy labor, but it had to be done, and even the elders were never idle.

"Saul?" he called out.

Phillip pulled Eliza away from the railing and made her sit in a chair on the porch, then joined Tom. "She won't say anything." He was equal parts baffled and worried, much like Tom.

"Stay with her," Tom told him, and limped into the house. It was dim and quiet, and everything appeared to be in its place. Of the three elders, Saul was the one with the most comfortable home, but that was because the man had pains in his joints. There were a few more rugs, cushions, and blankets.

The place smelled, as most of these Quaker houses did, of freshly cut wood. Another scent caught his nose, however.

It grew stronger as he made his way up the stairs. There were only two rooms up there; all these houses were alike. One was Saul's bedroom, and that door was standing open. The rug was askew where Eliza had likely kicked it in her scramble to get out of the house.

Tom knew the coppery smell of blood, and he knew that look on Eliza's face. Saul was dead.

Tom hadn't seen this coming. Saul had looked fine the day before, and he wasn't *so* old. He hadn't been sick. Had he just gone in his sleep? It wasn't unheard of.

He froze in the doorway.

Now that he was close enough, it wasn't just the blood he smelled: there was just the very first hint of rot as well. Saul was in his bed under the covers. The handle of a knife stuck out of his chest, but that wasn't what had Tom's attention.

The dead man's mouth was open and full of black feathers.

Tom had seen his share of violence, but never anything like this. Dark, dried blood marred the quilt, and some had pooled on the floor beside the bed. Light-headedness struck as he entered the room, and he put a hand on the dresser to steady himself. The night before he'd killed a man, maybe two, and he hadn't felt *this*. Last night, he had known exactly what was happening.

This, he didn't understand. An old man dying in his sleep was one thing, but it hadn't been Saul's heart or his lungs. It had been this knife.

Swallowing with a dry throat, Tom moved closer to the bed. The knife was the sort used for cooking.

He jerked the drapes aside, and the scene was no less ghastly in the light.

It wasn't just feathers in the man's mouth—there were twigs there as well, and maybe even parts of what might've once been a bird's nest.

Every bedroom in Friendly Field had a wooden cross hanging in it. Saul's was on the floor by the bed, broken into pieces.

Boards creaked; people were coming up the stairs. Jeremiah was the first through the door, Hattie O'Leary was with him, and Phillip tried to crowd in behind.

Hattie cried out and fell to her knees; Jeremiah tried to catch her, but just ended up going down himself.

Tom reached out to Hattie, but Jeremiah pushed him out of the way and lurched to his feet, mouth hanging open.

"God have mercy," he said.

Hattie let out of a sob; she didn't see Tom's hand held out to her, just Saul and that knife.

Phillip saw the body, but he only froze for a moment. He hauled Hattie upright and pulled her back to the stairs.

Jeremiah put his hands on his head, and he was starting to turn blue. Tom hit him on the shoulder.

"Breathe," he said.

Jeremiah did so, then set his jaw. The sound of his teeth grinding could probably have been heard in Connecticut.

There was more creaking from the stairs, but Tom didn't care who it was. There was something about the bloodstain that didn't look right, not that he'd seen *so* many men stabbed.

He jerked the knife out of Saul's breast, and Jeremiah made a choking noise. Tom drew back the quilt to reveal the wound.

There were two. The one that had killed him, and another just beside it, but perhaps less severe. Tom was no doctor.

That was enough. He put the knife down on the bed and turned his back on the scene before going to the window and opening it. The smell of the corpse ripening was weak, but it still made him ill.

Thaddeus reached the top of the stairs, gasping and sweating, and made it through the door.

"Oh, heaven," he said, and the words came out as faintly as a sigh.

Tom looked at each man for a moment, then left the bedroom and made his way downstairs. He didn't stop until he was on the porch, and there he sat on the step. The commotion hadn't gone unnoticed, and Phillip was trying to maintain some kind of order. Tom should've helped him, but he just looked up at the morning sky and the crows flapping around up there and cawing.

Even the ladies over at the White residence were on the porch, gazing across the grass as Eliza was led away, weeping.

The new lady, the housekeeper—it looked like she was watching from the window of Thaddeus' house, but Tom couldn't be sure.

It was fully ten minutes before Jeremiah and Thaddeus emerged.

"Everyone?" Thaddeus was asking, face gray.

"Yes." Jeremiah's voice was firm. Tom didn't look, but he heard the older man pause. "Go on," he said, and Thaddeus cast an uncertain glance at Tom before heading off into the grass.

"Friends," he announced, "everyone in the fields must come in. We must all gather in the church. Help me, George. Run out and find Sebastian and Hansel."

Tom didn't hear the rest; Jeremiah was standing beside him. Tom didn't have to look to know what kind of expression the other man had on. He gripped the banister and got to his feet.

"So the devil is here," Jeremiah said bitterly.

Tom snorted, and the other man looked over at him sharply.

"What?" he said. "Do you mean to say your outlaws are responsible?"

"No. But neither is the devil," Tom pointed out, and only after he said it did he remember whom he was talking to. There was no devil, no witchcraft—he knew that like he knew the sky was blue, but the Quakers didn't look at things the way he did.

"A murderer. Witchcraft," Jeremiah said, watching the people make for the church, more than a few of them turning to look back at the two figures on the porch. "I can hardly believe it."

He was telling the truth; his was the face of man questioning everything.

CHAPTER EIGHT

TOM WAS STANDING in the grass when he spotted
Asher approaching.

"Did you find it, kid?"

"What, Mr. Calvert?"

"What you were looking for. When we came here,"
Tom said as the last few Quakers disappeared into the
church. He and the kid were supposed to be there as
well, but he was dragging his feet. It would be time for
lunch soon, but in a few minutes food would be the last
thing on anyone's mind.

"I am not certain I understand you." Asher frowned
up at him, but he could sense that something was
wrong. He was wary.

"I guess I'm just glad we got to enjoy this place
while it was peaceful. For a little while. That was what
you wanted, wasn't it?"

"Peace is not what I came here to find," the boy replied. That was true; the kid hadn't ever said anything like that. *Tom* had been the one who wanted peace.

Tom snorted. "Fair enough. What *do* you want?"

"I will tell you when I find it."

That was as good an answer as any.

"What has happened?" the boy pressed.

"Someone killed Saul Matthews."

The boy took that in with surprisingly little difficulty. And why wouldn't he? Ever since he had met Tom, it seemed as though there'd been nothing but killing. Even Asher had been forced to take a hand in it, in a manner of speaking. After Tom was too far gone to see to things himself, the boy had hunted game for them, and cleaned and butchered the animals without assistance. He could handle a gun or a knife nearly as well as Tom could now. He wasn't as good a shot, but that would come in time—or perhaps not, not if Friendly Field suited him.

Tom wished Asher would just meet a girl he really liked. That had a way of changing things.

Mary was in that church, and any moment she'd find out what was going on. He swallowed.

"Mr. Calvert, who killed Mr. Matthews?"

"That's what I can't figure, kid. It wasn't the Porter gang. I can't think of a way that could be it. They used feathers, put them in his mouth. Same feathers as we saw on that thing you found. But if whoever made that was offended by us taking it, why not come for *us*? Why Saul? I don't know, kid. Let me think on it."

And they couldn't wait any longer. They went to the church and let themselves in, finding the whole pack of Quakers in shock. Tom pushed Asher toward the pews in the rear and limped into the aisle, making for the front.

Jeremiah and Phillip were up there, and Thaddeus

as well, but Thaddeus was off to one side, dazed. Jeremiah was the one doing the talking, but he paused at the sight of Tom.

Everyone watched as Tom limped past, sneezing; the air in the church always had a hint of sawdust.

The Quakers were all on their feet, and the men had their hats in their hands. There weren't many tears; they were all just stunned.

Tom made his way straight up to Jeremiah, who looked only mildly affronted.

"Yes?" the older man growled under his breath.

"The trouble only started when I got here," Tom told him quietly. There was no reason not to be blunt. "If you want me to say something or tell it all, I will."

Phillip's eyes became suspicious, and he stepped in close enough to join the conversation.

"No one has accused you, Mr. Smith."

"And I reckon they're too well-mannered to do it," Tom replied frankly. "But they'll all think it, as any reasonable people would, and you two as well. Hell," he muttered, and Jeremiah's eye twitched, but he didn't apologize, "I'm halfway suspicious myself. Secrets are bad business. We should clear the air, and if you all want me to leave, I will."

"Tom, are you a witch?" Jeremiah asked tiredly.

"I don't believe in witches."

"Did you murder Saul Matthews?"

"Of course not."

"Are you in league with these men in the woods?"

"No."

"Then if you want to leave, leave. If not, sit down," Jeremiah said firmly.

Taken aback, Tom straightened up. He swallowed, actually a little hurt. Then he ducked his head.

"Yes, sir. I apologize."

"None needed."

Shaken, Tom did as he was told and sat. Jeremiah motioned for the rest to do the same, and they did. The pews creaked, and the breeze caught one of the shutters that hadn't been tied. It banged against the wall, and a boy leapt up to go secure it. Phillip stood at Jeremiah's side, and they both surveyed the people gathered.

To Tom's eye, the Quakers weren't nearly shocked enough. Jeremiah had told them that Saul was dead, but he must not have told them that he'd been murdered. *That* was why Jeremiah didn't want Tom talking—or part of it.

Tom looked around, but Eliza, the girl who'd found Saul's body, wasn't in the church.

Jeremiah started to speak, but Tom didn't hear him. Someone had taken that object out of Thaddeus' house. Tom hadn't been bothered by that detail because he already knew that someone from Friendly Field had made it. Had he and Asher been seen finding it in the woods? How many people in Friendly Field had *known* that it was in that house?

Thaddeus, Jeremiah—likely Phillip, because Jeremiah seemed to tell him everything. Jeremiah's wife, Mrs. White, perhaps. Very little was lost on her. Who else?

Jeremiah was talking about Saul going home, being taken to heaven and so on.

No mention of murder or witches.

Tom let his breath out, discreetly watching the Quakers. He wasn't sure if Jeremiah's decision was shrewd or cowardly, but it was clear these people wouldn't take well to news of a murder in their village. He was a little surprised to hear the older man lie, but he couldn't find it in himself to disapprove. Jeremiah owed something to God, but he owed something to his people as well. If Thaddeus wasn't going to assert himself, that meant it was Jeremiah's choice to make.

There could be consequences, though.

Tom spotted Mary, who looked just as distressed as everyone else. And why not? Tom hadn't found Saul to have much presence, but he'd been reasonable and easy to deal with. These people had looked up to him.

"Phillip and I will handle the particulars," Jeremiah was saying. "We will hold service at sundown. May I lead a prayer now before we return to our tasks?"

There was a chorus of yeas, and Tom obligingly bowed his head, but he wasn't about to close his eyes.

There was a killer in Friendly Field—one who wasn't named Tom Calvert, no less.

These people had been a curiosity to him from the moment he first set foot in this place. Now he watched them as he'd never watched them before, and his eyes settled on one face in particular: that of Miss Adams, the girl newly arrived to be Thaddeus' so-called housekeeper. For a moment his heart stopped, but not because of her looks.

Tom had noticed her prettiness the first time he met her, more than a year ago. He'd noticed it again the *last* time he met her as well, aboard the *Newlywed*, where she had been plying her trade on the arm of a man Tom shot and killed a few hours later.

Her name was Holly, and though Tom had never known her family name, it probably wasn't Adams. He was startled to see her here with her head bowed. He was the last man to judge anyone for their means of

making a living, but one thing was certain: Holly was
no more a Quaker than he was.

D EATH WAS NOT new to Friendly Field. They'd been
in this place for nearly forty years.

The loss of Saul was different, though. It wasn't just
abrupt; he was also one of their leaders. A fixture. It
wasn't that he was well-liked; *everyone* in Friendly Field
was well-liked, more or less. Folks even found ways to
take Mrs. Heller in good humor. There was some dis-
approval of Holly—or Miss Adams—but if none of
that seemed to spill onto Thaddeus, then it seemed
likely that they would warm to Holly in time.

Assuming she planned to stay, and Tom wasn't sure
she did. He wouldn't know until he could talk to her,
and there was no telling when that would be. At one
time he wouldn't have thought twice about shirking his
chores to hold a conversation, but Jeremiah's rebuke in
the church had put him on his heels. This wasn't his
community; it belonged to the Quakers. He couldn't
just do as he pleased.

The distress in the sewing room was easier to understand this time, but the afternoon seemed to stretch
endlessly, and the service was even worse. Jeremiah
hadn't needed half the day to bury a body or prepare
some words; he'd needed it to decide if he was going to
stick to his lie.

He was; Tom heard that perfectly clearly, and it hurt
to see the other man this way. Saul's wife was dead, but
both his sons were still alive and married in Friendly
Field. Tom saw them trying to explain things to *their*
small children. He had shot more men than he could
reliably count; some of them had probably been fathers.

Tom had never known his own, and from what little his mother had told him of the man, that was for the best.

These people were different, and they were all out of luck. The Porter gang. This—this business with the feathers.

Saul must have had an enemy. But had he known he had one? That was the part that Tom couldn't stack up; unless he'd completely misjudged the man, Saul hadn't believed himself to be in danger. He hadn't seen it coming.

Τ HE HEAVY AIR over Friendly Field hadn't even begun to lift by the time Tom and Asher made it to Mary Black's door. Saul had been buried, words had been spoken, and there had been altogether too much praying. Tom didn't begrudge the Quakers their ways, but he believed Jeremiah needed to spend less time with his head bowed and his eyes closed, and more time with his eyes open looking for whoever had done it.

Saul must've known something about the business with the feathers. It was the only thing Tom could think of, but what could he have known that would have cost his life?

The sight of Mary brought him out of his thoughts. There was an exhaustion in her bearing and less color in her face. It meant something if she was suffering enough that she couldn't convincingly hide it, but that wouldn't stop her from trying. The food smelled heavenly; Mrs. Washburn had seen enough people come and go in her time that something like this wouldn't put her off her cooking.

Telling Mary she didn't have to try so hard wouldn't have helped any. It might've been better if Asher hadn't been there, because she certainly wasn't going to appear upset in front of him. On the other hand, it spared her the trouble of wondering if it was proper to be genuine with Tom. They liked each other plainly enough, but she had enough sense to remember that they'd only been acquaintances for a short time.

Good food was a waste on nights like this; no one tasted any of it.

"It was a strange look on your face," Mrs. Washburn said to Tom as they ate. "In the church today. Was it a dressing down that Jeremiah gave you?"

"It was. And I deserved it."

"What was your offense?"

"Being a busybody."

Mrs. Washburn's brows rose as she feigned surprise. "You, Mr. Smith?"

"Wouldn't be my first time."

Here it was; this nosy old woman wasn't blind. She knew something was wrong, and she wanted to know what it was.

"And into what manner of business did you try to insert yourself," she asked, "to find ire in Jeremiah White?"

"I expect his ire had less to do with anything in particular that I had done, and more with my habit of believing all the problems are mine to solve my own way," Tom replied. "I'm a stranger here, not well-known, and undeserving of the trust you've all placed in me already. It's not my place to tell anyone here what to do. It's presumptuous of me." That was a word he'd heard used but never used himself. He was fairly sure he'd used it right.

"But what did you presume to do?"

Stubborn old woman. He tried to think of an answer, but Mary rescued him.

"Mother, I believe you are prying."

"Who better to pry?" Mrs. Washburn shot back. "After all, Tom's the only halfway new thing to come to Friendly Field in a long time."

Holly was newer than Tom, but he couldn't point that out.

"Do you mean to say, Mrs. Washburn, that you know all there is to know about everyone else?" Asher asked mildly.

It warmed Tom's heart that he had two allies at the table. Not that Mrs. Washburn was his enemy; she was just every bit as much of a busybody as he was. He'd still play cards with her after dinner, if she was inclined—except no. *Was* she a busybody? Or was she just trying to get them talking to lift the mood, to bring some life to the table?

That was probably it. She was a clever woman, and Tom liked her more every day. He expected that he'd have liked her even if he wasn't courting her daughter.

"That is exactly what I mean to say," the old woman replied to the boy. "It's a small community, dear."

"I would concede that you surely must know the people," Asher said, his eyes on his plate. "What do you know of witches?"

Tom wouldn't have thought there was anything the boy could say that would have startled him as much it startled Mrs. Washburn and her daughter, but there it was. The question itself was hardly something one expected to hear over dinner, but more than that—well, it was the boy's *nerve*. That business was secret, more or less. The trinket, the feathers—he couldn't just go talking to the people of Friendly Field about witches. That was *Tom's* job. He'd fully intended to do it himself, but a good deal more discreetly.

Those thoughts went as quickly as they'd come, because Tom was far more interested in the two women. Mary had crumpled a bit, and a sudden vacancy had descended on her mother. It wasn't the surprise, or even outrage, that one might expect of pious folks confronted with such an ugly subject.

No, this was something else. Something more personal. It was the same reaction they'd had when they mentioned that hanging.

"My word," Mrs. Washburn said to Asher, though there was no surprise in her voice, just a bit of a chill. "Why do you ask?"

"I have heard things. When I was younger, from the preacher of our parish."

Tom didn't know if the boy was lying or not, and that was frustrating. Tom had been the one to coach him on his poker face, and there was no stopping him. Asher was taking it upon himself to fish for information, and Tom's pride at his initiative was locked in a fierce grapple with his fear that the kid would say something he shouldn't.

Jeremiah was irritated enough with Tom's meddling and his association with all this misfortune. Learning that Tom and Asher were the ones who got Friendly Field talking about witchcraft as well—that might even be enough to make a man of peace want to punch someone in the nose.

"He told us about the witches and signing the devil's book," Asher went on, still eating. "And it was very frightening. Business of candles and black feathers and strange rituals. I wondered if Friendly Field has ever seen anything to that effect."

"We have," Mary replied shortly.

To Tom's surprise, Mrs. Washburn had nothing to add. Mary took a moment with her hand on her tea before continuing. She had no choice but to continue; Asher was looking at her with such naked expectation that she couldn't do otherwise.

With a glance at her mother, she faced the boy across the table.

"There was someone here who practiced witchcraft. When it was discovered, she was hanged."

Asher took that in. "You did say someone had been hanged in the past. So that's who it was, then."

"Yes."

"I am surprised your ways allowed it," the boy remarked, and Tom realized he'd have to step in. He was just as interested as the kid was, but Mary didn't like talking about this, and Mrs. Washburn clearly liked it even less. They could get the same information from someone else.

"Let it go, kid."

"I apologize," Asher told Mary. "I found it fascinating, and I thought such a theologically minded community might have notions to share."

"I think of that time as little as possible," Mary told him, smiling. She noticed how shaken her mother looked, and frowned.

"Of course. It's unpleasant business," Tom remarked. "It must have been a shock to find something like that going on."

"It certainly was," Mary replied, and they left it there.

* * *

Asher took his leave after dinner, and Tom wasn't surprised when Mrs. Washburn did as well. She didn't want to play cards; Jeremiah's death and the talk of witchcraft had put her in a fouler humor than Tom had ever seen her in before.

The boy graciously apologized one last time before departing, and that was good of him. Mary was equally gracious, but that came easily to her. She followed Tom out onto the porch, and together they watched Asher stroll away across the dark field. It was all right for the two of them to be alone together this way, out in the open. Surely a few nosy Quakers would be watching from their windows. They had some degree of privacy, but no need to worry about anyone suspecting impropriety.

Mary drew her shawl close around herself and perched on one of the wicker chairs. Tom joined her without an invitation, maintaining an appropriate distance.

"The kid doesn't always have much sense," he said after a moment, and Mary waved a hand dismissively.

"It's all right," she said. "He couldn't have known." Her eyes narrowed. "How old is he?"

"I'm not rightly sure," Tom admitted. "He talks like he has the head of a grown man. Part of the time, at any rate. If he'd put on a little height, you wouldn't be able to keep the girls away. But he is odd."

She nodded, smiling. "She was a good friend of mine, you know."

"Who?"

"Vera."

"I don't know that I follow you."

Mary shook her head and hunched over a little, resting her chin on her hands. She glanced at Tom.

"She had the devil in her."

"Oh." Tom straightened up. She meant the woman who'd been hanged.

"She was the sweetest girl, and pretty. Pretty like him," she added, indicating Asher's retreating form with her eyes. "I never thought she would be spoken of that way."

Feeling something he didn't like in his belly, Tom waited in case she intended to go on. He didn't want to learn this from Mary; that wasn't why he was here. She wanted to talk, and he wanted to listen to her, not because of this terrible business, but because he liked her.

But he couldn't leave money on the table.

"The witchcraft with the feathers and such?" he asked uncertainly.

Mary nodded, and as she did, her eyes widened, as though she had just now begun to notice the cawing of the crows. It had been going on for a while; it was normal, a part of the day and evening. Tom had stopped noticing it shortly after arriving here. She swallowed.

"They say the black birds are the devil's fingers," she told him quietly. "I don't know what could have made Vera go to do those things. I can't even remember it anymore, what happened. Or I've tried to forget, I suppose."

"That would be hard to take. For anyone."

Tom couldn't let his skepticism show. He couldn't tell her she was a fool to believe in such nonsense, because that wasn't fair. She'd been born into this place. These teachings were all she'd ever known. There were things that Tom believed that were no less foolish. He could hardly fancy himself more sensible than anyone else;

the life he'd led wasn't something that anyone would admire.

She looked grateful. "Her in particular, though. I'm sure she never meant anyone any harm."

"You saw her hang?"

"No. I was . . ." And she sort of pointed up, likely toward her bedroom in the house. She sighed. "I didn't stop crying for a week."

"When did it happen?" Tom winced on the inside as he said it, but he couldn't help himself. He *had* to know. He was being a busybody, yes, but being a busybody wasn't *always* wrong. Was it?

She let out a long, shuddering breath, and he realized she was close to tears.

"You don't have to talk about it," he said quickly.

"No, it's all right."

Was it? Tom shut up and clasped his hands, keeping his eyes on her face.

"It's been a long time," she admitted, squinting up at the stars. "I've done a good job forgetting. I was young." Her voice was getting husky, but there weren't any tears in her eyes yet. "To lie down with the devil. I still wonder how it all happened."

The crows fell silent. The devil's fingers? Tom doubted it.

She abruptly sobered. "But it was years ago, and the devil has been gone from here since. It bothers Mother more than it bothers me. I was surprised she said as much as she did at dinner. She's more of a mind to tell you it never happened at all."

"I imagine a lot of folks feel that way."

Mary nodded. "It's in the past."

"I'm glad to hear it."

A little of the light returned to her eyes. "You are not afraid of him," she said, a hint of a smile on her face.

"Well, I haven't met him yet. I expect I will be if I ever do."

The smile grew. "That is very like you, Mr. Smith."

"My name isn't Smith. It's Calvert. The reason I don't go by it is because there's a chance, likely a very small one, that someone taking the potatoes to Des Crozet would mention it to someone, and that person might mention it to someone else, and it might come back to haunt me."

She looked taken aback. It couldn't have been a total surprise; surely Jeremiah or Saul or Thaddeus had spoken to her and her mother about Tom when they got acquainted.

"Are you such a villain that your name would be recognized?" she asked.

"I don't think of myself as a villain. If I have any notoriety, it won't be because of the wrong I've done. It'll be because of what I've done at the poker table. I'll risk sounding like a braggart, but the truth is I wasn't half-bad at cards when I was out and about."

She laughed. "I know that's no boast. I've seen you play with Mother."

"She's pretty good. Will she forgive the kid for bringing it up?"

"Of course."

"What about me?"

"You gave no offense," Mary said quickly.

"She doesn't mind a cripple courting her daughter?"

That brought a touch of color to her cheeks. Mrs. Washburn did not mind, but Tom wasn't really asking.

Mary kept her bearing. "I hope she will come around," she said gamely, "though she might remark that you appear to have misplaced your walking stick."

"I don't need it," he confessed. "I like it because the limp's not so obvious when I use it."

She looked sympathetic.

"What about you?" he went on. "What do you think?"

"I have no objections."

CHAPTER NINE

"I DON'T KNOW WHAT the hell this damn witchcraft-and-feather nonsense is supposed to mean," Tom grumbled to Asher as they sat at the rear of the church.

"I know what it means," Asher murmured back.

The church was full; if the community grew much more, they'd have to build a bigger one. Jeremiah was at the front, speaking. It wasn't his turn, but with Saul's death the day before, everyone wanted to hear from the elders. Thaddeus had already gone up there and read about a hundred verses from the Bible. Tom wanted to cut his ears off, then blow his brains out.

"Do you?" he whispered, glancing past the boy.

Holly was there, across the aisle. A family shared the pew with her, but several feet separated them. She was alone.

"A woman was hanged," the boy said. "*Someone* is not pleased about it."

"It happened years ago, maybe before you were born. If they're sore about it, why kill someone *now*?"

"Perhaps they only just found out," Asher whispered back.

Someone looked at them, and they fell silent.

"Friends, our blessings abound," Jeremiah was saying. "We have prospered to a measure that none of us would have thought to expect. The Lord has given and given, and we are occasionally reminded that he also takes."

Someone coughed, and someone else sniffled. All the windows and shutters were open, but it was overly warm regardless.

"If they cared enough to kill over it, they wouldn't wait ten years or fifteen years to settle it. They'd have found out in their own time." Tom was fairly sure of that.

"Perhaps they were lied to, and only now has the lie been exposed," Asher offered.

That was workable, but it didn't fit these people. They had their manners and their ways, but as Holly's arrival showed, there were still vices and difficulties. He wouldn't judge them for that.

They might not care for the notion of someone like Holly being brought to Friendly Field to provide companionship for Thaddeus, but that smudge on their values did not *threaten* them. Not the way that Saul's murder would.

Right now they were all but carefree. Sad for the loss of Saul, but otherwise well. Jeremiah wasn't lying; they were prospering. They didn't know about any of the trouble that might be brewing beyond their fields. As for back when that woman had been hanged, Tom hadn't been there. Things might've been different then.

Phillip stepped up beside Jeremiah and cleared his throat.

"I believe He reminds us not out of cruelty but because He sees our weakness. And He worries, as any parent would worry for their child or their kin. Mrs. Lester worries when she sees me pick up a kitchen knife because I've cut myself one too many times. He's no different, and I wonder if He worries that we are not so vigilant as we have been in past years." Phillip was what? Tom's age or a little older? He would've been fairly young when this witch had been hanged, but he'd remember it.

"It's a woman who killed him," Tom told Asher, watching the Quakers listen to Phillip and Jeremiah, rapt. "Vigilance" likely wasn't a word that came up often, and it had their attention.

"What?" The boy looked surprised.

"Who killed Saul."

"How do you know?" Asher hissed.

"Remember what those two said in the woods? They'd seen a woman up there where you found that thing. Whoever made it, whoever they saw—that's who stabbed Saul." Tom straightened a little and glanced toward Holly.

She was looking straight at him. He was a changed man, sitting in these simple clothes that the Quakers wore.

She still recognized him. He'd figured she would.

"You are certain? From only that?" Asher looked surprised.

"Not just that." Tom gestured at his chest, over his heart. "Easy and simple aren't the same thing, kid. Knives are simple, but they aren't easy. It's easy to point and pull a trigger, but to cut flesh—that's different. There were two wounds. The first wasn't much good, like she tried to stab him and thought twice, or thought it wouldn't take much strength. And then he woke up, and she stabbed him hard enough to put that knife in his heart."

Asher's eyes were wide. He swallowed.

"It's ugly, kid. Killing with a blade. I don't know that I could do it," Tom admitted.

The boy pulled himself together and sniffed. "I suspect you could," he whispered after a moment. "Provided you felt strongly enough about it."

"Maybe," Tom grunted.

"The devil has not come to this place for some time," Jeremiah said, giving those gathered an oddly direct look. "But we haven't forgotten him or his face. And we must not forget. We must remain vigilant, because he might yet return. I had very nearly forgotten him and what he's done, and who would blame me?" He spread his arms. "Do any of us look back on that with any fondness? Of course we don't. It still happened, even if I wish it hadn't. He came here. He came among us without us knowing."

"It could happen again," Phillip agreed. "We must be watchful."

"Smart," Tom said under his breath.

"To lie about what happened?" the boy asked.

"To put people on edge. We don't want them to panic, but we do want them to have their eyes open for anything strange. Let them worry a little. Someone might see something that matters, and this way they'll be more apt to tell someone. Jeremiah's got the right idea."

Tom fell silent as Mrs. White gave him a reproving look. Asher waited until she was looking away to reply.

"You do not believe in the devil?"

"Whoever killed Saul likely doesn't," Tom whispered. "She's just using him. She had her own reason for murdering Saul, and the feathers were just for show. To send us down the wrong trail."

"If that's true, why was that thing in the woods?" Asher countered, and it was a fair point. "That thing" hadn't been meant to be found.

Tom scratched his chin irritably. "You're right," he conceded.

"What if it's true?"

"What if what's true?"

Jeremiah was praying, and a hush had fallen. Tom and Asher waited patiently in silence. Phillip started reading from the Bible, and Asher gave a little shrug.

"The devil. Suppose he *was* here all those years ago, just as they say."

"And?"

"And now he has returned," the boy said.

"You got more sense than that, kid."

"Let's rise," Phillip announced, and Tom woke up. Not because everyone was standing, though that was happening as well. He woke up because he'd suddenly understood what just happened. His stomach did a flip.

"Did you see that?" he muttered.

"What?" Bewildered, Asher stood up beside Tom.

"Phillip Lester just became the new Saul Matthews."

The boy didn't get to reply; the hubbub of the Quakers had filled the church, and they were all moving around, shaking hands and such. It was a strange thing; they worked long, exhausting days—but they still took breaks; they still had their evenings to spend more or less as they pleased. They had time to mingle this way whenever they liked, yet they *still* did it during services. They would be doing this for twenty long minutes or even more—they seemed to enjoy it so much, and Jeremiah would likely let it stretch on, on account of Saul's death and because he wanted to cheer folks up.

Tom stood like a statue, his eyes fixed on Phillip at the front of the church, embracing Sebastian.

There really wasn't any question that the Quakers' notion of no leaders was nonsense. Jeremiah, Thaddeus, and Saul—it had been those three, and everyone had seemed content.

Had Phillip *not* been content? What did he have to gain from taking Saul's place? What did the leaders have that the others didn't? They ate the same food; they lived in the same houses. There was some . . . prestige associated with it, Tom supposed, but most of these Quakers really were more interested in what God thought of them than what other people did.

Thaddeus had the privilege of hiring a girl like Holly to keep his bed warm, but it seemed unlikely that Phillip would envy an arrangement like that. He was married to a fine woman, and he had children.

What if it wasn't Phillip behind it, then? What if the murder hadn't been to make a new leader but instead to remove an old one? Had Saul been on poor terms with Jeremiah and Thaddeus? Was this their doing? Why? Surely there was another way to be rid of Saul if that was what they'd wanted.

It didn't make sense to kill him, particularly for people who were, rather pointedly, not inclined toward killing in the first place.

No one wanted to shake Holly's hand. She startled when Tom pulled her behind one of the beams. For a moment she was tense, but upon seeing it was him she relaxed. That was an odd reaction; she'd been aboard the *Newlywed* when Tom lost his temper and threw his life away.

"You aren't afraid of me?" he asked.

"No. I've got your measure." That was why he'd liked her back when they first met. "You look different," she added quietly.

"I like to think I *am* different," Tom replied, leaning in so they could speak quietly. "How much is Thaddeus paying you?"

"You want to make me a better offer?"

"I just want to know he's treating you all right."

"He's harmless. Five dollars a day."

Tom balked. That was—well, that was a problem for two reasons. First, it was an immoral expenditure of Friendly Field's money. It *was* Friendly Field's money. It came from the men in the fields. The boys as well, and Asher. Tom didn't begrudge Thaddeus some company— it was a fair enough thing to want—but to pay that much for it when the money wasn't really his?

Tom could see Thaddeus up there at the front of the church. Tom had to be honest with himself, even if he wouldn't be with other people. He was more inclined to see Thaddeus as a fool than as a villain. It was more likely this was an act of stupidity than of callousness. Thaddeus wasn't young anymore, and Tom had begun to see that Friendly Field really had had only two leaders. Now it had two again, and Phillip would probably be a decent one.

That was, provided he hadn't murdered Saul Matthews. And Tom was fairly sure he hadn't, at least not with his own hand.

And there was the second thing. Holly? Five dollars a day? Tom had spent a mere two nights with her, and if his memory served, it had cost him considerably more than that. Admittedly, he was always generous with girls—but the point was that Holly could have made a hell of a lot more money just about anywhere else.

"How long you been here?" she asked him bluntly, searching his face.

"Just a couple weeks," he replied, staring back just as hard.

"It's good to see you, Tom. I'm glad you're alive."

Tom had questions, but he'd spotted Mary—and she'd spotted him. He remembered himself and hurriedly drew back from Holly. The instant he moved, Mary did too, but Tom wasn't about to let her run away. He'd seen what misunderstandings had done to his life in the past, and he'd be damned if he'd let that happen again.

Threading through the Quakers, he pursued her to the rear of the church, where she opened the door and went out into the sunlight, or at least tried.

She was frozen in place, though, and he nearly ran into her.

He saw what had made her stop. There was a mare in front of the church, and a man feeding her sugar from his hand. He looked over as the door opened and smiled. The sun was bright on his perfect white shirt, stitched with blue flowers. He was Tom's age, and clean-shaven. His sleeves were rolled up, revealing tanned, muscled forearms, and his boots were black.

Tom did what he'd done a thousand times before.

He put on his poker face, moving past Mary and limping out into the open.

"Good morning," he called out. "Peace be with thee."

The man smiled. "Well, uh—same to you, partner."

Tom reached him and put his hand out. The other man shook.

"My name's Tom," he said. "Welcome to Friendly Field."

"It's good to know you, Tom. My name's John."

It was true; his name was John Porter, and Tom knew his face from the posters. He was worth ten thousand dollars.

PART TWO

DEAD OR ALIVE

CHAPTER TEN

Tom was a little surprised he hadn't run into more outlaws in his time playing cards. After all, men chose to rob banks because banks were where the money was. Well, there also tended to be a fair amount of money where good poker players sat down together.

No one had ever tried to rob Tom or a game he was playing in. He'd heard of those things happening to others, but that misfortune had never come his way. He liked to think he'd have killed anyone who might try anything like that, but it was just as well not to have to.

That luck had just run out.

With a grin that sparkled, John turned in a full circle, taking in Friendly Field. It wasn't much of a settlement, but the impeccable neatness of it all still made it something to look at.

"What a thing," he said. "I never knew you all were here, so close to Des Crozet."

"Is that where you ride out of?" Tom asked, stifling

a yawn as Mary disappeared back into the church. She would bring Phillip and Jeremiah—or possibly everyone— but there wouldn't be any cause for alarm. John Porter was an outlaw, but they didn't know that. Only Jeremiah knew of what had happened in the woods, and this man was perfectly dressed and groomed. The sight of him wouldn't be enough to bother anyone. The sense of friendliness came off him like heat from a rock in the sun.

"It is," John lied. He hadn't come from Des Crozet. "Friendly Field, huh? That kind of name makes you want to visit, don't it?"

"You won't believe it, but I know a kid who drove a wagon more than six months to come here, knowing not a thing more than the name." Tom folded his arms. "What brings you to us?"

"Well," John replied, taking off his hat. He squinted, turning it over in his hands. "I'm a banker. And when I learned there was a town without a bank, I had to see it for myself. Of course, 'town' ain't quite the word."

"God has more sway here than the taxman. I can't see that we'd get much use out of a bank," Tom told him frankly. He scratched his head and shrugged. "Unless the bank's meant to hold potatoes."

"Potatoes," John echoed, gazing past Tom toward the fields. "I see that. Well, I don't suppose you might have met my friends. A tall fellow named Ben, and one about my height. Both of 'em very crude and disagreeable."

"Does the shorter fellow wear a . . ." Tom trailed off, gesturing at this throat.

John's eyes brightened. "He *does*."

"Course, yeah. Here, come with me." Tom put a friendly arm around the man's shoulders and led him away from the church. "Pious folk, you know. Quakers and all. They're worshipping in there, and a man passed yesterday, so they're a little touchy."

"Ain't you one of them?" the man asked, snorting.

"Lord knows I'm trying to be, but I've only been here a couple weeks. I'm not much good at it yet. So your friend—and just like you said, another fellow, real tall—well, they turned up a couple nights back, drunk from head to toe. The tall one couldn't even speak. And they were none too pleasant. Now, my nephew put them to bed. And the strangest thing happened."

John Porter was rapt. "What?"

"They weren't there in the morning. Neither was the silver, and a blanket, and a fair amount of dry beef. And," Tom went on as John opened his mouth, "my neighbor's daughter told everyone she was sure there was someone at her window that night. So I tell you what, John. I don't know you well, but I reckon someone ought to have a word with those friends of yours."

John let out an incredulous breath and gave an exaggerated shrug.

"I'd *love* to do that," he said, and Tom was inclined to think he meant it, "if I could just figure where the hell they went to."

"They didn't go back to Des Crozet?" Tom rubbed his cheek. "They didn't have mounts, but you could walk it. It's all they could've done. We looked for them ourselves on account of they were so sick from drink, they could do themselves harm. I was sure they must've walked to Des Crozet."

"I don't believe they did." John folded his arms and bit his lip, gazing out at the fields. "*Where* would they go to? There isn't anything else like y'all around here, is there? Another camp I ain't heard of?"

"No one nearer than Des Crozet, surely."

"I didn't think so." John snorted again and crammed his hat back onto his head, glancing past Tom. The church doors were opening, and Jeremiah was coming out in the lead with Phillip—and it was just the two of them.

Tom could picture what had happened. Mary had gone to Jeremiah, who had in turn told everyone to stay in their pews. There had been a murder here, and he was wary now. Wariness didn't come easily to him, but he was capable of it. Saul wouldn't have known danger if it had been chewing on his leg, and Thaddeus wasn't any better. Jeremiah was like Phillip, though. He could be counted on.

"Gentlemen," Tom said, waving them over. "This is John. He's come to visit us. He's a friend of those two we met the other evening that were so sick with drink, then vanished in the night. I know I've asked you both before, and you didn't know where they'd gone, but I wonder if you've heard anything from anyone. Have we seen those two fellas?"

Jeremiah couldn't hide his displeasure, but that was all right. *John* didn't know that it was displeasure at being dragged bodily into a lie—he'd think Jeremiah was angry because Ben Garner and Scarf must've been terrible guests.

John might've already found one or both of the bodies, or he might have Scarf home safe—and heard his story. Tom couldn't predict every outcome or make provision for every possibility, but he was doing one thing very well: confusing the hell out of John Porter.

And praise the Lord, Jeremiah and Phillip had the sense not to undercut him.

"I don't know," Jeremiah said, and most of the bewilderment in his voice was real. "Peace be with thee."

John grimaced and nodded. He tipped his hat. "Well, I'm real sorry to disturb y'all. Just looking for my friends."

"No disturbance," Tom told him. "Stay and eat with us. Service is about over. We'll be cooking here any minute."

The man looked genuinely tempted. After a long moment, he sighed.

"I'd better not. But if'n I can impose just momentarily, let me speak to your mayor. Or your lawman. I know my friends are a pain in the ass on their best day, so . . ." He trailed off, pointing at them knowingly. "I got a notion of what you been through. I'd like to apologize."

Jeremiah spread his hands. "No apology needed. And God is our mayor, sir."

"No apology? They stole from you," John pointed out, frowning.

"What?" Phillip couldn't help himself.

Tom waved if off. "Asher's candlesticks. Some food. It's nothing that's going to harm anyone."

"Oh."

"That's awful Christian of you," John said.

"Well, we do try. You sure you don't want to eat with us? These folks know more ways to fix potatoes than you'd believe," Tom told him truthfully.

The outlaw smiled. "No, I'd best be going. I can't eat when my friends could be in trouble. It's real good to make your acquaintance."

"Will we see you again, John?" Tom asked as the other man climbed into the saddle and patted his mare's head.

"Oh, I'm sure," John replied. He tipped his hat again, cantered just enough that the hooves wouldn't kick up the dirt onto the three of them, then pushed to a gallop.

"Son of a bitch," Tom muttered.

CHAPTER ELEVEN

"Mr. calvert, i have never wished to put my hands on another man before," Jeremiah growled as he followed Tom into the house. He'd probably never growled before, either.

Tom didn't care; he wasn't afraid of any Quaker, let alone one twice his age.

He was afraid of a notorious band of outlaws, as any reasonable man would have been.

Phillip shut the door of Jeremiah's house behind them and didn't say a word. His nerves were evident from the tremble in his hands and the wild look in his eyes. Phillip had a head on his shoulders and it was a cool one, but he was still a Quaker. Yes, he'd come to Friendly Field ten years ago as a young man—but Tom had learned that he'd come *from* another pack of Quakers to marry a Quaker girl. He'd had no more dealings with outlaws than Tom had, and the notion clearly terrified him.

"I had to learn things from him, and lying was the best way to do it," Tom replied, waving a hand. "That was John Porter, for God's sake."

"Now *we* are a part of your lie," Jeremiah said. "Deceit is *never* the best way."

"You want me to tell him the truth? That I shot both his men in the woods?" Tom shook his head. "No, I don't think that'd have done us any better."

"Why would you *do* such a thing?" Phillip's voice came out slightly shrill.

"Because, while I can't speak for John Porter, I *know* that those two had designs on Friendly Field. I heard it from their own mouths. I told you this. And, more immediately, I had to protect the kid. They might well have done for us right there if I hadn't shot first."

"Do you see a pistol on my belt, Mr. Smith?" Jeremiah asked tightly. "God protects this community. *We* do not take lives, even if it is for our own protection." He was going to go on, no doubt to talk about how the son of God wouldn't even lift a finger in his own defense— even Tom knew that part—but they didn't have time for that.

"Don't you?" Tom raised an eyebrow. "I bet that witch you hanged would have a question or two about that. And where was God when someone was stuffing feathers in Saul's mouth?"

That shut them both up, but not for long—these people might not know how to fight, but they sure as hell knew how to argue. They never let Tom see it, but he wasn't stupid.

"I would rather die doing God's will than live and carry the weight of that sin," Jeremiah said, though it was very nearly a snarl.

"And I'm not insulting you or trying to say otherwise," Tom fired back, raising his voice enough to cow the older man, "because I'm already carrying all that, and I don't like it much. I don't want your blessing, and I'd think less of you if you gave it. But I don't have the same faith you have. If I did, I wouldn't feel the need to do things myself. But here we are." Tom spread his hands. "God didn't save Saul, and I don't have a single solitary reason to think He'll save you. You don't have to like it. And you don't have to like me, but I like you. That's why I'm not about to let John Porter make himself at home here."

"You're doing this because it's the only thing you know how to do," Phillip snapped. "And you've put us all in danger."

Someone moved past the window, and they all turned to look. Tom reached over and pulled the curtains irritably.

"You were already in danger. What I've done is let you know it's coming."

"I already carried word to Des Crozet, and I believe that word will be our salvation." Phillip had some of his confidence now. "If you don't have faith in God, have faith in greed. These men are worth money, aren't they?"

"They are, and I have complete faith that someone will come. What I don't know is when—" Tom was cut off by a knock at the door.

Jeremiah opened it to reveal Mrs. Lester, who appeared concerned.

"We need a little time," Phillip told her over Jeremiah's shoulder.

Three men standing in a dim house with the curtains

drawn and no lamp while everyone else was outside eating—well, Tom didn't care what it looked like. He had bigger problems.

"Please," Jeremiah added.

She nodded, even more worried, and shut the door.

"Is this what you want?" Phillip asked. "Chaos?"

That took Tom off guard. "What?"

"Outlaws in the woods. Feathers and skulls. Saul." The big man threw up his arms in exasperation. "It's all to do with you, Tom."

"Maybe it's you who should be under suspicion—you're the one who got a promotion out of it."

Phillip balked, and Jeremiah's eyes widened.

"A—a promotion," Phillip echoed. His hands became fists.

"He must've had an enemy," Tom told him frankly, "because your friends don't put a knife in your heart and feathers in your mouth. And there isn't any damn witch. I think you both know it. Someone used those feathers because they knew about the woman you hanged and thought it would throw us all off. It was real smart to hide it from everyone, but it doesn't make the problem go away. You still have a murderer here and no idea who it is. But I'll tell you something—it's not me or you," Tom said, pointing at Phillip, "or any man. The one who did it is a woman."

Jeremiah narrowed his eyes. "How can you know that?"

"Because the outlaws saw a woman in the woods. She's who made that *thing* we found, she's who stole it back out of Thaddeus' house, and she killed Saul. Who is it? Who didn't like him?" Tom looked back and forth between the two of them. "Was it Eliza?"

"What?"

"Did Saul take advantage of her? Did they have an arrangement? Like Thaddeus has with Miss—Miss Adams?"

Jeremiah's face went beet red, but he caught himself. Then he shook his head. "No. No, Saul never did that."

"How do you know? Can you see through walls?" Tom pressed. "I don't know who this woman is, but I know something about her. She's angry. She's been wronged."

Jeremiah and Phillip shared a long look. The older man sighed and went to the table, pulling out a chair to sit. He put his elbows on the rough wood and clasped his hands.

"That hanging happened before I even came here," Phillip pointed out. "More than ten years ago, closer to twenty, I thought. Eliza's hardly older than my daughter. Even if Saul did something wrong to her, she can't remember that witch, let alone think to *use* that business in this way. She is a sweet girl. She isn't disposed to scheming."

"Someone could've told her," Jeremiah said, rubbing his eyes. "Saul—I never thought he would do that."

"It might not have been her. It could've been any woman with a pleasing figure. The outlaws commented on that. They didn't see her face, but they liked what they did see." Tom leaned against the mantel. "And maybe Saul didn't put his hands on anyone. There's more than one way to give offense, and I didn't know the man well. But he offended *someone*. You see that, don't you?"

"Yes, yes." Jeremiah groaned.

Tom hesitated, then joined him at the table. He took

a moment to let some of the irritation go, then softened his voice.

"Listen, fellas. I spent a long time by myself. Always plenty of people around, other players and such. Always a pretty girl for the night. But it was really just me and the next stagecoach. For a *long* time," he repeated. "It's not the same here. I got the kid to think about, and it's no secret that I'm sweet on Mary Black. I liked your way of doing things, at least when there wasn't any trouble. But it's different now."

"What if I told you that you were no longer welcome in Friendly Field?" Jeremiah asked.

"I'd leave," Tom replied easily. "Of course, you aren't the mayor. And it's not your way to turn folks away."

"As you reminded us, exceptions have been made," the older man ground out.

Tom didn't blame him for this; in fact, he was glad of it.

"Something tells me you aren't likely to say that. I've already told you what I've done. I know all about that weight you're afraid to carry. That's the trouble." Tom made sure he caught Jeremiah's eye. "I *can* carry it. It might make me miserable, but I'll still be standing at the end of the day. What I can't do is just sit here and wait for the Porter gang to ride into a town of Quakers with no leader, no lawman, and no means to defend themselves. Not when that kid is here, not with Mary here. It's not that I won't let it. It's that I can't."

"What are you planning to do? Kill them?" Phillip asked, now more tired than angry.

"No. Even I wouldn't try to draw down on a whole gang, unless it's an awful small gang, and I gave you my gun anyway. I'll do what I'm good at. I'll lie to them."

Tom leaned back with his hands behind his head. "I figured my bluffing days were over, but I guess the joke's on me. Again." He gave a little shrug. "I'll talk them into moving on to someplace else. There's no sense hoping they'll do it of their own accord. You heard it from John Porter's mouth. He'll be back."

"You make it sound simple."

"Let me worry about that. You got your own worries," Tom pointed out. "I'm guessing this woman killed Saul to settle a grudge. Now, provided that was her only grudge, things ought to go back to how they were. But I've been wrong before. You'd better find out who did it."

"Are you the mayor now?"

"No. But if I were you, I'd sleep easier knowing what really happened and that it wasn't likely to happen again. And if I am wrong, anyone could be in danger. Suppose it *is* a woman who believes in witchcraft and the devil. Or take it further and suppose it *is* the devil who's got a hold on one of your people—you can't just let it lie and hope it'll go away."

"I know all of this, Mr. Smith." Jeremiah straightened up, and Tom saw that it was true. It might've appeared as though he seemed content to simply move past it all, but he wasn't. He hadn't stopped thinking about it. The trouble wouldn't be finding Saul's killer—the town was too small for her to stay hidden for long. Once someone started asking questions, it would come out.

The trouble was what they'd do when they found her.

CHAPTER TWELVE

A LIE WAS LIKE a saloon, a card game, or a bear trap: getting out was never as easy as getting in.

Tom was used to being the object of curiosity in the sewing room. It had begun this way, with the curious looks and the polite silence. Then the women had gotten over that and questioned him ruthlessly to satisfy their curiosity about the outside world.

Now they were back to the silence.

The whole village had been in the church, watching the three of them speak to John Porter. As far as they were concerned, the man was just a traveler who'd gone on his way, and no cause for alarm—yet these people weren't blind or deaf. They knew something wasn't right. Jeremiah had given it away with his words during the service; apparently it was unlike him to preach that way, and Tom wasn't surprised.

Everyone in Friendly Field knew something was

wrong, but they couldn't ask about it because they didn't know what to ask.

When the day's work was done, the sun set on a lot of uneasy Quakers, more than a few of them casting worried glances at the road. But the road led south, and Porter had used it to give the impression that was where he was coming from. He and his gang were more likely somewhere to the east, and after talking to a few of the men around Friendly Field, Tom had a fairly good idea where. The men didn't often go far beyond their fields, but they had the lay of the land, and it sounded as though there was a valley among those hills that would make a comfortable place to camp awhile: plentiful game, a stream and a pond, and even some trees with nuts.

Charming.

Mary's windows were wide open, and the house was brightly lit. That was unusual for her, but Tom was too exhausted from the day to be curious. He knocked, and Mary answered. Rather than ushering him in as she usually would, she stayed in place, blocking the doorway.

Tom could smell the food, fresh rolls chief among the scents. Sometimes worry and nerves could take his appetite away, but not tonight.

"Mr. Smith."

"I wish you'd just call me Tom."

"My mother's gone to stay with Mrs. Beckett and Mrs. McHenry." She was visibly troubled. "She tells me it's because she's in a foul humor and doesn't want me to have to suffer it."

"But you're worried she's ill." It didn't take a great mind to work out that much.

"Yes," she admitted, scowling.

Tom sighed. "I guess you can't be alone with me, can you?"

"We could eat outside," she suggested.

That was a relief. It wasn't until he sat down with her on the porch that he realized how wound up he'd become. It wasn't as though he'd never felt nerves before, but never quite like this. And it wasn't just nerves; it was his temper. It was the injustice of it. By all accounts, Friendly Field had been nothing but peaceful over the past several years. Why should all this happen the moment he got here? It wasn't fair. He was willing to sit and sew. In fact, he was getting along well enough without his stick that he might even be able to make a go of working the fields. He was willing to sit in service, and willing to sit with Mary on the porch to eat a meal because they couldn't be alone together behind a door. Balancing a plate on his knees and trying to eat like he had some dignity was one of the most difficult things he'd ever done, but Mary made it look easy.

All of that, he could live with.

But he saw Saul in his mind, the knife still sticking out of him. He remembered the Pinkerton in his hotel room, back when he and the kid had still been with the wagon train. Tom hadn't stabbed the Pinkerton; that man had fallen on his own knife. All his fear and tension came back at the memory of it, and the smells as well—of the room, of the outhouse where he'd gotten rid of the body.

"Tom?"

He grimaced. "I'm all right. I apologize."

"You don't seem well."

Mary was no gossip, and Tom trusted her. But it wouldn't have been right to give up Jeremiah's trust or to give her that burden.

"It's better if I don't talk too much," he said honestly. "Jeremiah's trusting me to be discreet. I know you'd never tell. But I shouldn't."

She didn't look happy, but she understood.

"There's always something," Tom went on. "I shouldn't be mixed up in it. It shouldn't be my business, but it seems I do that. I never got to be a busybody when I was on my own because there wasn't anyone around I cared to meddle with. Then the kid came along, and now I'm just in everyone's business."

"Better a busybody than cold and selfish."

"Oh, it's selfish," Tom said, laughing quietly. "It's all for myself in the end, I'm sure. Does your mother often go to be a guest of the McHenry house?"

"Now and then. She's grumpier each day." She gave Tom a grateful look. "Playing cards with you gave her something to look forward to."

"For me as well. I'll be just as bad-tempered when I'm her age."

"I'm sure."

The crickets filled the silence, and Tom looked out at the Ford house, where Asher was eating dinner. He could hold Mary back, but he couldn't lie to the kid about what was coming.

It was *possible* that it could all be settled without the majority of the Quakers ever being the wiser. That would be the best outcome, but Tom couldn't guarantee that, and he knew it. Less fuss would mean less ire from Jeremiah, and that would be good for his prospects. He had to try to clean all this up quietly.

"Where are you?" Mary asked softly. "Where is your mind?"

"Oh, off in those hills," Tom replied, pointing northeast. She laughed. "It's pretty country," he added, shrugging. "But I'd rather be here with you. If I had it my way, I might not ever leave this porch."

"I think you'd want to come in when the snow starts," she replied, laying down her fork and knife. "To get warm."

Tom didn't have to wait for the snow; he wanted that now. Instead of saying that, he smiled.

"It's warm enough. And it'll get worse before it gets better." He peered into the evening. "I'd wager your summers aren't easy."

"Not in the fields," she replied. "And it's no better in a stuffy room."

Tom wasn't sure which would be worse. But even so, there was no desire to do anything else. A few months ago he never would've been able to convince himself that he wouldn't spend every waking moment thinking about cards. Now they seldom crossed his mind. He didn't *want* to leave Friendly Field and go back to all the hotels and saloons. He'd need his gun back for that, and he'd have to . . . wake up. He'd have to start watching his back again.

It was odd, because that had never bothered him when he'd been doing it, so why should it feel so much better now that he didn't have to? Or maybe he should be more careful; after all, he could easily be wrong about everything to do with Saul's death. For all Tom knew, someone was going to stick a knife in him next.

Well, they could try.

Mary took his plate from him, but didn't stand up.

Tom didn't know what to say, and even if he did, he wouldn't have known how to say it. He was overwhelmed, and Friendly Field had never been quieter. The tranquillity was like a silk sheet just draped over the town, keeping everything else out so he could be alone with Mary. It was exactly what he wanted, and he couldn't imagine anything better.

But he couldn't forget Saul Matthews or John Porter. It couldn't be done.

That irked him.

"I don't know you," Mary said.

"I know." Tom sighed and leaned forward, clasping his hands. "But you know I'd tell you anything."

"You won't, though." She returned his smile, and she had him there. She was completely right, and he was ashamed for saying it.

Tom could hold his ground. Would she fault him for it? Maybe, but . . .

"Trust," he said, shaking his head. "Bluffing's just lying. I did it so much, and I still do. You ever done something so much that you forget how to do anything else?"

"Smiling," she replied, smiling.

He snorted. "Yeah. You still want to ask me things, even when you know you won't like what you get?"

"I'm not making any demands, Tom."

"But you'd like to. And you've got a right to do it."

"Your life before you came here is not my business."

"It is if you think I might become a part of your life."

"No," she replied, shaking her head. "Would you consider yourself entitled to every detail of mine if I were to become a part of yours?"

"No, but I have no call for concern about you. You're a good woman. You've led a good life. I'm different, and you've got a right to be suspicious of me. I'm a professional liar. And I'm not a criminal, but I am a killer."

There was only a twitch to indicate that had struck

her. Tom hadn't kept that a secret from Thaddeus and the others, but it hadn't been advertised. He'd certainly never come out and said it this way to her. He should have, much sooner.

"Have you done soldiering?" she asked.

"No," he replied, gazing straight at her. "I never killed for this country or any other one. I've done it to protect myself. I've done it to protect the kid." He straightened up and glanced around at the other houses. "And I've done it because I lost my temper."

For a moment there was just quiet. She started to take a breath, like there was something she wanted to say, but Tom beat her to it.

"And one more reason," he said. "I did it because I couldn't let a loose thread hang. I killed a man because if I hadn't, he'd eventually have come after me and the kid. Can't leave a job half-finished," he said, sniffing and rubbing his nose. "That's what I thought at the time. But I wish I hadn't done it. There was probably another way. . . . I've been thinking about it ever since, and I can't stop."

"How many have you killed?"

Tom felt his brows rise. He opened his mouth, then shut it. He shrugged and gestured vaguely.

She swallowed, eyes wide.

He licked his lips. "For a long time, it was two," he said. "And then I met the kid, and . . ." He shook his head. "Things started happening. It's not his fault. I expect in the end it's mine."

"He's not your nephew."

"No, he's just some kid. He made a mistake, and I helped him. Then I made a mistake, and he helped me. I tried to look after him, and he ended up looking after me. He's the only reason I'm still alive."

"You helped him first?"

Tom nodded, smiling at the memory. He'd caught Asher trying to rob a cabin on the riverboat. The kid had been terrified in that moment. How had he changed so much in less than a year? The boy had a much cooler head, and he wouldn't have any trouble in a pinch like that now. Asher could fend for himself.

"Why?"

Tom leaned back. "I don't know. Why not? Do you want to know about Miss Adams?"

That took Mary aback, but she shook it off. "I'm more particular about the killing, I think." That was what she said, but, yes, she did want to know.

"Fair enough. I've met her before. In the church, I was asking her what brought her here."

Mary nodded, and it wasn't necessary to say more about that. He still hadn't answered her real question. She wanted the truth, and not the truth about his past. That stood to reason; she was a sensible woman, so of course the present was a more pressing concern. Tom had already made up his mind.

"It's Saul," he told her, lowering his voice. There was no one about, but sound wanted to carry in this quiet. "He didn't die in his sleep. Well, he did—but someone killed him."

Several moments went by, and she looked at him as though she expected him to say something more. When he didn't, she frowned and glanced at her hands, folded on her knee.

"Murder?" she asked hesitantly.

"Yes. And that man outside the church? He's an outlaw. And I worry that he and his men may come here and make trouble." Tom held up two fingers. "Those two things are what have me troubled."

Mary took that in.

"That's the truth. Are you sorry you asked?"

She shook her head, grimacing. "Saul was *murdered*?" It came out in a whisper. "There has never been a murder in . . ."

"I know." Tom rubbed his chin. "I don't have it figured yet myself, but he must've done something to someone. It's the only thing I can think of. Look at Thaddeus. Nobody's perfect. Not me, for certain. I suspect he made a mistake, and it caught up to him. If we work out what he did, we'll know who killed him."

"And then what?"

"I don't know. I'm not the sheriff."

Mary tried to smile but couldn't. Tom didn't blame her.

"I'm sorry," he said.

"You did warn me," she said, and there was an encouraging hint of dryness there.

"I hope you'll keep that to yourself."

"Of course." She wasn't thinking of telling anyone; she was just trying to make sense of it all. "And outlaws," she murmured, and by her voice she might as well have been talking about creatures from fairy tales.

"I know. As though a murder isn't enough."

Her knuckles were white on her apron. "What do they mean to do?"

"I don't know. And I hope we never find out."

Mary nodded but stayed silent. Tom did too. He'd said enough or even too much. It was selfish to risk the secrecy this way, but he cared about Mary a good deal more than he cared about Jeremiah. What she thought of him mattered. Jeremiah's good opinion? Tom could live without it.

A few lights were going out. It was too early for

Tom, but these folks worked hard. It was the smart ones who made a point to get their rest. And Tom? He didn't want to rest. He wanted Mary, and he wanted to tell her so, but he couldn't. He wasn't shy, but it wouldn't be right. It wouldn't be fair to put her in that position.

It was getting cooler, and he rolled down the sleeves of his shirt.

"Do you think you could trust me?" he asked. "One day?"

She hesitated a moment; then that look was in her eyes, the one that made her seem like anything but a Quaker. It was the kind of confidence that Tom had seen in good cardplayers. A sort of calm.

"I believe I could," she replied, and it was fairly convincing.

But Tom read people for a living, or he had once. She wasn't lying. She meant what she said, but the confidence underneath it—that was a little much. She was trying too hard.

"You don't need to be afraid," he told her. "What happened to Saul—it's got nothing to do with you. I know it's awful, but you're not in any danger." Anyone would feel unsafe if someone they knew was killed. It was normal for her to feel this way, mere minutes after hearing the news. "And those outlaws—you don't need to worry about them."

"Oh?"

Tom nodded. "No one's going to bother you, Mary. I promise."

CHAPTER THIRTEEN

THE FIREFLIES WERE out, and the purple in the sky was all gone. Night had come to Friendly Field, and it was getting too chilly for Mary. Tom didn't want to leave her porch, but he couldn't let her freeze. He remembered chasing after the kid, if "chasing" was the word for his ragged limp, when those Shoshone had him. He'd dragged himself through the snow in spite of his weakness, falling and clawing his way upright over and over.

Getting up and saying good night to Mary felt even more arduous than that.

She went into the house, and the longing look she gave him before she did it was equal parts gratifying and frustrating. Mary wouldn't have minded a stolen kiss, but she'd have regretted it. If the judgment from the others didn't get to her, her own guilt would. Tom didn't think it was anything to feel guilty about, but he knew he had a lot of work to do before he could see things the way the Quakers did.

He wanted to, though.

Phillip's door opened, and he emerged, coming purposefully off his porch. He met Tom in the middle of it all, hooking his thumbs into his suspenders. He must've been watching from his window and waiting.

"Peace be with thee," Tom said as he approached.

"And also with you. Can we talk, Tom?"

"You don't have the wrong idea, do you? I never even went in the house," Tom said, glancing back toward Mary's place. "I've been very proper."

"I know you have. I'm worried."

"About Saul or John Porter?"

"Both."

"So you should be." Tom folded his arms and faced him. This was as good a place to talk as any, here in the middle of the field. They were far enough from any of the houses that there was no danger of anyone overhearing. "Tell me the truth, Phillip. Don't lie. Don't try to protect anyone. Tell me what Saul was doing. Tell me who had reason to hate him."

Phillip scowled in the dark and shook his head. "Tom, there's nothing. Saul was a good man."

Tom sighed. "There's no such thing. We *all* do wrong. Now, what did *he* do?"

"I don't know! The worst I saw of him was to take the Lord's name in vain when he hit his thumb with a hammer! You're wrong about him, Tom. I think you're wrong about a lot of things, for all the good it can do us now."

Tom waited, but apparently Phillip was finished. The big man was just looking at him expectantly.

"Come with me." Tom beckoned and started toward the house he shared with Asher.

There were no sofas in Friendly Field, just as there

were no stuffed armchairs. Apparently those humble comforts were too distracting from God. What they did have were wooden benches, which they would then cover in so many pillows that they became more or less like sofas. Tom's house had one, and Asher was sprawled across it outrageously. The boy had been the same in the back of the wagon, always arranging himself in strange ways, curling up or draping himself over things morosely when he thought he was alone. He'd always sit with a straight back when anyone else was around, but on his own he was like a house cat.

He'd been lying back with one hand covering his eyes, but he looked up, surprised to see Phillip.

"Mr. Lester," Asher said quickly, sitting upright.

Tom pulled a chair away from the table and spun it around, sitting down to rest his arms on the back.

"Here's how it'll have to be," he said.

"Did you listen to a word I said?" Phillip asked.

"As a matter of fact, I did. Kid, listen up. Until one of you thinks of a better idea, I want both of you talking to everyone. Old, young—it doesn't matter. Find out everything you can about Saul. *Someone* will know something."

Asher frowned and spoke up before Phillip could. "What will you do?"

"I'm leaving."

"What?" Phillip and the boy said as one.

"Any one of us could ask around and sort out Saul," Tom said, pointing from himself to the boy, to Phillip. "But I reckon I'm the only one who can stop John Porter from bringing his gang here. So you'll do that for me, and I'll do this for you. Phillip, it's the *least* you can do," he said, cutting the other man off. "You're the new Saul Matthews. You're a leader, even if you don't call yourself one. It's dangerous enough to have a murderer in your town and not tell people. You can't hide it from them *and* do nothing."

"We don't know that it's one of us," Phillip hissed. "For all we know, it could be your outlaws."

"No," Tom replied frankly, "it couldn't. The timing makes no sense, and what would they have meant with the feathers? Porter might steal, or he might hurt somebody, then offer you protection in exchange for payment. But that isn't what happened to Saul. "

"You intend to kill him," Phillip said.

"I already told Jeremiah that I don't. I won't even take a gun with me." Tom took the derringer out of his pocket. Ignoring Phillip's look of horror, he handed it to the boy. "Watch your back, kid. There's no telling, but it's always possible that once the killer knows you're looking for her, she might come gunning for you. Keep your guard up. Follow your gut. And, Phillip, I expect you to do the same. It's all right if you want to count on God to protect you. You count on Him to provide for you, don't you? But you still work the fields and grow the potatoes; you don't wait for Him to come down here and pick up a shovel."

Something in Phillip's jaw twitched. "How do I know anything you say is true?" he asked.

"Men lie to get what they want," Tom told him frankly. "The only things I want are Mary and some peace and quiet." He squared himself and met Phillip's eyes. "That straight enough for you?"

"I guess it'll have to be," the other man replied grudgingly. "I can't stop you. Can't we just wait for the law?"

"If I knew when they were coming, that's what I'd do." Tom rubbed his hands together tiredly. "But it could be a while. And I can think of too many ways that John Porter could do us harm in the meantime."

Phillip fidgeted with his suspenders, and Asher got up to toss more wood into the fireplace.

"What do you think he would do?"

"I can't say for certain, but, having met him, I think he'd try to make a deal with you for whatever it is he and his gang might want from you. And you might agree, having no other recourse. But then he and his men would start to push and take liberties, and things would get bad. That's how things are with men like that." Tom put his hand out, palm up. "Their word isn't worth much."

"What about yours?" Phillip asked.

"I've been known to bluff, not lie."

"What's the difference?"

"I suppose there isn't one. What do you want, Phillip? Do you have some better idea of what should be done?"

The other man shook his head. "Of course not."

Tom already knew that. Jeremiah and Phillip and particularly Thaddeus *wanted* to wait quietly and hope for the best. And Jeremiah and Phillip at least knew that wasn't wise. They needed someone to push them, and Tom was happy to oblige. He knew what *he* would have done in John Porter's shoes, and he wasn't about to let it happen.

"Mr.—," Asher began, but caught himself before saying "Calvert." "You—you want to *approach* these men?"

"Worry about your own job, kid."

The boy looked down at the derringer in his hand and swallowed. "It seems imprudent," he said.

"When have I ever been prudent?"

The kid wasn't in the mood for jokes. Well, Tom didn't like this, either, so he could hardly blame Asher.

"Get some rest, Phillip. Tomorrow you start learning everything you can about Saul. Start with Jeremiah and Thaddeus. They knew him the longest. Mrs. White as well. And Mrs. Washburn. Could be an old grudge. And if I'm wrong, we'll know soon enough."

"Tom, we welcome everyone to Friendly Field, but you can't come here and—"

"What? Raise hell and then bully you? I *know*, Phillip. If I could think of a better way, I'd take it. If I'm not welcome here when I come back, that's another day's problem. That's my piece. If you think of something better, I'll listen. Until then, let's call it a night." He looked meaningfully at the door.

Phillip took a deep breath, then walked out. He didn't slam the door.

Tom listened to the steps creak as the big man left the porch.

Asher ran his hands through his hair. "Do you mean it, Mr. Calvert?"

"Of course. It makes sense this way. The cripple sews and the able-bodied man works the fields. You two can ask questions, and I can tell stories. We do what we're good at."

"Are you much experienced at dealing with outlaws?"

"Hardly at all. Should make it interesting."

"I do not think this is wise."

"I didn't ask your opinion, kid."

"Let me accompany you."

"No. I won't slight you. Your poker face is good. You've come a long way." Tom smiled at him. "But you aren't ready to play at this table."

"Well, how can you say that *you* are if you have never done it before?"

Tom opened his mouth, then laughed. "Trust me."

"Why should I?" Asher grumbled. "No one else does."

"I think Mary does."

"You really do like her."

"I certainly do."

The boy gave up. "When will you leave?"

"Oh, in about ten minutes."

CHAPTER FOURTEEN

H E REALLY WAS getting around better.

Using the walking stick had become a habit; he reached for it automatically each day and never gave any thought to if he really needed it. Tom had a limp, and it was a noticeable one. He'd have it for the rest of his life, however long that might be, but it no longer bothered him, maybe because it didn't seem to bother Mary.

And it didn't bother her because she didn't think her prospects were very good. She just couldn't see herself clearly, though that wasn't entirely her fault. As in most things, there was an element of luck in play. She hadn't remarried because there was no one precisely eligible. The only unmarried men were the older ones like Saul and Thaddeus who had outlived their wives, and Mary likely wasn't inclined toward them— or the *young* men coming to marrying age, who were not inclined toward a woman both thin and plain who was almost twice their age.

It wasn't true, of course. In the right clothes, she would be slender and elegant, not bony. Tom *liked* her face, and even if he hadn't, her bearing would've drawn him in regardless. She stood out from the other women just by the way she carried herself. On the trail, Tom and the kid had read a book about wealthy English women trying to marry in the countryside, and there was a great deal in it about manners and what made a lady. Well, Mary might have spent her time working on handkerchiefs for potato farmers, but she was a lady. It would take more than a too-strong nose to change that.

Tom knew this probably wasn't the best time to be thinking about her, but it was getting harder to think about anything else. At any rate, he was moving faster on his bad leg even without his stick—and more quietly too. So quietly that John Porter's man didn't hear him coming.

Tom knelt beside him, and the man startled, then froze in the act of grabbing for his pistol.

"Don't do that," Tom muttered, squinting past him through the shrubbery. "I'm unarmed. Good morning, neighbor. Peace be with thee."

The man was probably ten years Tom's junior. He was decently dressed for an outlaw on the run, and didn't even smell particularly bad. He was sitting here, hidden in the bushes as the gray light of morning started to filter through the gloom. The road to Des Crozet was about twenty feet away.

"What the hell do you want?" the lookout asked, resting his hand on the grip of his gun.

"I want to talk to you." Tom put his hand out. "My name's Tom. What's yours?"

"It don't matter."

"Fine." Tom cleared his throat, then groaned and sat down, patting his bad leg. "I need a rest. I've been looking for you all night."

It was partly true—Tom had been out in the woods all night, but he hadn't been searching for this fellow. He'd had a pretty good idea where he'd be. John Porter was smart enough to be cautious, so he had to have left someone behind to watch the road. What Tom didn't know was if this man was meant to report on anyone leaving Friendly Field or to *stop* them from leaving.

"Where's Ben Garner?" Tom asked.

He didn't even need the lookout to give voice to his answer; his face made it clear. The gang didn't know where Ben Garner was, and that meant Scarf had never made it home alive, and neither body had been found.

"How do you know Ben Garner?" the lookout asked suspiciously.

"He came here drunk. And lit out again before anyone knew what to do. The trouble's that he was recognized. John Porter has you here to make sure that if *he* was recognized, no one went running to Des Crozet to fetch the law, right? Well, we already did that." The lookout's face went hard, but Tom kept on, making sure his voice came out easy. "But we didn't say anything about John Porter because we didn't know. We just knew Ben Garner— It's my fault. I saw his poster. Course, when word reaches the law that Ben Garner's been sighted here, like as not they'll figure John and the gang are close. You see? We need to warn John that they're coming."

"Why the hell you want to warn anyone?"

"Because I owe him one, that's why. Now, will you take me to him or tell me where he is?"

Tom had never done so much bossing people around in his life. First Quakers, now outlaws. He didn't care for it; it was just as well that he'd spent his adulthood shunning honest work.

This fellow didn't like it, either, but he liked the idea of a noose around his neck even less.

"Just take me to him," Tom told him tiredly. "And don't be so jumpy. I got a bad leg and no pistol. I'm a Quaker, for Chrissakes."

"You don't talk like no Quaker," the lookout said, squinting at him.

"What the hell do you know about Quakers?"

The lookout kept his hand on his gun, but he was thinking. His eyes strayed to the road. He was reluctant to leave his post, but if someone had already gotten word out, his post had no meaning. That was what anyone with any sense would have concluded, and he did after a minute. Muttering curses, the lookout nodded, then rolled a smoke. He'd been abstaining so the glow wouldn't give him away, but now he didn't care. He put it in his mouth, lit it, then pushed to his feet and picked up his scattergun from where it had been lying in the leaves.

"What you got in there?" he asked around the cigarette, eying Tom's satchel.

"My lunch."

Without a word, the lookout reached out and gave the bag a shake. Finding it much too light to contain a weapon, he let go and turned to stomp off through the woods.

Tom cast a glance back toward Friendly Field, then

followed. His nerves stirred, but that was all. This wasn't his first time going all in. And what was the alternative? To trust his fate, and Mary's, and everyone else's to luck. In all his days as a gambler, he'd never trusted anything to luck. Why would he start now? You might have one thinking man in a gang. Or two. Even three.

But they wouldn't all be too smart, or else they'd start a real business. Tom had given a fair amount of thought to how it might be done, trying to keep a band like Porter's under control. The wilderness was a good place for hiding, but not for keeping busy. Staying quiet and out of sight was the best plan, but how would someone like John Porter convince his boys to go along with it? Tom was a patient man, and he liked to think an intelligent one—but he knew he'd be driven out of his mind by the idleness of hiding.

He had pictured a few tents in the woods. He hadn't given the Porter gang enough credit.

Each of the two massive stills stood taller than he did, towering over the leaf-strewn floor of the ravine. They had tents, but they were big ones on wood frames. They'd built chairs and hung hammocks. They must've been here for months, and all the while working these rickety stills.

Tom was impressed.

There was another thing he'd wondered about: how many of them there were. He'd figured it had to be at least seven. With Ben Garner and Scarf sent down below, that would have left five or so.

But there were fifteen men, including the lookout, and within a minute of entering the camp, he'd heard mention of at least one more fellow out there somewhere. If the authorities knew how big Porter's gang was, it might take a while to gather up a big enough band of men willing to chase him.

Tom had once faced down four armed men alone. Those hadn't been hardened gunmen; they'd just been fools.

This would be a little different.

He had to shield his eyes. The sun was up now, and there wasn't a cloud in the sky. It was half a day's hike from Friendly Field to the camp.

John Porter was perched up on the left-hand still, a copper cup in his hand. He gulped the contents, tossed the cup to one of the others, and climbed down. "My friend from Friendly Field! And Andy. Andy, Andy."

"I had good reason," the lookout muttered, the hard look on his face never flickering.

"I'll reckon you did." John strolled over and put his hand out. Tom shook it, but John wasn't looking at him. "It's making me itchy, though. You know what I mean? Nobody watching that road."

"It don't matter," Andy told him, gesturing meaningfully at Tom.

John looked taken aback. Everyone else was staring, and Tom sensed there weren't strangers in this camp often, if ever. He was probably the first. He stopped trying to count the pistols, rifles, and knives. These men were better armed than the Army. There were horses tied to trees up the hill a little, and the cooking pot over the fire was the size of a barrel. Speaking of barrels, there weren't any.

Tom realized with a start that the gang wasn't storing whatever was coming out of the stills; they were drinking it. You *might* convince some rough men to go without diversion or company, but you'd never keep them out here without something to drink.

"I think Harry had better hear this. Harry! Harry, come out and meet my good friend Tom from Friendly Field! Something's up!"

The flap of a tent lifted, and a sour-faced man emerged. He was older than John, but only by ten years or so. He too had a cup in his hand, which was shaking. Wearing a fierce scowl, he ambled over. He had to be Harry Peckner, but Tom was sure he'd never seen that face on a poster.

"Now, Tom—just you being here makes me puzzled. What'd you bring with you?" John looked curiously at Tom's bag.

"Provisions. Even Quakers eat." Tom shrugged it off and held it out. John peered inside, then handed it back, shaking his head.

"Make it clear for me, Tom, if you would."

"I ratted you out. Well, not you. Ben." Tom hung the bag on his shoulder and shrugged. "I didn't know he ran with you. He came to us like I said, drunk. After he'd gone, my friend rode to Des Crozet and let them now. I recognized him from his poster." The camp had gotten very quiet, and Tom just kept talking. "I figure a lawman out there might know Ben Garner rides with you. There's a good chance they'll put two and two together and come for you."

As he listened, Harry Peckner's grip on his cup had loosened. It had tipped somewhat, and the firewater ran down his fingers and dribbled to the ground. He didn't seem to notice.

"I wanted to tell you. So you weren't taken by surprise."

It wasn't even evening, but John had clearly had a cup or two already. It took him a moment to find words.

"You ratted us out," he said finally, gesturing slowly with a finger. "And then you came here to tell me that you did it."

"As a favor," Tom supplied helpfully.

"As a favor," John echoed.

Most of the men looked more confused than alarmed, but not Peckner. His face was getting darker by the second.

"And I didn't rat *you* out," Tom corrected. "I wouldn't do that. It was an honest mistake. I ratted out Ben Garner, but I think it might come to the same thing. You understand?"

"Have we met before?"

"Just yesterday, but you did me a favor once," Tom told him.

"Did I?"

"You killed Mike Dern."

"Mike Dern," John echoed, frowning.

"He was in the bank you did in El Paso. My brother had debts—you don't want to hear me talk." Tom waved a hand. "You helped us out when you killed him, that's all. Quite a bit."

"Huh," John said, chewing his lip and glancing at Peckner. "You hear that, Harry? We did a public service in El Paso."

The other man didn't react at all; he just gazed at Tom.

"How long?" John grunted.

"How long ago did we give word in Des Crozet? About two days."

John looked thoughtful and glanced at the cup in his hand, then at Peckner. "Word's probably found old Russell by now."

"If he's telling the truth," Peckner grunted.

"I reckon he is. And if he ain't," John added, pointing southwest, "there ain't nobody watching the road, so they might as well be going to Des Crozet now."

"You're mighty easy for a Quaker in a camp of thieves," Harry Peckner growled.

John wasn't nearly as relaxed as he wanted to appear, but Peckner wasn't even trying. He was downright hostile, and he couldn't be blamed for that. Tom hadn't brought good news.

"I got no desire to get friendly with the law," Tom told him truthfully. "My neck's on the line too."

"Why would anyone want to put a rope around *your* neck, Tom?" John put up a hand to halt one of the outlaws.

They wanted to be a part of the conversation. A couple of them were shifting nervously, and there was some whispering.

Tom realized he hadn't brought entirely bad news; some of these men had to be itching for a reason to leave. "The name Fulton mean anything to you?"

"Fulton Ranch?" John asked, raising an eyebrow.

"That's the one. A couple of them were along on a wagon train I was part of, and I shot them down. I had cause, but you can't kill men like that, even justified." Tom plucked at his suspenders. "You could say I'm in hiding myself."

"Well," John said, eyes wide. He glanced at Peckner again, who looked even more suspicious of Tom.

"Which ones'd you kill?"

Tom sighed. "Eli, Rodney, Norman, and . . ." He trailed off and groaned. "And Jake. I shot Jake too. I shouldn't have done it."

"You killed four men? I think you're spinning lies," John said. "You ain't the type."

"No, it's too damn crazy not to be the truth," Peckner countered, lifting his hat to scratch his head. "You hear that, boys?" he asked, raising his voice. The outlaws were all around: in front and behind, up on a slope looking down, and under the makeshift pavilions. "We got trouble coming."

CHAPTER FIFTEEN

JUST THE SMELL of the spirits from the stills was enough to make Tom light-headed, and the outlaws drank it like water. There was one named Otis who never drank a drop but appeared to spend every waking moment tending to the stills. He was a skinny fellow, and young, but the others helped him when he needed it.

Tom watched him work, perched on the worst excuse for a bench he'd ever seen. When they'd come here, the outlaws must have had a wagon with them. Very nearly every piece of furniture they had constructed was built from wagon parts, and Tom couldn't help but wonder how they'd done it. It was foolish enough to have horses in these hills; it was inconceivable that they'd driven a wagon this deep. Had they broken it apart and carried the pieces in?

It was easier to think about something like that, something that didn't matter, than what would be go-

ing on in Friendly Field right now. Was the kid being
smart? Was Phillip letting people wonder where Tom
had gone, or had he done Tom a favor and told them a
story? What did Mary think? Tom's greatest worry was
what he'd told her. Would she be alarmed at his depar-
ture? Enough to let something slip? He wished he'd had
the courage to say something to her before he left.

Maybe it had been a mistake to tell her the truth. If
so, he couldn't change it now.

"You look like you need it," a man said, appearing
at his side with a flask.

"I can't," Tom told him apologetically. "It'll put me
to sleep and make my head hurt."

"Your loss." The outlaw sat beside him, following
his gaze to the tent where John and Peckner were pre-
sumably conferring. "You really kill them Fulton
boys?"

Tom sighed. "Afraid I did."

"You'll swing for it if they get irons on you."

Tom nodded. "I know."

"Then why'd you run to the law? Tom, right?"

Tom leaned over and put out his hand. "You?"

"Creel. You seen my poster out here?"

"Not that I can recall."

The man looked relieved. "Well, answer me, then."

"Because I didn't want trouble. I figured I'd lie low
when the law came around, and they'd keep the Quakers safe. There's a lady there I'm sweet on. Those poor
folks have enough problems without anyone's help."

Creel nodded and rubbed his face, which was full
of freckles.

"I did those things," Tom added. "But I don't want
to do them anymore. If I can help it."

"You think you can just hang it up?" the outlaw asked curiously.

"If it was that easy, I wouldn't be here."

Creel snorted. He reached into his shirt and took out a folded piece of paper.

"I hear you," he said, opening it up. On it was a startlingly skilled portrait in charcoal. The girl was pretty. "I want to hang it up too, and I would have if we didn't have to wait here so long. I'd've been back to Sacramento to get her and go back East months ago. But we got to wait."

"Why not just get over the border?"

"Because we all got people on *this* side."

"You could just come back."

"That's what John said." Creel sniffed and scratched his nose. "Harry don't like it, though. A few of the boys are sore at what you done, but I'm more inclined to thank you. If the law's coming, we might as well know. I think John feels the same."

They were interrupted by a man doubling over behind them and being violently sick. Tom flinched and glanced back, then politely looked away—except his view was blocked. A mountain of a man stood in front of him, glowering fiercely.

Creel stiffened a bit. "Easy, Quincy," he said. The words came out casual, but his flask was halfway to his mouth and just frozen there.

"Easy," the giant echoed, his gaze fixed on Tom. His beard was as impressive as the rest of him; there was more muscle in one of his arms than in Tom's whole body. A hatchet was tucked into his belt with a blade the size of a wood ax. "The hell I will be." He didn't speak loudly, but Tom had heard that tone of voice before. He'd heard it from his own mouth, and it told him clear as day what was coming.

"All right," Tom said quickly, rising and putting his hands up. "Please. I'm unarmed."

The giant looked genuinely baffled, as though he didn't comprehend why that should matter. He took Tom by the throat so quickly that there was nothing anyone could've done about it. His hands were so big that he only needed one.

Tom struggled futilely, and Creel got to his feet. He didn't look happy, but neither did he look especially bothered.

"Leave him go, Quincy. He don't know what he done."

"I know what he done. Throw half a year of my life down a well's what he done."

With that, he squeezed tighter. Everyone was watching now, and Tom would've liked to say something, but he couldn't breathe. He gripped Quincy's wrist, but he might as well have tried to fight a steel bar.

"You hear me, you stupid son of a bitch?" Quincy shook Tom like a rag doll. "They're supposed to think we're dead or gone. Now you told them! You *reminded* them! *Now* how long we got to wait afore we can go home? *Now how long?*" he roared.

That was enough to bring John and Peckner out of their tent, and Quincy loosened his grip, hesitating.

"Quincy," John said, more surprised than bothered.

"Help me out, John." Tom's voice was a croak at best.

"Looks like a fair fight to me," Peckner said, taking a drink from his cup. "Old Quincy ain't even brought his gun."

John frowned. "He's got a point, Tom. And I don't think I could stop Quincy if I wanted to, short of shooting him. I'd hate to shoot my friend."

"I thought *we* were friends," Tom pointed out in a rasp.

John shifted awkwardly. He cleared his throat and looked away. "Well . . . ," he said uncertainly.

Quincy flung Tom to the ground, and it was the worst tumble he'd ever taken. The leaves weren't deep, and there were plenty of rocks. He rolled through the dirt with a cry of pain, coming to rest and not even trying to get up.

"That ain't language for a Quaker," Peckner noted as Tom swore.

"Get up," Quincy snarled.

Rubbing at his throat, Tom sat up just enough to catch John's eye.

"You won't stop him?" he demanded, his voice hoarse and thick with disbelief.

"Think about it, Tom. I don't know you. And if I hafta have one fella for an enemy, would I want you— or him?" He gestured meaningfully at Quincy.

John's friendly airs made it easy to forget what he did for a living. If he wouldn't help, no one else would, either. Chances were good that Tom was already dead, and he just didn't know it yet. He'd known that was a possibility; he just hadn't pictured it coming about like *this*.

"Well, suppose I don't *want* to die today?" Tom snapped.

"Why are you asking me?" John touched his chest, looking hurt. "I ain't the one aiming to kill you."

Stars fluttered and bloomed against the leaves and the trees, and the men gathered around. Tom shook his head and looked up at Quincy. His face was so dark that it was nearly purple, and his hands opened and closed, itching to grasp Tom's neck.

If that happened again, it would be the end. Tom

still couldn't breathe right, and his throat would be black with bruises. Bruises. What were bruises going to matter if he was dead in five minutes?

Quincy started toward him, and Tom threw out a hand.

"All right," he gasped. "All right. Fair fight." He shook his head again and got to his feet, but staggered. He brought himself around, blinking rapidly and wavering. He still couldn't breathe without pain, and there were black spots in his eyes. He raised his hands, but they shook as he took another step to his right. "I'll fight you. I don't want to, but I will."

That was good enough for the giant.

Quincy barely took a step before a shot crashed through the forest, startling everyone. There were sixteen men present, and nearly all of them froze for an instant. Several of the outlaws went for their guns, but no one cleared leather—it had been Peckner who fired.

He still had his Schofield in his hand, pointed at the sky.

Quincy stared at him. "Harry?"

"Quiet, Quincy."

"Why do you want to stop me?"

"I expect I just saved your life." Peckner lowered the gun and gently opened it, tossing away the empty shell and replacing it with a fresh cartridge.

"How'd you figure that?" John asked, trying not to laugh.

Tom wobbled but stayed on his feet. He kept his fists up as though to fight, but Quincy didn't move.

"Look where he's standing," Peckner said quietly, pointing at Tom. "In front of that beam. Quincy'd have brought the whole still down. And this one"—he jerked his chin at Tom—"woulda had that ax and used it. I seen him look at it and make his odds. He ain't standing there by chance. He's a wily Quaker." With that, Peckner went back into the tent.

John looked impressed. "You wouldn't do that, would you? Tom? You wouldn't hurt old Quincy."

"I only kill ranchers," Tom croaked.

"You see, Quincy"—John yawned and followed Peckner—"Tom's all right."

The murder had already gone out of the giant's face. He was still angry, but his hands were steady. His teeth ground.

He stalked off, disgusted. Tom sagged against the beam holding up the still, then sank to the ground, rubbing at his throat.

As much as they ground on his nerves, he was beginning to miss the company of Quakers.

CHAPTER SIXTEEN

ASHER HAD BRAINS, but just about every other part of him had *seemed* to be wrong for poker. He was a fair liar out of necessity—Tom had found him attempting a grift on that riverboat, after all. But he was softhearted and, oddly enough, *too* attentive to other people. In poker you had to keep your eyes open, but the kid took it a step further. He was always worried about folks, and sometimes it wasn't even their well-being; it was their feelings. Card games were won by knowing how the other players felt, not by *caring*. The boy cared. He cared about people he didn't even know.

Tom couldn't even imagine what that was like. He knew that not everyone was as cold as he was, but he was also sure that not everyone was as warm as the boy. Even so, with enough hours spent and a reasonably good teacher, Asher had become competent enough to hold his own at the table. Skill wasn't everything in poker, but it went a long way. It went a long way with cooking too, and the Porter gang had been honing its skills for quite a while.

John put a bowl of soup in Tom's hands and grabbed him under his arm to help him to his feet. It was late, and Tom had been wondering when this was coming. His hope had been to light a fire under the gang to get them running scared, but that hadn't happened. John and Peckner clearly had too much sense—and confidence— to be spooked into reckless flight.

The sun was down, and it was getting chilly, but the outlaws were used to it. They had a few fires built, but John and Peckner had nothing in their tent but a pair of lamps and a map.

"Join us, Tom." John wasn't asking; he pressed Tom to sit.

"It was thoughtful of you to tell them all not to put a bullet in me," he said, tasting the soup. It lived up to his expectations; he hadn't eaten all day, and he'd spent the past hour smelling it simmering.

"I didn't say anything like that. Did you, Harry?"

Peckner rested his chin on his fist and gazed across the table. "You're a wily one, Tom. It's taken me all day to get it into John's head that we can't believe a single word you say." He paused for another drink. "I reckon he's got it now."

"You wouldn't lie to me, would you? Tom?" John's cup was empty. He poured more.

Tom blew on his soup. "Course I would," he replied, taking a sip.

"Have you lied?"

"Not about my distaste for the law. Not about what I've done. Not about sending a man to Des Crozet to take the word that there were outlaws nearby. That's all true."

They were both looking straight at him, but there was nothing to see through. It was the truth.

"I want to be a Quaker. I want you all to leave us in peace."

"Now, see," John said, snapping his fingers and pointing at Peckner. "I reckon that's true, 'cept it can't be. Because it all fits together nice, Tom—but how in the hell did you think you were going to leave here alive?"

Tom shrugged. "I don't know for sure. I figured there was a chance you wouldn't see any money in killing me."

"If we leave, then you can tell folks where we went."

"Then kill me and go." Tom took a drink of soup. "How difficult is that?"

Peckner nodded sagely, glancing at John. For a moment none of them spoke. Someone near the tent was being noisily ill again.

"You wouldn't mind that?" John asked.

"Course I'd mind."

"I just can't understand you, Tom."

Tom rubbed his sore throat. "By my count I've died twice already, John. If you want to try your luck, there isn't a thing I can do to stop you."

"He just don't care, Harry."

Peckner raised an eyebrow. "Is he drunk?"

"He ain't. The smart thing's to kill him and go, just like he says," John pointed out.

"I'm starting to like him, though."

"Well, I liked him from the beginning."

"Was I right?" Peckner asked, and when Tom didn't answer quickly enough, he reached across the table and took him by the hair, pulling Tom's head up to meet his own eyes.

Tom jerked free and swatted Peckner's hand away. "About what?"

"About Quincy. What you had in mind?"

"More or less."

Tom *had* put himself in front of the still, but he hadn't had any intention at all of going for Quincy's ax. His hope had been that the still would crush the other man when he crashed into that beam. Had there been a fair chance it would have crushed him as well? Tom had been playing the hand he'd been dealt; it wasn't always a *good* hand. It was fine if these two wanted to think that he'd somehow had the upper hand.

"Do you give a damn or don't you?" John snapped, taking out his revolver and laying it on the table.

"I wouldn't have come if I didn't. But I've shown my cards now," Tom shot back, annoyed. "If it goes well for me, good. If not, then that's how it is. I got to die of something."

Peckner chewed his lip. His eyes darted to the left as someone outside the tent shouted, but with that many drunken outlaws, there was bound to be trouble now and then. Shouting and brawling weren't a problem; that was likely an ordinary night. It would take gunshots to get Peckner's attention.

John picked up the revolver and snapped it open. He tipped the bullets into his palm, selected one, and slipped it into a chamber. Tom drank the last of his broth as John closed the gun and placed it back on the table.

"You got a one-in-six chance, Tom." John looked curious. Peckner looked skeptical.

Tom set the bowl aside and picked up the pistol. "You mean for me to point this at myself?" he asked.

John nodded encouragingly.

"First you won't help me with that big fellow. Now this." Tom shook his head in disgust and turned the gun on himself. He pulled the trigger, and the hammer dropped with a click. He rolled his eyes and tossed the revolver back on the table. "You're awful rude, John."

"Well, I do rob banks."

"Boy, you didn't think twice," Peckner remarked. *He* looked surprised.

Both men had expected Tom to try to talk his way out of it. The only advantage Tom had was that he could keep them guessing. He was used to watching for cheats, and he knew every trick that could be done by sleight of hand, so of course he'd seen John palm the bullet before closing the revolver. He didn't mind pointing an empty gun at himself. And even if he hadn't known, feigning boldness was the winning move. A one-in-six chance to die meant a five-to-one chance he'd live; those were good enough odds to gamble on, and provided he came out on the other side still alive, he'd want his fiction intact to keep him that way.

Tom rubbed his eyes and let them see all of his exhaustion. It was authentic, and there was plenty of it.

"If you don't kill me, I figure Quincy likely will. I wouldn't dare go to sleep."

Peckner snorted, and John leaned back in his chair, folding his arms.

"He won't." The smile on John's face was all amusement. "Quincy's never killed anybody."

"Like as not he'll apologize to you in the morning." Peckner just pinched the bridge of his nose. "He don't belong here."

"No, he does not," John agreed sagely. "Well, Tom, you're a poor excuse for a Quaker. That's all I can say to you. Killing ranchers, trying to kill old Quincy—who wouldn't hurt a fly—and then trying to kill yourself. I don't know Quakers, but that don't sound much like one."

"A good Quaker would graciously accept your insult," Tom replied. "A bad one would want to get up and fight."

"You want to fight me, Tom?"

"You want to fight a cripple, John?"

"You seem to get on."

"Well, I do. Just not very quickly." Tom started to massage his throat again. It was just as sore as it had been an hour after Quincy let go.

"That's nasty," John said sympathetically. "Maybe you can borrow one of Billy's scarves when he comes back. Cover that up. Like I was saying, I believe there's a way for you to see tomorrow still drawing breath, Tom. You ain't much of a God-fearing man, but you might make a half-decent banker."

A banker was what John had called himself in Friendly Field.

"You're smart," Peckner said grudgingly, yet also in that disinterested way that he liked to talk. "That much is for sure."

"We're cooking something up, Tom. Something tricky," John said with relish. "A delicate job," he went on, wiggling his fingers. "And we could use a man with brains for the planning." His eyes strayed to the empty pistol still lying on the table. "And guts for the doing."

CHAPTER SEVENTEEN

T OM HAD ALWAYS tried to be like the people he admired when he was young. There had been an educated man who always dressed well and spoke well. Women had liked him, though he stubbornly would not marry. Tom had always been impressed with that fellow. And there'd been another, a rancher with a big family and an even bigger property. He'd always had plenty of money to throw around and nothing to stop him from doing more or less what he felt like. And of course there'd been that cardplayer, the one he'd watched gun down two men in self-defense.

None of the men Tom had tried to style himself after had been outlaws. Maybe that was why breaking the law had never really crossed his mind. If someone had asked him where life would take him after he found himself in a little community of Quakers, joining a gang likely wouldn't have been his first guess.

They didn't trust him, but it didn't matter. The Porter gang knew these woods so well that even with two good legs Tom wouldn't have had a prayer of getting away. They weren't concerned about a cripple being able to flee.

He didn't want to flee, though. He wanted to watch, because every second he spent doing that, he learned something new. The most important detail was that there was no Porter gang, not really. There were really two gangs: Porter's and Peckner's. They'd joined forces to do a job, and when that had gone well, they'd stuck together, but there was no mistaking that some of these men were loyal to John, and others didn't give a damn what he had to say.

Peckner was the one who kept the same scowl on his face all the time and spoke quietly, but he was still an easier read than John. John would play as though he wore his emotions on his sleeve, but all his showmanship was hard to penetrate. There might have been an idiot in there or a man with some sense. His success so far suggested the latter.

The bandits weren't as hospitable as the Quakers, but it might've been worse.

There were two cots unused, thanks to Tom's aim with the derringer, and someone dragged one under the tent where they ate for Tom to sleep on. It was built of sticks, not lumber from the wagon, and there was no blanket or pillow, but it was better than sleeping on the ground.

A few lamps would burn through the night at Friendly Field, so even on a cloudy night, there was a light or two in the dark. Here in these woods, once the sun was down, the blackness was so deep that when Tom's candle went out, he wouldn't be able to see his hand in front of his face.

He perched on the cot, which creaked and rustled. The camp was quiet; these men had spent the day drinking, and they had nothing to entertain them in the night. They retired when the sun did, but there were no fewer than *four* sentries. What was more, all four were sober. Worse even than that, Tom knew the locations of only two.

No, he wasn't going anywhere. Even if he could slip away, Friendly Field was the first place John would look. The purpose of all this was to keep these men *away* from Friendly Field. Giving them any reason to go that way would make it all pointless.

Tom listened to the handful of voices in the dark, but they were just murmurs. He couldn't make anything out.

A light approached, and he turned, leaning over to peer out from under the flap. The man holding the lamp was just a shape, but he was so big that it could only have been Quincy.

"If you want to kill me, would you make it quick?" Tom asked tiredly.

Quincy just brushed the flap aside and ducked under, then straightened to loom over Tom. Face stony, he gazed down at him in the lamplight. Maybe he was looking at the black and purple marks on Tom's neck.

"I should not have attacked you," he rumbled at last.

"I'm counting myself lucky you didn't kill me." Tom waved a hand. "So I thank you for that."

"I was angry," the big man added, and his voice was so deep and rough that at first the embarrassment hidden in it had gotten past Tom. Now he noticed it.

"I'm all right. I'd have been angry too," Tom assured him.

"Harry says you'll ride with us."

"Well, it's that or be shot." Tom shrugged. "I like getting money as much as the next fellow. And I'm not superstitious."

"I do not hold you accountable for what you done."

Tom nodded hesitantly. "Well, thank you."

"I might have done the same."

Quincy seemed to get on with the other men, but there was something different about him, and it wasn't that he was a head taller than any of them.

"Is there somewhere that you need to be?" Tom asked after a moment.

Quincy nodded.

"And I'm keeping you from it by interfering with your plans."

"Yes."

"You should blame Ben Garner. And I wonder if your boys had gone to Friendly Field and made trouble if that would not have brought about the same result," Tom suggested cautiously.

"Maybe," the giant grunted. "Will you shoot me in the back for what I done to you?"

"Mister, I got no plans to shoot anybody at all," Tom told him. It was the truth.

Quincy nodded and put out one enormous hand. Tom shook it, then got to his feet. His mind had been slow to put it together, but he had it now.

"You're no bank robber." Tom gave him a sympathetic look. "How'd you get roped in?"

"I needed money. For my little ones."

"How many you got?" Tom asked, stifling a yawn as he sat down again. Quincy sank onto the bench a few feet away. To Tom's surprise, it held him.

"A few of my own, and a few more."

"More?"

"Seemed like half the town got it. I don't know what the doctor called it." Quincy counted on his fingers. "My brother, our dad, my wife, our cousin Longfellow."

There wasn't much feeling in the way he said it—of course there wasn't. He'd spent months sitting in the woods, thinking about it. And his hands around Tom's throat—that had been the pot boiling over. Now it was all done, and there wasn't much left.

"It's just me and my brother's wife left now to care for all them little ones. Ours and those who lived. John and Harry needed a man who could lift something heavy."

"Of course. You do what you have to for your kin."

The giant didn't look convinced. Or maybe there was something else distracting him.

"Are you ill?" Tom asked.

Quincy shook his head, taking in a deep breath through his nose. "Trouble is, I can't get them the money."

Tom had been wondering about that, and there was his answer. He didn't know how much the gang had made off with, but it appeared they were still sitting on it. If the law found out about *that* detail, they'd likely have been here a good bit faster.

Tom opened his mouth but didn't let the words out. His brain still worked, and he wasn't going to fall into the trap of thinking he had another man figured. That would get him killed, if he hadn't done that already.

"Quincy, John mentioned he was planning a job. Do you know anything about it?"

The giant's brow furrowed. "Job? I ain't heard nothing about no job."

CHAPTER EIGHTEEN

M EXICO," THE OUTLAW said derisively, leaning over to spit in the leaves.

Tom was only half listening. Less than a year ago, he'd stood on the deck of a burning paddle steamer. Thanks to his anger that night, he'd made a snap decision that ended his old life. In some ways he really had died back then. Not in any melodramatic sense. Just that everything he knew of cards, that way of life, those people—that old Tom Calvert had disappeared from the world.

He'd made a decision in half a second, then had months on months to spend regretting it.

He didn't want to do that again. So instead of seeking out John, he just sat with the outlaws by the weak little fire meant to ward off the chill of morning. They enjoyed their breakfast of spirits, and the night sentries dragged themselves back to camp to go to sleep. More went out to take their places. Tom suspected there

hadn't been quite so many men keeping watch before
Ben Garner and Scarf went missing.

The outlaws spoke of Mexico and its people in crude
terms and such a way that Tom doubted any of them
had been there. He kept waiting for an opportunity to
step in and say something that would nudge them the
right way, but it didn't come.

Quincy was on watch, and Otis never stopped tending the stills. Tom had learned a few more names, but
even the outlaws who weren't openly cold to him were
never quite friendly. A few of them seemed to have
people they wanted to return to, but Quincy appeared
to be the only one who truly didn't belong. He'd made
his living in timber before all this, and that was what
he meant to get back to.

Tom didn't look over his shoulder. John and Peckner weren't in their tent this morning. They were up
the west slope, looking down into the shallow ravine
where the tents and the stills were. What were they
doing up there? Just smoking? If they were talking,
they were doing it quietly. It bothered Tom that neither
of them was holding a cup.

Or maybe it was that there was no coffee that was
troubling him. No, it wasn't that. It was Tom's gut, and
he knew better than to ignore it. John wasn't a fool,
and though he seemed to speak without care, the truth
was that he was very careful about exactly what information he allowed other people to have.

Tom wasn't anywhere near having John's measure.
It had nearly been too late last night when he finally
realized it was Quincy's mouth that was moving but
John's words that were coming out. Quincy hadn't
been lying, but he hadn't decided on his own to come

and talk to Tom. He wasn't the type to do that any more than Tom was. That was why it had felt as though neither one of them knew what they were doing. Tom hadn't wanted Quincy's apology, and Quincy hadn't particularly wanted to give it, let alone tell a stranger about his circumstances.

But that had been the job given to him by John, the same John who had told Tom but no one else that there was a job.

What had John been fishing for? What did he really want from Tom? He wanted to use him, of course; he and Peckner weren't lying about *that*.

It had to be the money. These outlaws figured everyone was like them. Quincy had been meant to let Tom know that the money was here somewhere. John must have wanted to know if Tom would ask about it. Tom had caught on and held back from doing so. He wasn't guilty of what John suspected, but the details didn't matter; what mattered was John's suspicion. Trust wasn't easy to come by anywhere. That thought wanted to push Mary's face in front of his eyes, but Tom resisted.

"I liked Mexico," he lied with a shrug. "I wasn't down there long, but it was all right. Some good cooking and good-looking women. Things didn't cost much."

A couple of them glanced at him, but he didn't say anything more. As expected, no one asked what he'd been doing there. He'd have thought of something, but lies were best kept simple. What he'd said about Mexico? That was word for word what he'd heard another poker player say once, so there was a fair chance it was true. It was good to mention women as well. Quincy was the most intent to leave, but they were all itching to. While a few wanted to see their people, the rest wanted to spend their money. That was reasonable enough; Tom would've felt the same way in their place. In their own way, they'd worked hard for it.

At any rate, he couldn't try to talk them into going to Mexico. He could only try to plant the seed.

"You look mighty comfortable for a prisoner," an outlaw named Isaac noted.

Well, at least they weren't confused about the place Tom occupied in their outfit.

Tom patted his bad leg. "I'm always glad to be sitting."

The other man snorted and went back to his drink. Their nerves were thick in the air. Yesterday, Tom had brought the news that they were no longer safe here, yet here they still were. There had been no order given to break camp, no hint let slip about what was next. The outlaws all knew they were leaving, but they were starting to twitch as they waited to hear when and for where.

They had done as good a job with their camp as anyone could possibly hope to do. They'd made this dark little cleft in the hill as cozy as it was capable of being. But now they *wanted* to leave, and the sooner they got moving, the more of a lead they'd have on whoever might try to follow.

John and Peckner just stood up there, murmuring to each other. They didn't look happy. There was none of John's big smile and big words.

At the same instant, they turned and began to pick their way back down. Tom just held his hands out to the fire, though there wasn't much of a chill this morning.

"Otis," Peckner called out as he passed. "Leave it set and come on."

"You as well, Tom." There it was: the friendliest words from John's mouth.

"Your pardon?" Tom asked, glancing up.

"You heard." John beckoned.

Tom rose with a groan and limped after them into the biggest tent.

"You'll excuse us," Peckner said amazingly politely.

The outlaw at the table picked up his cup and left, while John undid a string and let the flap fall completely shut. He put his lamp on the table and took a wad of papers out of his waistcoat.

"Boys," he said with an ironic smile, "join us."

They sat at the table, where John was spreading his papers out. One was a real map, and another appeared to have been drawn by hand.

"Will it be Lorne or Bixby?" Peckner asked, the question directed at Otis. "That's the question, son. If it's Lorne, he'll ride into Des Crozet and then to these Quakers, and come from here." He pointed at the map, then took out a piece of charcoal and drew an arrow. "He's old, and he ain't smart enough to do nothing better than that."

"He's too old to think of a smart play *himself*," John countered, tapping his empty cup on the table. "But if there's a fella with sense in his posse, he might listen. Now, the *best* way to get us would be from the north." He pointed. "With them rocks and them thorny bushes. You can't see a damn thing. Someone could follow the river to the bend, then in through the trees—we wouldn't know until they was tucking us into bed."

"Well, that's no threat," Tom said, holding a hand out. "They'll come on horseback. They *have* to follow the river before they come in. We can watch that."

"We surely can," John replied, smiling. "Would you expect that, Tom?"

"I don't know. I've never led men before or gone looking for"—he waved his hand—"anything like this."

"Well, you found it. Otis?"

The young man's mouth was twisted in a line as he thought hard. Finally, he shook his head. "From the north is the way that would give us the most trouble," he said slowly. "But I reckon we are the only people in this world who know it, because we *been* here. Lorne and Bixby ain't never been to these woods. *They* don't know. So I wouldn't expect them from the north. I'd expect them in a straight line, from the southwest." He tapped the map. "Either one of them."

"That's provided they're willing to camp and they don't insist on a warm bed," Peckner replied.

Tom followed, more or less. He knew who Lorne was supposed to be—some bounty hunter from California. Bixby, he'd never heard of—but he was likely a lawman with ties to the things the gang had done.

"Anyone else comes, they'll come from Des Crozet," Otis was saying.

"All right, then." Peckner drew two arrows. "Northwest. When we leave, that's where we go. We can take the long way around for the horses, go straight to the river, and move out. That's where we shake the trail."

"Don't make it too easy now," John chided, shaking a finger. "Give them something to chase."

"Go have Sven scout it out," Peckner ordered. "Tell him to go now, figure out our course, and think about provisions."

Otis nodded and left the tent. Tom was done.

"Well, what the hell'd you need me for? I don't

know these woods or the people who want you." He didn't bother hiding his irritation.

John cocked his head. "Now, Tom, are you bored by our talk? Surely a fella with brains like you approves of making plans. You got to have a plan, Tom. You can't do nothing without a plan."

"Make your plan, then. What I approve of is knowing what's coming."

"Hell, that should be obvious," Peckner grunted. "What do you think?"

"I think you're getting ready to leave and you want to make sure you don't run headfirst into the law that's coming for you."

John leaned back, making a face. "See? Why you gotta ask, then? You already know."

"Because I don't see what part in it I play."

"You have a trade with them Quakers, Tom? Or did you just spend your days praying?" John asked idly.

"I sewed pillowcases."

"You what?"

"I sewed pillowcases," Tom repeated, "on account of my leg, though I think I'd fairly soon have been in the fields. I'm getting around better without my stick. As you see," he added.

"What happened to your leg?" John asked.

"A bullet."

"Who shot you?"

"A man named Dan Karr."

"I've heard of him." Peckner lit his cigarette. "I suppose the details ain't none of my business."

"He shot me because I did something stupid. I'm not sore about it. When do we leave?"

John frowned and turned to Peckner.

"Well, since Tom can't bear to be idle and his religious beliefs preclude him from standing watch, I reckon we might as well leave now. How's that suit you, Harry?"

"Might as well."

CHAPTER NINETEEN

TOM WISHED HE had his walking stick back. Bad leg and all, he'd never shied away from moving around. The trouble was that when the walking was his idea, he had a way of choosing terrain that suited him. These hills had little sympathy for him, and the outlaws had even less.

Worse, he couldn't account for everyone. There were only eleven of them slogging through the woods. John and Peckner had sent one man to scout ahead. That left a few more—where were they? Stranger still, a couple of the *outlaws* seemed puzzled by their absence.

Puzzled but not alarmed. The only thing that troubled them was that there was a limit to how much firewater they could carry in their jugs. They weren't worried about being found by the law; they were worried about running out of spirits and getting thirsty. Tom couldn't understand that. He'd been forced to try the stuff, and even just one swallow of it had left him with no feeling in his mouth and a headache for an hour.

The path they took was chosen more for the horses than for the men, and it worked—it was past midday and none had been lamed yet despite the treacherous loam and unsteady rocks. It was bad country; when the trees and thorns weren't too thick to block the view, the hills were in the way. It wasn't just the strain of the journey that made Tom's chest tight and kept his lungs from getting enough air. The Porter gang was all around him, and he remembered the beautiful views from any porch in Friendly Field. There was none of that here; he was boxed in.

It didn't matter, though. As long as they were going *away* from Friendly Field, he could manage any discomfort that might come his way.

Someone had miscalculated. The sun was getting low, but they hadn't reached the river yet. There was a fair amount of grumbling among the outlaws, and Tom had half a mind to join in it. He kept on limping, though even his good knee was on fire. He'd found a good branch to use as his walking stick, and he was looking forward to trimming it a bit if they ever stopped to rest. There wasn't any shame in using a stick, or if there was, Tom didn't care. He needed the help.

John dropped back from the front to join him when he started to lag behind.

"Thinking of having us cut you loose because you can't keep up?" he asked mildly.

"Wouldn't work," Tom grunted. John put his hand out, and Tom took it, letting him pull him over a fallen tree. "I already know your course. You couldn't leave me alive."

"You got a bleak way of looking at things, Tom. Don't you see how we done bent over backward to keep you with us?"

"You didn't do much bending when Quincy had his hands around my throat," Tom pointed out, stopping himself from reaching for some creepers. If he tried to grab those for purchase, they'd come loose and he'd fall in the dirt. Instead, he planted his hands on his stick and forced himself forward.

"You're a tough one," John replied, as though that were an answer. "What do you see in them Quakers?"

"I like the way they try to get along."

"How do you mean?"

"I mean they've gotten so used to giving one another a hand that they just do it. They don't stop to think about it. It's just what you do, even when they don't like one another."

"They don't like one another?"

"They're people, John. Of course they got problems. But even then, they still do it. There's this woman there no one approves of, but they were still giving her things when she showed up. Same as they did with everyone else. Hell, they gave me a *house*. Well, they didn't so much give it to me. I don't own it. But that's how they are. And compared to what I come from, it's nice."

"You told me they didn't have no lawmen." John paused, then pointed to a thorny vine half-hidden by the leaves. Tom stepped over it. "So does that mean there ain't no lawbreakers?"

"There are," Tom told him grimly. "In fact, there's a murderer."

His mind spun; he had to keep his lies straight. He'd told Ben Garner that there *was* a lawman in Friendly Field. He *hadn't* tried that lie with John, not with Jeremiah and Phillip standing there. A day ago he might've hoped that John wouldn't catch a slip like that, but now—

now Tom was fairly sure the other man didn't miss anything. At least, not anything he knew to look for.

"Really?" The outlaw sounded taken aback by the notion. There was irony in that, yet it wasn't every day you heard of a Quaker taking a life.

"I'm fairly sure."

"What'll they do about that?"

"I can't say. The last time they had a real problem, it sounds as though they hanged them." Tom wished he had something better than his sleeve to wipe the sweat from his face. "But that was different. They say that was the devil."

"The devil?"

"A witch. Sounds like when it's a witch, they say they aren't hanging one of their own. They're hanging the devil. Makes it easier for them."

John snorted. "You think the devil'd let you hang him?"

"I had that notion myself, but it isn't my place to"— Tom searched for the right words, shooting the other man a wry smile—"*challenge* them, not when I have so much to thank them for."

"You're such a decent fellow, Tom. Is that why you came to warn me? Decency?"

"I'm done explaining myself, John. I'm sick of it."

"Oh, don't be like that. If there's no lawman, who decides to hang the witch? Who'll decide what to do with your murderer?"

Tom waved a hand. "There're a couple fellas who are the mayors, even if they don't say they are. At the end of the day, what they say goes."

"The others don't mind?"

"Mind?" Tom raised an eyebrow. "They don't know

what the hell to do. They're nothing but pleased to have someone else giving the orders."

"Folks are like that," John said, nodding. "Suppose your murderer don't want to swing?"

"I don't know what they'd do. If they ran, I don't know that anyone would chase them. Maybe that's why I'm not more upset to be here," Tom said wistfully. "God knows what's going on there now. They're looking for the killer. Have they found her? Has someone else been hurt? I don't know." He coughed. "I don't know that I want to."

"You think it's a woman?"

"I'm certain of it."

"Can't they shoot her if she runs?"

Tom snorted. "I expect they'd let her go. It's what I would do. It solves the problem without them having to do anything God might not look kindly on. Of course, it's just as easy to say that God *would* look kindly on hanging a witch. It's godly to destroy evil, and it's godly to forgive. Reckon they just go with whichever seems easier at the time."

"The Almighty is convenient that way, ain't He? You twist it enough, just about anything'll sound righteous. We did God's work robbing them banks. We brought salvation to the people who had the money. That's in the Bible, you know. You'll get a camel through the eye of a needle easier than a rich fella into heaven. Them rich folks should be thanking us for saving their souls. Hell, maybe I should get ordained. Guess I'd have to learn to read."

Tom didn't argue with him. He needed all his breath for making his way, not for talking. A day on the move like this would have been difficult even before he'd spent all that time in the wagon, wasting away. Just holding up his end of the conversation felt like entirely too much work.

"You gonna make it, Tom?" John asked worriedly.

Tom wasn't sure that he would, but as usual, there was always a way for it to get worse. The report of a rifle sent all the birds scattering from the branches and a storm of swirling leaves down into the shade.

John had his revolver in his hand fast enough to make Tom's head spin. He darted into the trees ahead, where there was a commotion among the men.

Tom put his back to a tree, waiting for the next shot from the lawmen—only nothing came. It didn't come because there were no lawmen; that shot had been fired much too close. They weren't under attack; this was something else.

For a moment he was torn. It was a good distraction, but would it give him enough of a lead to get away? No. No, not without something more.

Disappointed, he followed John.

There was a cheer from some of the outlaws, and Tom swallowed.

John pushed past Cyril to get a look.

"Damn it, Simon, I *told* you not to fire," Peckner snarled.

"That's the first I seen in three weeks!" the man protested, shaking his rifle. "He weren't but twenty feet away and didn't even move, hearing all us coming. Woulda been against God's will *not* to shoot him, boss."

John briefly considered the dead buck lying in the loam, then let out a bark of laughter. "Can't go giving in to temptation that way, Otis. The Quakers won't like it."

There was laughter from the others.

"Well, go on." Peckner shook his head and glanced upward. There wasn't much light left, and a few leaves were still floating lazily to the ground. "Make him into stew, then. Let's hang it up, boys. We'll go on to the river tomorrow."

There really was no hurry, then. Tom stood rooted to the spot, his heart thudding. A knife came out of a sheath, and he swallowed and looked away, suddenly queasy. It was all he could do not to throw up right there.

John was still chuckling, and Tom reached out and stopped him as he was about to walk past.

"John," Tom said, his mouth dry.

"Hope you're hungry, Tom."

"Are you ever going to tell me what job you want my help for?"

"Be patient, Tom." John shook him off and took out his tobacco pouch, moving on. "Otis makes a hell of a deer stew."

No. No, John wouldn't ever tell him. He didn't need Tom's help—not anymore.

Tom had already helped him, and he hadn't even realized he'd been doing it.

CHAPTER TWENTY

GRIFTERS CAME AND went. They were everywhere and had been every step of the way. That was just part of living in the world. This was still the first time one of them had ever gotten the best of Tom, and that upset him. He would've thought that being reduced to a sickly cripple, helpless, on death's door, would have done away with most of his pride, but apparently there was enough of it left to bruise.

He was starting to see how John Porter had gotten so many lawmen riled up. And how he'd gotten so many other men to follow his lead. He was every bit as sly as Tom was, and, just like Tom, he liked to plan ahead.

The outlaws had gone ahead and shot two more deer, so there was no shortage of stew. It smelled mouth-watering, and Tom's belly rumbled as he sat in the gathering twilight, unable to let his anger show.

John's distinctive laugh echoed up and down the valley.

"I recall it," he said to Otis, shaking his head. The two were by the nearest fire, consulting one of their maps. "I recall it was damp and smelled funny as well."

"We cross water twice to reach it," Otis pointed out hopefully. "If we stay in the cave, the trail goes cold. We'd be well hid if they came round."

"We'd be hemmed up is what we'd be," John replied, making a face. "A bunch of—a bunch of . . . What do you call 'em, Otis, folks who live in caves?"

"Trolls," Peckner grunted. He was lying a few feet away, his hat pulled down over his eyes, but he wasn't sleeping because there was a smoke in his mouth, glowing in the gloom.

"That ain't right," John said disdainfully.

"Trolls live in caves," the other man mumbled around his cigarette, though he still didn't open his eyes.

"Trolls live under bridges," Otis supplied.

"Then who lives in caves?" John asked, irked.

"Troglodytes," Tom supplied.

"What the hell is that supposed to be?" Now Peckner opened one eye.

"People living in caves."

"You sure?" John peered at him suspiciously.

"Fairly sure," Tom replied, rubbing his eyes.

"Did you eat, Tom?"

"Not yet."

"I don't want to sleep in no damn cave," John snapped at Peckner.

"Don't sleep, then. Go stand watch instead of Sven."

John just suppressed a belch and settled back, trying to get comfortable. Quincy helped himself to more stew, and a couple of the men were already curling up on the ground. They'd gotten used to lying around, and a day marching wasn't much easier for them than it was for Tom.

Then John sat up. He shook his head as though to clear it and looked at Tom. "Come talk to me, Tom."

"You come to me. I'm the one with a bad leg."

John's brows rose, but he got up and ambled over, putting his hand out. Tom took it and let the other man pull him upright.

"Take a walk with me. I have a little proposition for you."

"You finally going to tell me about this job?"

"Well, I think so." Did John really think Tom hadn't seen that just now, the way he had caught Creel's eye? Did he think Tom was blind? And stupid?

It was proof that something had changed. He remembered clearly what it had felt like when he had gone through temper and come out the other side, months ago on that riverboat. It didn't happen here, and he'd been half afraid that it would.

Tom was as calm as he'd ever be.

"I'm worried," John confessed as they walked a short distance away from the others. "I'm real worried about your Quaker friends."

"Are you?"

"You make them sound downright helpless." The outlaw folded his arms, scowling. "Defenseless if the wrong folks were to come along."

"They certainly are. It worries *me* how easy they trust a man they don't know," Tom admitted. "But that's just their way, I guess. Don't seem to have come to any ill yet that I can see."

John nodded sagely.

"How are you going to do it?" Tom asked bluntly.

"Do what, Tom?"

"Convince the law that you're gone." He gestured at the ground. "Walking us and the horses through the woods to make the trail is all well and good, but are you sure they'll find it?"

"I think they will. And if they don't, can't nobody complain about *that*," John replied easily. "I've shook them off before, and I will again. That's what'll convince them, Tom. Don't tell me you already know about the job. If you do, how come you been asking so much?"

John stopped, and they were barely out of sight of the camp. It was dark, and getting darker. There weren't any fireflies in these woods, and precious little moonlight would get through the leaves above.

"I think you showed your hand when you asked me those questions," Tom told him frankly.

"Did I?" John was smiling, but it wasn't real. He was uncomfortable, and Tom knew why.

"You did. It was plain as day. What I can't see is why you didn't tell me straight."

"Tell you what?"

"That you never planned on leaving. That you meant to lie low until the law moved on, then take up at Friendly Field."

"Supposing I had," John replied carefully. "What would it matter?"

"Well, I might have talked you out of it," Tom replied, rubbing his face. "It's a bad idea. In fact, it'll get you killed."

"The law ain't gonna wait around forever," the outlaw pointed out. "They'll follow our trail, lose it, and think we're going for the border like anyone else would."

"Why not just do that, John? Why not go? You can't move your boys into Friendly Field without bringing down the law on you. They're a good few miles from Des Crozet, but it's not an island. People come, people go. Word'll get out, and when it does, it'll be no different than it is now. Men riding to find you, and the Quakers couldn't hide you even if they wanted to."

"Hell, Tom. You make it sound like I want to settle down there forever. I think we'll just enjoy their hospitality for a short while before we go on. Even bankers need provisions."

The two of them just didn't see things the same way. To Tom, it was appallingly impractical. Why would the gang go out of their way and take on so much additional risk just for—what? Some stolen food, the chance to sleep in beds, and unwilling women? These were poor rewards for such an effort.

The outlaws saw it differently. A place almost provocatively helpless. It would strike them as unjust *not* to take advantage of it. No, John couldn't move his gang into Friendly Field for long, but he didn't want to. He'd just use it up and move on.

He'd planned this from the beginning, and there was probably an element of pragmatism in it—he had to keep the men happy, and this was what they would want, not a grueling flight to the border and more time in the wilderness.

It had taken Tom much too long to figure out John's intent in keeping him alive. It was to probe for information, and he'd thought perhaps to *use* him to somehow facilitate his takeover of Friendly Field. The Quakers would become hostages in their own homes, forced to play host to these men and their whims. The outlaws wouldn't think twice about killing anyone who resisted. Just listening to a few of them talk, Tom gathered there were at least a couple among them who enjoyed killing enough that there'd likely be some even if no one resisted.

"It'll end poorly," Tom predicted.

"Now, Tom." John cocked his head. "You don't think I brought you out here to shoot you, do you?"

"It crossed my mind. Course, it seems more likely you brought me to ask me to talk to Jeremiah and Phillip. And Thaddeus. Those are the names of the three men who run the place," Tom explained, waving a hand. "I figure that *you* figure that I can convince them easier than you can. And if someone was going to shoot me, I guess it wouldn't be you. It'd be him." Tom indicated his left with his eyes; they could just hear the muffled sounds of someone vomiting in bushes up the slope. It was Creel, who had been following quietly.

John scowled. "He ain't supposed to be drinking tonight," he muttered. "And he was just to keep an eye on us," he added, doing an excellent job of hiding his annoyance. He *was* annoyed, though. He didn't like having his hand read accurately, and it was distracting him.

"I believe you," Tom said, and he did. John hadn't meant to kill him tonight; Tom was still more useful alive—at least for now.

The sounds of Creel being ill turned to coughing. Common enough sounds in the gang's camp, at least when there had been enough firewater for them to drown in. Now they were traveling with only what they and the horses could carry. Would they ration the drink? Or just guzzle it all tonight?

Did they realize there were no spirits to speak of in Friendly Field? Would they build new stills to make their own? No, they didn't plan to stay long enough for that. What, then? Did they think they would send the Quakers to get liquor for them? Because *that* would arouse suspicion.

Tom liked to think of himself as a clever man, but he'd made foolish decisions. John was the same. He *was* clever, but making a play for Friendly Field was a mistake.

Nothing would have convinced John of that, though. His success had fooled him into thinking he was right about everything and invincible. He was wrong on both counts.

Instead of replying, John reached out and leaned on the nearest tree.

"You're a smart one, Tom," he said, swallowing. He put his hand on his abdomen. "I wonder if that meat was bad."

Tom doubted it; the deer were fresh kills. John leaned over a little, a distant look in his eyes as he dealt with what he felt in his belly. Most likely that was a result of the mushrooms that Tom had poured into the soup pot from his bag.

There must have been a particularly nasty moment of discomfort, because John didn't even seem to notice when Tom plucked his gun from its holster.

He did notice when the handle of it struck him on the head. John thudded to the ground like a sack of rocks, and the look on his face was more one of bafflement than of alarm, but just for the brief moment before Tom put a bullet in his head.

CHAPTER TWENTY-ONE

THE SHOT BOOMED through the trees, and as much as Tom would have liked to believe all the outlaws who'd partaken of the poisoned soup were too ill to hear it, that likely wasn't the case. He turned and lifted the gun, cocking back the hammer as Creel's head appeared above a thicket up the hill; eyes unfocused, he was in the act of wiping his mouth.

Tom shot him between the eyes and limped up the slope. His ears rang, but he heard the shouts of alarm and the other sounds that John had missed in his discomfort. Quite a few of them would have been affected by the mushrooms by now. If John had been paying attention, he'd have noticed the change in the air.

Well, he wouldn't be noticing much of anything now. You couldn't say he'd tried to get the best of the wrong Quaker, because Tom wasn't one. John Porter *had* set his sights on the wrong village, though. He'd probably realized that in his last moment or two.

Creel's gun was still in its holster, and Tom bent to pick it up. It was an English revolver that felt strange in the hand, but Tom wasn't particular. As long as it was loaded, it would do. He stepped behind the nearest tree, leaned out, and raised John's Colt as an outlaw with a rifle came crunching through the loam to investigate. He looked more or less alert. Tom lowered the gun and whistled.

The man whirled; he hadn't seen John's body yet.

Tom pointed. "They're up there," he hissed.

The outlaw lunged to the nearest brush and dropped to one knee. "How many?" he asked.

"Five at least," Tom replied.

"Five from the north!" the man called out. He meant to add something else, but Tom went ahead and put him down with a bullet between the shoulder blades. The outlaw never saw it coming, but as he slumped over, his rifle went off, sending a bullet into the night sky.

There was very little chill in the air, but Tom's leg pained him anyway. It was hard to avoid the thorns and branches in the dark, but there was still work to do.

Peckner was with the horses, pulling his rifle out of a sheath on his saddle. Others kicked dirt over the fires and found their weapons. There was more than enough swearing going on to cover the sound of anyone moving around.

Tom took aim at Peckner, but he moved past the horses.

An outlaw named Evan was staring straight at him. Tom shot him instead, then the man beside him as he pulled his own gun. Both men went down with cries of pain.

Tom looked over his shoulder on principle, and

there was Simon, just up the hill—he was one of the usual sentries. The shooting had brought him back, and he hadn't eaten yet. He was fast. Tom dropped to one knee, but he felt Simon's bullet go by and a sting from the bark it knocked loose from the tree. Tom's aim was better than Simon's, but now John's revolver was empty.

"There! There!" That was Peckner's voice, and it was followed by a rifle round.

Tom scrambled under the branches and scuttled into one of the makeshift tents. It was empty, but a pack was there, and a sheathed knife. He got down flat and peered under the flap.

Otis was on the other side of camp, clutching his rifle. He still faced north, as though he hadn't figured it out yet. Tom tossed John's empty gun aside and shifted the English one from his left hand to his right. He laid the barrel over his wrist and fired a shot into Otis' unprotected back.

As the outlaw's body thudded to the dirt, Tom was snatching the knife.

A pair of bullets punched through the tent, and he got down lower, forcing the blade through the canvas and sawing down. He pushed through the tear and tumbled into the loam.

More shots crashed through the dark, but they were aimed at the tent, not at Tom. The outlaws didn't know he'd slipped out, and he wouldn't be easy to spot in the gloom.

There were five shots left in the English revolver. Tom didn't know what kind of cartridges it took or even how to load it.

But he knew how to fire it, and he did at the shadowy figure trying to make its way down the slope toward camp. An outlaw named Shane went down with a cry, and Tom crawled, but he barely made it ten feet before the others were in the tent.

Several shots ripped through the canvas, throwing up leaves as the men fired blindly around the hole he'd cut.

Tom rolled onto his back and went still.

"Patrick!" Peckner called out. "Go around."

Someone was being violently sick nearby, but Tom preferred not to shoot at a man he couldn't see.

"He ain't back there," someone else reported in the dark.

"What the hell's going on?" another outlaw called out breathlessly from the hillside on the other side of camp. That would be another returning sentry—his name was Liam.

There was a second tent nearby, but Tom didn't hear anything from in there.

A twig snapped, and he looked to his right—there was someone back to the east, maybe another man who'd gone to investigate those first few shots. Now they were back toward where Creel's body was lying.

"It's that Quaker!"

Tom didn't feel a need to point out to that if he were actually a Quaker, he wouldn't have a gun in his hand and eight fresh graves on his bill. He just kept still and quiet.

Patrick staggered into view less than twenty feet away, putting his back to a tree. He was more interested in the hillside, not even looking in Tom's direction.

Tom waited.

There were footsteps behind him as well. Someone else was making his way around the thick shrubs and the second tent. Tom eased the English revolver under his thigh so the moonlight wouldn't catch on the polished barrel.

Peckner. Patrick. That was probably Cyril coming up behind Patrick.

That left who? Liam was out there somewhere. And Hollister. Where was he?

Who else?

It was hard to keep track, and he didn't get time to think about it; the loam rustled not even ten feet away. Who was it? It was impossible to know without seeing him or hearing his voice. Tom strained his eyes, but he couldn't see everything without turning his head, and that would give him away.

He stayed rigid.

There was a groan from the direction of the big fire, which was now completely out.

"There ain't nobody else," Peckner said. Tom couldn't see him. "Ain't no lawmen. It's just him."

Another moan of pain came from up the hill—that had to be Simon. He wasn't dead. Did he still have enough strength to hold a gun?

"Help me, Pat," Simon groaned.

"I'm coming."

"Be careful," the man behind Tom hissed, just as a third figure materialized not far from Patrick. It was Cyril, moving in a half crouch.

A boot sank into the leaves not even a yard from Tom. It was Sven, the quiet one.

Tom grabbed his ankle, and the tall man looked down in horror to see the muzzle of the revolver.

He froze.

Slowly, Tom rose to his feet and put a finger to his lips, keeping his gun on Sven all the while. He gently took Sven's Colt.

The other man's eyes moved, and Tom followed them. Patrick was looking in their direction, and Cyril was right there with him—and the dark wasn't enough to hide who Tom was.

Tom shot Sven through the heart and Patrick in the belly. Cyril returned fire as Patrick crumpled to the ground, and Tom dove behind the nearest tree, scattering leaves.

Behind him, with a dumbfounded look on his face, Sven fell backward and rolled into the ditch with a sound like a wheeze. Tom got Cyril in the back as he tried to get behind a tree, but a blast from Hollister's scattergun sent bark and branches flying. Tom winced but took his own shot, and he had better aim than Hollister, who got a startled curse out before his body hit the ground.

Tom inched to his left, trying to get as much of the tree between himself and them as he could.

He had lost count with the English pistol, but it had to be empty. He dropped it and hefted Sven's Colt, an old Dragoon.

A hushed conversation was taking place. Who was left? Peckner, Liam—and there had to be at least one more. Tom squeezed his eyes shut, trying to think.

Peckner didn't call out again. He didn't try to shout anything at Tom.

John would have, but Tom's bullet had put an end to John's bullshit for good.

"Isaac done ran away," Liam said in the dark, and Tom snorted. Like hell he had; Peckner had put Liam up to saying that, and it meant Isaac was creeping around somewhere nearby, trying to get a clear shot, but he wouldn't—not in these trees and this darkness.

Tom let himself down to a crouch, listening.

Nothing moved, and that suited him. He'd wait till dawn if he had to. They still outnumbered him, and boldness alone wouldn't get him out of this alive.

A cry of pain floated over the breeze. Maybe if he waited long enough, sickness from the mushrooms would kill the rest of the gang and save him the trouble. Shane had been watching to the south, and Liam up to the northeast. Isaac had been standing guard to the west. Like as not, that was the way he'd be coming from.

Tom squinted, but it was too dark for him. He didn't let himself sigh; such a stillness had fallen that someone might hear it. He didn't want to do it, but he didn't see that he had a choice. A fight was never his first preference, but a fight was what he had on his hands. He couldn't give up control of it, or he'd lose.

"I'm leaving now," he announced loudly. "Don't try to follow me!"

With that, he got down lower, ears primed. He leaned over to peek back toward the camp, but nothing moved. Slowly, he crawled away from the tree, staying as close to the ground as he could.

Sven hadn't gotten a shot off. There were six cartridges in the revolver and no guarantee that anyone else would come near enough for Tom to rob them.

There it was—a groan from the other side of the tent.

Tom made his best guess and fired a shot through the canvas at Isaac; then he scrambled up and slid behind the thicket.

Two deafening booms came so fast that it was almost a single shot, from Liam emptying both barrels into the spot that Tom had just escaped. Liam ducked out of the way, but Tom fired back and got him in the arm before he could get behind his tree.

Liam's scattergun was empty and his arm was shot.

Tom hesitated, but only for a single breath. He lunged forward, limping for Liam's tree as fast as he could.

The outlaw let go of the scattergun and went for his pistol, but Tom was there, swatting it out of his hand. He struck Liam squarely in the face with a closed fist, dashing him against the tree. Tom spun him around and locked his arm across his throat, putting the muzzle of the Colt to his head before Peckner could pull his trigger. He stood there between the two tents, his revolver pointed at them—but Liam was Tom's shield, and he was a good one, because he was just enough to give the gang's remaining leader pause. A pause was all Tom needed.

He shot Peckner through the throat. The older man jerked his trigger, but his bullet went wild. He fell to his knees, and Tom threw Liam to the ground and shot him as well, then brought the gun back up at the ready.

Seconds passed, and the sounds of the gunshots fell away, leaving only Tom's heartbeat.

Peckner gurgled in the night. Tom went over and put him down, then listened after that echo faded. Isaac was still breathing on the other side of the tent, and Tom finished him off as well.

Simon wasn't making any noise on the slope now. If he had the strength to move, he was using it to run, not to fight.

It was quiet. Tom let out his breath and lowered the Colt. The air was choked with gunpowder, and Otis' body smoldered where it had fallen on the remains of the fire. Tom coughed and covered his nose, trying to count in his head. It wasn't a snapping twig or a crunching leaf; it was just the scuffing of dirt that made him turn around.

But Quincy was already swinging his ax.

PART THREE

UNFINISHED BUSINESS

CHAPTER TWENTY-TWO

ASHER HADN'T EVER gotten to know the real Tom. Sure, he'd had plenty of opportunity to read between the lines, but he'd never seen Tom as he had been back when he was on his feet and playing cards. All the same, he knew enough that the very notion that Tom would *want* to return to Friendly Field, *want* to remain there—that would've been difficult to swallow.

Most men wouldn't look kindly on trading piles of money for potatoes. Trading silk handkerchiefs for linen pillowcases. They wouldn't want to sit in a parlor instead of in a saloon. They wouldn't choose a plain older woman with a sense of propriety over a beautiful younger one who made her living by being good company. They wouldn't give up good friends and allies for stuffy Quakers and stuffier churches.

That was what anyone might've thought, Tom included.

Of course, given the chance, Asher would've also had something to say about what Tom had done. He wouldn't have been able to help himself; he would have had to comment on the peculiarity of raising hell and killing more than a dozen men, all in pursuit of peace and quiet.

Asher was the type who couldn't let something like that lie. Of course, maybe Tom didn't know Asher quite as well as he'd thought; he'd been wrong about a thing or two himself, and here and there things had turned up that he hadn't seen coming.

Quincy's ax, for example.

Thoughts tumbled, but not in the same way they had when his brain had been on fire with fever. It was different and, in Tom's estimation, not as bad. It still hurt, though.

He groaned in the dark, though he barely had the breath to do that much. He was being crushed, and pushing against it didn't do any good. He was sticky all over, and his arm was numb. The hand he could still feel was wrapped around the grip of a pistol.

The numbness became a tingle. He needed to cough but couldn't.

In the end it was the smell that gave him the will to heave off Quincy's body. It wasn't much of a heave, but the giant rolled, ever so slightly, freeing one of Tom's arms. With pins and needles in his fingers, he clawed at the ground and dragged himself free in the grainy light of dawn.

No longer muffled by the corpse and filled with his own feeble attempts to breathe, his ears were suddenly full of rustling tree branches and the birdsong of early morning.

The pain in his chest was worse than the pain in his

leg, but he was glad just to be breathing. He crawled out of the miasma and sank to the ground, sucking in deep breaths and blinking away some of the stars. His fingers were still claws, locked around the empty pistol, which was caked with dried blood. With a shaking hand, he pried the empty gun free and shoved it away.

He'd had only one bullet left when Quincy came at him, and he hadn't missed. But a dead giant hurtling toward him was almost as dangerous as a live one.

Tom probed at the back of his head, which must have struck a rock when Quincy's corpse crushed him to the ground. There was so much dried blood all over him that there was no hope of telling his own from the dead man's. His shirt had started out white, and his days with the outlaws had introduced some yellow and gray to it. Now it was just brown, like rust. So were his sticky, tacky hands.

He rolled onto his back and fumbled with the buttons, then just tore the shirt open and struggled out of it. Tom climbed to his knees, peering down at the bruises on his chest. They hurt just to look at. He coughed, and that hurt too.

When he looked up, his eyes fell on the horses, tied up on the other side of camp. They peered at him suspiciously.

Scowling, he dragged himself to his feet and shuffled over, taking the canteen from John's mare. He got his hands and face mostly clean and drank the rest. Then, reluctantly, he turned and looked at the camp. It was littered with bodies, and there were more he couldn't see in the forest. The night had been mild enough that they were already ripening.

His head swam, and he shook it, then threw the empty canteen aside and steadied himself on the nearest tree.

It was warm, but he felt cold without a shirt. He wasn't above wearing something a dead man had worn, but there likely wasn't one lying about that didn't have blood on it. He rummaged through John's saddlebags and came up with one that looked all right. He donned it gingerly, then put his suspenders up, trying to work some of the stiffness from his neck and shoulders.

The smell made him queasy and he leaned over, but his stomach was empty except for water. Coughing, he untied the horses, one at a time. Just that felt like a lot of work, and when it was done, he tottered over to a rock and perched on it, breathing raggedly.

Something struck his head, and he looked up to see squirrels running along the branches above, shaking nuts loose. He leaned over to pick up Liam's fallen hat and put it on. Another nut struck the brim and rolled off. Tom sighed and got up, taking the hat off and tossing it aside. The shirt was all right, but that was all. The law was still coming to Friendly Field, and he didn't need to be found with anything that belonged to the Porter gang. With his luck, folks would think he really had been a part of it.

There was a part of him inclined to look for the money, but it wouldn't be here. It was hidden somewhere, and he wouldn't have taken it in any case. What would he spend it on? He couldn't think of anything, and if he did, there was still a few hundred dollars tucked away in the house he shared with the kid.

And that money that the outlaws had stolen—well, they'd stolen it. So it wouldn't have been Tom's just because he could get it. The right thing to do would have been to return it. He sighed; another right thing to do would have been to bury all these bodies. Or, the kid might have said, the right thing would have been not to shoot them all in the first place.

But Tom knew when a man had already made up his mind, and John had. John had wanted to use Tom as his key to Friendly Field. "Low-hanging fruit" was what some would have called it. It was one thing to be defenseless; being *disinclined* to defend on principle—that was something else.

There hadn't been any hope of talking the gang out of it. Or tricking them. If the news that the law was on the way wasn't enough to deter them, what was? They'd been fearless, ironically enough. Tom had *told* John this would get them all killed. John hadn't listened.

Tom wished he had. Or that John had been telling the truth about leaving. The notion upset Tom; he hated to think about going on the move, every step taking him farther from Mary—but he'd have done it. If the outlaws had wanted to run for the border, Tom would've gone along. He might even have pulled his weight on that imaginary job of John's if that was what it had come to. He'd have done whatever was necessary to stay alive and get free.

His gaze lingered on the massive shape of Quincy's corpse for a moment, and he weathered another wave of nausea.

Enough. He couldn't stay here any longer. The sun was rising, and it was high time he got on his way. With nothing in his hands and nothing in his pockets, and wearing a dead man's shirt, Tom limped away. He wasn't superstitious, and it was clearer than ever that he was no Quaker. He wasn't going to bury anyone; the Porter gang probably hadn't even brought a shovel. Why would they have? That was a tool for honest work.

Tom didn't like honest work, either, but he'd do it if he had to. Just like he'd sit in church if need be.

Maybe now, with all these men dead, he could have some peace. There wouldn't be any more quiet sewing, though. If he was well enough to take on a notorious gang of bank robbers, he could move a little dirt around to cover up potatoes.

He stepped over Harry Peckner's body and headed home.

CHAPTER TWENTY-THREE

FRIENDLY FIELD DIDN'T look like much, but after such a long time in a wagon, it had been attractive enough. Tom felt that way again as he dragged himself out of the trees and into the field. It was evening, and as he came out into the open, the workers were just beginning to collect their tools and start to head in. It took a few minutes for one of them to notice the lone figure raggedly shuffling toward the village.

William Beaumont waved to him. Tom didn't like Beaumont much, but he was glad to see him. He waved back, and one of the boys took off running. Several of the workers hurried out to meet him, and it wasn't long before people were gathering in the field.

Tom had been gone three days. He'd taken the time to clean himself up in a stream, but he knew he looked as rough as he felt. He was fiercely hungry.

Phillip jogged out to meet him, and he must've said something, because the other men stayed back.

Tom just put up a hand to stop him before he started talking. He didn't want to listen or even to talk—he just wanted to eat. Then sleep in his bed, if he could.

"It's done," he said.

Phillip just looked puzzled. "Done? Tom—," he began, but Tom cut him off.

"I mean it's done," he repeated, not angrily. He was too tired to be angry. "The gang won't come here. You're safe from them. What about you all?" Tom glanced past him at the others, and the rest beyond the workers—women and children were outside their houses now, looking on.

Mary was among them.

"What about our troubles here?" Tom pressed. "Is everyone safe and well?"

Phillip nodded, and Jeremiah arrived.

"Did you really go looking for those men?" he demanded abruptly.

"Peace be with thee too," Tom shot back. "I did, and it's settled. I convinced them not to bother us."

Jeremiah would know it couldn't be that simple, but Phillip might not.

"Can I eat?" Tom asked, spreading his arms. "I haven't in a day. I'm very tired."

"I feel as though there are things that should be said," the older man told him.

Thaddeus was hurrying out to reach them, but he didn't move very fast.

There was no sign of Holly.

"I feel as though if I don't eat, I might say something I'll regret," Tom replied honestly.

One more wrong assumption had been that Jeremiah and Phillip would come up with a narrative to explain his absence; it appeared they hadn't, and they'd merely left the others to wonder where he'd gone. The kid hadn't talked, of course.

"You can eat with me. And with Phillip," Jeremiah said frankly. And Thaddeus, no doubt, but he was red-faced and breathless.

Tom didn't argue with them. The day had been long, but it was over. The sun was sinking, and Tom's desire to argue had already left him.

"No lawmen ever turned up? Or anyone to ask about Porter?" he said as he followed Jeremiah back toward the houses, returning a wave, then pausing to rub his sore leg.

"We've had no visitors," Phillip confirmed.

Then there was at least one thing that Tom hadn't been wrong about. He'd known the law wouldn't come quickly enough to a place like Friendly Field, even with all those bounties on the table.

He spotted Asher, who looked tired but also stony. Tom waved to him, and the boy returned it. Was he cross? Of course he was.

Tom managed to catch Mary's eye, and at least she didn't appear upset with him. He'd have a job ahead of him to patch that up, but her safety came before her good opinion. It had been better to take the business to the outlaws rather than allow them to come here in a position of strength and *then* have to figure out what to do about them.

Tom's way *had* been better. It had worked, hadn't it?

He entered Jeremiah's house, and Mrs. White tied her bonnet and left without a word. There was no telling what kind of rumors and gossip had gone about while he was away, and Mary would've had to weather all of it in that sewing room. Her days must have been just as miserable as Tom's. Worse, probably. After all,

Tom had known all along that if he needed to, he could simply kill his tormentors.

Mary didn't have that thought to comfort her, and those other women could be vicious. He would make this up to her somehow.

With a groan, he sank into a chair at Jeremiah's table. He tore a piece of bread from a loaf and took a bite, eying the three men. After a moment, he gestured at the chairs.

"A generous invitation," Jeremiah said dryly, folding his arms. "In my house."

"God's house," Tom corrected, swallowing. "It's all His anyway, isn't it? Before you get to scolding me, have you made any headway? Did you find out who killed Saul?"

"No," Phillip replied, scowling. He took a chair as well and straightened his suspenders. "It's been a strange couple of days, Tom."

"I'll bet. You should've told them a story about me going instead of letting them wonder."

"Lie, you mean." Jeremiah sat as well, and Thaddeus followed, mopping sweat from his brow.

Tom sighed. "No. No, I suppose not. I'm sorry. I should've told the lie."

It *hadn't* been fair to expect that of Jeremiah. *Of course* he didn't want to deceive his people—except that was precisely what he'd done in the church when he concealed that Saul had been murdered.

Pointing that out wouldn't make anything better.

"Where have you been?" Jeremiah asked directly.

"Where I said I was. I told you." Tom looked straight at Phillip. "I went to take care of the Porter gang."

"And do we still need to fear these men?" Thaddeus asked.

He'd been there, after all, when John Porter came to Friendly Field. He might have been softer hearted than Jeremiah, but John had made him uneasy. Why was that? He hadn't been suspicious of Tom at all. Was it Saul's death that had put him on edge? Of course. It was the first murder Friendly Field had ever seen. No wonder Thaddeus was rattled.

"No." Tom could say that confidently. Dead men weren't going to give them a lick of trouble. Better yet, no one—*no one*—knew what had happened out there. There wouldn't be any lawmen to complain, nor any friends or family of those men. Even if someone took offense at what had happened to them, they wouldn't know who to blame.

The job was done and done well.

"It was like I thought," he went on. "John Porter came here to feel us out, and he liked what he saw. I went to them and told them that we had already told the law." Tom pointed at Phillip. "As you did. I'd hoped that would be enough to make them leave, but it wasn't. See, you aren't like other towns. There're no lawmen, you got no guns, and even if you did, you wouldn't want to use them. To a man like that, you're asking to be taken advantage of. He and his men have been in the woods for months. It was just like I thought and just like I told you. They wanted your food, soft beds to sleep on. They wanted your women." Jeremiah twitched, and Phillip tensed. "That's not my thinking. It's the truth. And in their minds, there wasn't a thing to stop them from taking it all. So their notion was to hide, wait quietly for the law to come, let the law think they'd moved on—then come here. And I have an idea of how they planned to go about it, but that's not important anymore."

Tom waved a hand and helped himself to more bread. "In the end I had to feed them some of those mushrooms. I put them in their soup. They were real brave, thinking they'd just sneak past the law. They weren't so brave after that. I'm sure they'll still be sick this time next year."

"You poisoned these men?" Jeremiah asked calmly, eying Tom's throat and the other bruises on his face.

"I gave them a good reason not to do something foolish," Tom replied.

It was a terrible story; it didn't make sense, but these three would probably swallow it. Even Jeremiah. Because as odd as Tom's false narrative was, it would still be more palatable to the Quaker mind than wholesale slaughter.

"What if they seek retribution?" Phillip asked worriedly.

Tom shook his head. "They can't. I told you, they were brave before—but now they're in bad shape. They won't stay around here with the law coming. They could handle themselves in a scrap at their best, but they can't put up a fight now. They don't have a choice but to run."

Seconds went by. Jeremiah leaned on the nearest chair, still scowling.

Tom spread his hands. "I won't apologize," he said. "I know that you don't care for this. And I wouldn't blame you if you don't like me much. If you don't want me here, I'll go. I'm content to head to Des Crozet and write letters to Mary until she agrees to come marry me. I know that I do things that are hard for you. I thought I could change." He shook his head. "I can't. And I won't ask you to put up with me if you don't want to. I know if someone tried to tell me not to do what I thought I had to, I wouldn't take kindly to it. So

I can't very well try to tell you that you're wrong." He shrugged at them. "That wouldn't be right."

As he said it, he thought about the gang of outlaws rotting in the forest. He could talk about what was right until they nailed him in his coffin, but the truth was that he wasn't sure he'd know the right thing even if it was shouting in his ear.

CHAPTER TWENTY-FOUR

Tom left the house, and no one followed him. The village had settled for the evening, though no doubt every dinner table was abuzz with the strangeness of it. The fireflies were out, and they seemed agitated. Friendly Field always smelled good at dinnertime; the only time it smelled better was on Sunday, when they ate outdoors after service.

Tom hadn't taken his leave until after eating his fill of bread and jam, and he didn't feel much guilt for depriving the White household. The way he saw it, providing a little refreshment was the least Jeremiah could do.

Asher sat cross-legged in the grass, a polite hundred feet from Jeremiah's house. He had a stick, and a firefly had perched on it. He saw Tom come out and shook it off, getting to his feet.

Tom didn't have to look back to know that Phillip and Jeremiah were watching from the window.

"You are injured," the boy observed.

Tom touched his neck, which was still red and sore. "I've had worse."

"You found them."

"That was the easy part."

"What did you do?"

He sighed. "Same thing I always do."

"You got the best of them?"

"I suppose." Tom worked his shoulders and neck, hearing some alarming pops. He sighed.

"What's wrong?"

"It's always the same, kid. I think I know what I'm doing, and then, when it's all said and done, I start having second thoughts. Like there's always a better way, but I can't figure what it would be. There're some people you can't talk to."

"What you did, you did for these people," Asher said, and Tom couldn't believe his ears. Was this even the same boy he'd met on the Missouri River? "I would think that would count for something."

"I don't know, kid. All I think about is her." Tom glanced past him at Mary's house. "Maybe I did it for me. To keep them out of my way."

"Are you in love, Mr. Calvert?" The boy looked bemused.

Tom folded his arms and frowned. "I like to think so, but I just killed more than a dozen men. I wish there'd been a different way, but I know if it came to it, I'd just do it again. I guess I always thought love was for nicer people. I used to think I was in love with Miss Ayako, but now I barely think about her. There's just Mary."

"Mr. Calvert, there are some people who need killing." The boy said it without any particular emotion, like he would mention that he'd seen a hawk in the sky. "And I imagine there are few who would argue in defense of a gang of thieves. If those are the words."

"That may be, but I don't know that Mary would approve."

"I did not approve when you bossed me on the trail or went off to . . . to what?" the boy said, gesturing vaguely at the woods. "To fight an entire gang. But it seems I will benefit."

"I'm responsible for you."

"What?"

"I'm not responsible for her."

But Asher didn't seem to hear that. He was still hung up on the first part. "Mr. Calvert, you are *not* responsible for me."

Tom wasn't going to argue with him. "Fine. I thought of myself as being responsible for you. Does that suit you?"

Asher just swallowed; then he scowled at Tom. "I am older than you think," he said a little waspishly.

"But you still got no idea who knifed Saul?"

The boy blinked, then shook his head. "Mr. Calvert, you suggested that someone used the feathers to mislead us. Someone like that is cunning and may not be so easily uncovered."

"You might be right." Tom ran his hand through his hair; he'd left his hat in the woods with the outlaws and he needed a new one. "Well, I'll find them in any case."

"I thought it was your reckoning that Mr. Matthews must have done something to deserve what happened," the boy said.

"Oh, I think he must have." Tom paused to sneeze,

then shook his head. "I keep telling you, kid, they aren't all as pious as they act. But even if Jeremiah tells me to leave, I'll still sort this out first. Can't have a murderer just going free."

"What about you, Mr. Calvert? Can you go free?"

"I . . . ," Tom began, then stopped himself. He glared at the kid. "What is it? It's like you don't *want* her caught."

"You said you were certain it was a woman who was wronged who had done it," Asher accused. "Why not let her have her justice in peace?"

"Because I can't be *certain*. What if I'm wrong and she wants to hurt Mary next?" Tom spread his hands.

"And if you knew? What then?"

"I don't know, kid."

The twilight was fading, and the boy's flash of frustration seemed to go with the light. He let his breath out and smiled. "I am glad you are well, Mr. Calvert. I am glad you were not killed by those bandits."

"Me too," Tom grunted.

"How did you do it? Kill all those men?"

"With my bare hands," Tom replied, holding up his fists.

Asher snorted. "I suppose you will go to call on Mrs. Black."

"I owe her an apology."

The boy nodded. "You certainly do."

"Don't go taking her side, now, kid."

"The side of decency. You must have an idea what was said after you left. It is no secret that you love her and that she is partial to you," the boy hissed. "For good Christians, some of these women are downright cruel."

Tom grimaced. "I figured."

"But they are jealous," Asher relented, waving a hand. "That is why they bully her."

"Jealous of what?"

"Of Mary. Because of you."

"I'm a cripple."

"A handsome cripple. At least when you shave. Go on, then. I will not keep you. 'I would by no means suspend any pleasure of yours,'" the boy quoted dryly from that silly book of his, turning and starting back toward the house.

Tom watched him go, trying not to laugh.

"I found you a girl once, kid," he called after him. "I can do it again."

Asher just waved without looking back.

Tom grinned and started to limp toward Mary's house; he was too drained to do anything more than that. Which would be worse: staying in Friendly Field or going? There was guilt now; he didn't belong. Would it be any better if he went to Des Crozet? He'd have to make a point there not to be recognized, so he'd always be on his guard.

He didn't want to be on his guard all the time.

Well, his future in Friendly Field was in Jeremiah's hands. And Phillip's. Thaddeus probably didn't have much to say. Maybe Holly was wearing him out. At least Friendly Field was getting its money's worth out of her. These Quakers—well, they weren't any stranger than anyone else. In fact, they seemed more ordinary the longer he spent here.

The porch creaked as he climbed the steps, and Mary opened her door before he could even knock.

Tom went to take his hat off, only he wasn't wearing one. She didn't *look* angry.

"Evening, ma'am."

"Sir." She rolled her eyes and came out onto the porch, pulling the door shut. "Would you like to sit?"

"Yes, please." He sank into one of the wicker chairs, and she perched elegantly in the other. "I wish I could do that," he noted, gazing at her.

"What is that, Mr. Smith?"

"Sit up straight that way."

"I think you could if you were inclined."

"Not tonight."

Her expression softened as she gazed at his neck. "Mercy. What in the world have you been doing?"

"I went and talked that gang into leaving."

Her brows rose. "Did you really?"

"We won't see them here," he assured her. "So that's one less thing to worry about. But it's been a long couple days. I'm sure it has for you as well."

She wasn't the type to go looking for pity, but Tom would've known even without the kid to tell him. She'd weathered some things while he was gone.

"I'm sorry," he said.

"You might have told me where you were going."

"I thought you'd worry."

"I did worry."

He sighed. "I thought you might worry even more."

"I might have. Why would any sensible person do that, go looking for those men?" she asked.

"I thought it was better to make the first move," Tom said truthfully, "rather than let them do it."

"Weren't you afraid?"

"I was. But if I'd stayed here and waited, if I'd just hoped the law would come in time, I'd have been afraid then as well. More afraid, even."

Mary shook her head. "I cannot fathom your mind."

"You wouldn't want to."

"I would, though."

"Jeremiah might ask me to leave," Tom said bluntly, and Mary was taken aback.

"Would he? Why?"

"Because I keep making trouble."

There were more diplomatic ways to put it, but that was what it came down to. There'd been an awful lot of trouble lately, and Tom had had his fingers in all of it. In Jeremiah's shoes, he'd have thrown himself out of Friendly Field a while ago.

"I am sure your intent was to help."

"I believe it was," Tom replied. "But intent doesn't put supper on the table. It isn't worth a dime. There's been a lot of trouble since I came here. I reckon you'd have had most of it whether I came or not, but still . . . I know how it looks, and they aren't used to it. Jeremiah and Thaddeus. Having dealings with men like me and John Porter. And Saul." He drummed a finger on the arm of the chair. "It's the worst time to lose him. I don't know if he was much of a leader, but it still worries me. Jeremiah and Phillip are steady enough, though. They won't steer Friendly Field wrong."

"We don't have leaders," she reminded him gently, smiling.

Tom was tired, but when Mary was in front of him, he couldn't possibly pay attention to anything else. He sensed that something wasn't right. Instead of speaking, he just looked at her. That wasn't enough, though.

"What is it?" he prompted. "What are you thinking?"

There was a flash of frustration, but it was gone almost at once. She looked away from him, glancing out at the fireflies in the field. Then she made what might have been a shrug.

"I'm angry," she admitted finally, and she looked a little surprised that the words had made it out.

Tom swallowed. "I don't know what to do but to apologize," he told her honestly. "I'd like to make it up to you—"

"Not at you," she said, cutting him off. "Or not just at you."

He followed her gaze.

"Is it Holly?" He was taken aback; he'd thought that he'd gotten that straightened out.

"No," she grumbled. "It's not *her*. I know she's only doing what she . . . what she does." She fell silent, then looked at her hands, which where clenched on her knees. "You know that after Obadiah died, he solicited me."

"Thaddeus did?"

She nodded, and for a moment Tom heard what might have been her teeth grinding.

"Right away?" He couldn't help himself; he had to ask.

"No, no." She scowled. "He waited before he made his offer of marriage."

"Was he a leader at the time? But you said you have no leaders— Was he a . . . spiritual elder at the time?"

Mary gave him a flat look. "Thaddeus, Jeremiah, and Saul have been leading Friendly Field since I was a girl."

"And you turned him down?"

She looked affronted. "Of course."

"He has *all* the money that the village brings in. All of it. If you'd married him, *you* would have had it."

"For mercy's sake! I don't want money." She glared at him. "And he didn't want a wife. He— You know what he wanted."

"Of course," Tom replied. "I want it too."

Her eyes flashed. "No, Mr. Smith. You *do* want a wife. He wants a . . ." She trailed off, snorting. "A doll."

Tom watched her sit there, seething. She *was* angry. She saw him looking and tried to glare, but her heart wasn't in it. Her posture changed, becoming a little less perfect.

Mary groaned and glanced upward. "Thaddeus does this in front of God and everyone and then preaches virtue on Sunday. And someone's done murder. And we can't even sew without needling one another as much as the cloth."

Tom gave her a sympathetic look. "It's frustrating. But I'm no better."

"At least you tell the truth."

"I don't, though."

"Not even about yourself?"

He shook his head. "I lie like I breathe. Those men I talked into leaving? It's not true. I tried to do that, but it didn't work. So I killed them."

Even in the dark, he saw the color leave her face.

"It's true," he added, answering her unspoken question.

"Why?" The word came out sounding weak.

"They meant to come here. And I believe they would have done a lot of harm. So I made my choice. Then I came here and lied to you about it because"—he sagged in the chair—"because I knew you wouldn't like it. But I don't like lying to you. So I guess I can't win."

For a minute they were both quiet.

"What does it feel like, to have done that?" Mary asked finally.

Tom frowned. "There's a couple in the past that I regret." He scratched his cheek tiredly. "Not this bunch, though." He pointed at the bruises on his throat. "Suffice it to say they'd have done the same for me. And they would have, when they were done with me. John Porter never had any plans to let me live."

Someone blew out a candle in the next house over. There weren't many windows still glowing.

"Seems like ever since the boat, I just make a mess wherever I go." Tom sat up. "I'm sure Jeremiah and your mother are afraid I'll just lead you into sin. They're right."

"That does not concern me," Mary replied, joining him in looking out at the night.

Tom was surprised. "It doesn't?"

"If everyone else is free to just talk about following God instead of doing it, why shouldn't I be as well?"

CHAPTER TWENTY-FIVE

Tom had never given much thought to the notion of things turning out all right, maybe because he didn't have a good idea what all right was supposed to look like. After all, everyone liked to talk about all the things they'd do when they got a chance or after some obstacle was overcome—but there was always something else. The fellow who thought he'd have everything he needed when he had ten horses would inevitably realize what he *really* needed was twenty. Some other problem would come along, some other reason not to be content.

So what was the point? Why chase something that wouldn't ever be real?

He could think of a couple of reasons, but there were more important things to consider. It was odd that gossip worried him more than outlaws and murder, but there were a number of things about Tom's life that he thought people might find odd.

It was early enough that it was still dark outside, and that was good. It meant there was still time for him to make a stealthy escape. He didn't *want* to; in fact, leaving Mary's bed was the last thing he wanted to do. Even opening his eyes was a struggle, but he did it anyway.

She was gone.

Frowning, he sat up and listened, but the house was dead quiet. He touched the sheets where she had been and found them cool. Tom threw off the covers and got up, nearly tripping over the clothes strewn on the rug. He dressed quickly, then picked up Mary's clothes and folded them. He doubted anyone would come up here and see the room, but anything was possible. He wasn't worried about his own good name because he'd never had one, but Mary's still mattered. Where had she gone, though? He didn't want to steal away without saying goodbye, but Mary would probably prefer that to being discovered. She'd been pretty bold the night before, but she'd also been angry. Things tended to look and feel different in the light of morning.

There would be Quakers up and about even this early, mainly wives baking bread for the day. Tom slipped out of the house and hurried away in the dark. He didn't simply make his way back to the house he shared with Asher; that would be too obvious if someone saw him. He struck out east, making a wide loop around the houses. Now if someone saw him limping along, they would think he was just returning from one of his morning strolls.

To his surprise, he found Asher awake, perched on the bench that wanted to be a sofa. The boy was dressed for the day, and it looked as though he'd already bathed.

He looked up, startled, as Tom came through the door.

"Morning, kid."

Tom started the business of making tea. Asher had probably noticed that Tom hadn't come back last night, and he could be a worrier. Maybe he'd thought that Tom had run off again. Well, there was no danger of that. Not unless Jeremiah decided to throw him out of Friendly Field. Even then Tom wouldn't go far. He'd stay close to Mary as long as she didn't object.

"Have you eaten?" he asked.

Asher shook his head, then seemed to pull himself together. He was always a little off in the morning, when he was still groggy. Of course, if bathing in cold water hadn't woken him up, nothing would.

Tom prepared some eggs. They had a few of Mrs. Heller's biscuits, which were a day old but still good. With plenty of money to throw around and no shortage of good hotels, he'd eaten some good meals, but the Quakers ate well too.

Mary could be upset over their hypocrisy. Tom couldn't blame her for that, but things weren't any different anywhere else. Why wouldn't Quakers have weaknesses and vices? Well, it wasn't the vices that she held against them; it was that they wanted to pretend they didn't have them, and judge the people who did. This community had hanged a woman years ago, and now they wanted to act squeamish at the idea of outlaws being strung up.

Of course it bothered Mary. It probably bothered them all.

He was still a little hurt that she'd left without saying anything, though. What did she get up to in the mornings? He didn't know; she might have some responsibilities like feeding chickens, or maybe this was when she bathed. That seemed plausible.

"Are you well, Mr. Calvert?" Asher asked the words dryly.

"Well as I'll ever be. I think I'll be working the fields with you soon."

He knew perfectly well that Jeremiah wouldn't ask him to leave. Tom kept telling people it was a possibility because he didn't want to look like he was taking Friendly Field's hospitality for granted.

"I look forward to it."

"How do you like farming?"

"Compared to driving a wagon?"

"Sure."

"I like it a good deal better," Asher replied, "though I suppose that might be because I no longer have to worry about you succumbing to fever, Mr. Calvert."

"I'm glad I'm not worried about that as well." Tom shook his head. "I did hate not being able to think clearly."

"Are you thinking clearly now?"

"For a minute or two before I met Mary, I like to think I was."

They ate, tidied the house, and ventured out. The kid's head was somewhere else, but Tom was no different. The sun was out, and so were the Quakers.

"Peace be with thee," he said to the fourth person that morning, returning another wave. They weren't all as angry with him as Jeremiah, and even Jeremiah wasn't angry at *him*. He was angry about all of it; Tom was just one piece of this mess. Maybe Jeremiah could live with compromise, but all this lately had made him face it. Maybe his anger wasn't much different from Mary's.

One couldn't be cross about anything on such a pretty day, but Tom suspected it wasn't so much the day as the night before that had him in a good humor.

He spotted Mary, wearing the same sort of dress as always, but looking particularly radiant. She was with Mrs. Young and Mrs. Heller, making for Mrs. White's house to get about the day's sewing.

She saw him and froze, but only for a moment. The look of panic came and went so quickly that Tom might've missed it, but she mustered her courage and, with impressively little pink in her cheeks, detached herself from the others to join him.

Tom rolled up his sleeves and walked out to meet her, stopping several paces short.

"Peace be with thee," he said mildly.

"And also with you," she replied.

There were too many people, and it wasn't an option to go somewhere private.

"Are you well?" That was what the kid always said; it seemed appropriate.

"Very well," she replied. "Mr. Smith, have you ever done anything that left you surprised at yourself afterward?"

"Too many times," he admitted. "I got my share of regrets."

"I don't mean regret," she replied, and he let his breath out in relief. "But on occasion I feel as though I should take time to breathe."

Tom put his hands on his hips and took a breath. "I wish I was smart enough to do that. Ma'am, I won't be joining you today. I think it's high time I went to the fields. I'll miss the society," he added quickly, seeing her look of concern. "But I have to do my part."

"Of course," she replied.

"Would you like to have dinner with me and the kid this evening, if your mother's still taking her leave of the house?"

"I would. I think it might be best if the two of you called on me," she suggested.

"We accept. I just didn't want to impose."

"You're very polite, Mr. Smith."

"The kid gives me lessons." He tipped his hat.

So it was embarrassment that had made her flee. He *had* to leave the sewing room; she'd just have been self-conscious with him there.

Phillip was by the barn with some of the others, handing out tools. Tom yawned and headed that way, wondering what was waiting for him. He'd seen the men doing this work, but he'd never done it. It didn't *look* hard. They were just hilling right now, weren't they? Making sure the potatoes were covered with soil so the sun wouldn't get them?

That couldn't be very difficult.

"Would you let me go out? Peace be with thee," he added.

Phillip didn't reply for a moment, instead handing a spade to another man. He opened his mouth but didn't speak. Something had caught his eye.

Tom turned to see a girl he knew only as Laura hurrying out of the trees. She was a long way off, but Phillip wasn't blind.

"Something's wrong," he said, but Tom had already started off at as close to a jog as his limp would allow. Laura didn't appear to be injured, but there was naked desperation in the way she ran, not even bothering to hold up her skirts.

A second figure came out into the open—it was Holly, and though she wasn't running, she was every bit as pale. Was Laura running from her? No, that wasn't it.

Tom reached Laura, seizing her hands, which were locked into shapes like claws by her panic.

"Miss," he said, looking at her very directly. She didn't resist, but none of the tension would leave her, and her wide eyes were glassy. "You're safe," he said, looking past her at Holly.

Phillip arrived, and Tom passed Laura to him, striking out for Holly. She didn't rush toward him; she just walked stiffly. Rather than wide, her eyes were down, and her fists were clenched.

"Someone killed him," she said before Tom could even open his mouth.

"Killed? Who?" His hand was suddenly on his belt where his pistol should've been tucked into it—but he hadn't seen that gun in weeks.

"I don't know his name," she hissed, staring at the ground. Of course. She'd arrived only recently, and she didn't give a damn about these people.

"Did you see who did it?"

She shook her head.

"Where is he?"

"Right there. Just there." She jabbed her finger toward the trees.

Tom stepped aside, and Holly hurried back toward the houses. For a moment he stood, skin hot, a ball of queasiness sitting in his belly like a stone. The birdsong that normally filled the air all sounded miles away.

The body lay no more than ten paces past the tree line in the shade.

Some things got easier the more you practiced. Being wrong wasn't one of them.

When Tom had been lying in that wagon and thinking he would die of his wound or the fever, he'd been so careful not to talk himself into a lie. Not to tell himself that it would be all right.

He'd wanted to be ready to die, and being ready meant being honest.

Tom had convinced himself that he was right. That Saul Matthews had done something wrong, and some woman in this community had gotten justice and that was that. Had he been sure? No. He'd just *wanted* to be sure.

The leaves were kicked up, and the blood was all dark and dry. Jeremiah had been lying here for a while.

CHAPTER TWENTY-SIX

J EREMIAH'S EYES WERE open, and the pain and terror were fixed on his face so ferociously that Tom could see why Laura had looked that way. It struck even him, and he was no stranger to death.

This time the feathers weren't in his mouth; they were just scattered around his body.

Tom startled as Phillip appeared next to him, white and shaken.

"My God," he said.

The knife buried in Jeremiah's breast had been used several times. It was so dim that Tom couldn't be sure, but it looked as though there was also a wound on his abdomen. He'd been stabbed in the gut, then in the heart. The murderer's hand had been sure this time.

Jeremiah held no weapon, of course. It looked to Tom as though he'd fallen, and then his murderer had swooped down to finish him.

Tom found himself looking at the trees, watching as though there might be someone out there. Who? One of John Porter's outlaws? No, that wouldn't have made any sense. This was the work of the—well, the *witch*. Why? Why Jeremiah?

No one was perfect, but Jeremiah was *genuine*. He really had been. Tom could have seen Saul doing something in a moment of weakness, wronging someone. Jeremiah, though? The people of Friendly Field found it in themselves to like Thaddeus despite his vice.

They *loved* Jeremiah. He was a shade worldlier than the other two leaders, but that was good sense, not evil. They'd known that and taken comfort in it. *Tom* had taken comfort in it. He'd known Jeremiah wouldn't throw him out of Friendly Field because at the end of the day, even if he didn't like how Tom had gone about it, he was *glad* that he wouldn't have to deal with the Porter gang. And maybe he *had* believed that God would protect them, but he saw the benefit to having someone like Tom around in case that didn't turn out to be true. Friendly Field wasn't perfect—nowhere was— but it was a decent place and filled with decent people. Jeremiah had known that, and he'd known it was worth his while to do whatever he had to for its protection, even if it left a bad taste in his mouth. He had been a *good* leader.

What reason could anyone have had to kill this man? It almost wasn't an act of murder; it was more like a declaration of war. Taking away their best leader was an attack on all of Friendly Field.

Could that really have come from within?

Tom swallowed and turned his back on the corpse, rubbing his eyes. He'd felt obliged to figure out who'd killed Saul, but he hadn't felt *urgency*.

"Hell," he muttered, but Phillip didn't even hear him.

Tom lifted his hand, intending to give the other man a shake, but no—no, that wasn't the way to do it. Phillip was a solid man, but one killing in Friendly Field, let alone two—it was like the sun falling from the sky. Phillip didn't know what to do. And Thaddeus was likely very good at saying what the Quakers liked to hear and taking care of money and potatoes, but he didn't have much in the way of a spine.

Or a strong stomach.

Tom left Phillip there and hurried out of the trees. A couple of men from the field were making their way over; a commotion was brewing, and it wasn't clear where Holly and Laura had gone. Probably to their homes. Word would have been spreading.

"Sebastian," Tom called out, "find a bedsheet and run it out." He pointed. "And a blanket. Hurry." He kept on limping. "And you, Mr.—uh—Mr. Simmons?"

"Simcox," the man replied worriedly. "What's the matter?"

"Something bad has happened. You need to gather everyone up right away. I'm going to go get Thaddeus. He and Phillip can tell everyone what's happened."

"And what *has* happened?" the man pressed, clutching his spade.

Tom hesitated, standing in the sun. He was sweating. "Someone's killed Jeremiah White."

Laura was already talking. There was no hiding this. Jeremiah had concealed the first murder, and now—yes, it was time for everyone to know. They had to know.

The words were out of his mouth, and they couldn't go back in.

Mr. Simcox just looked blank.

"Did you—," he began, and Tom cut him off.

"No," he snapped. "I didn't kill him. We found his body just now."

"Could it have been an accident?"

"I don't think so." Tom meant to go on and tell him to do as he'd been asked, but Simcox was still talking.

"Over there?" he asked, pointing. "Why's he out by the lily pond?" That was what they called the pond where the women went to bathe.

Tom had been wondering about that himself, but all hell was about to break loose in Friendly Field. It would be bad no matter how it played, but it would be worse if someone didn't at least try to control it.

"Gather them up," Tom repeated more firmly, and Simcox flinched. "Get everyone in the church, and do it now. They need to know what's happened."

He didn't argue, and Tom got moving.

"What's the matter?" Mrs. Heller demanded the moment he was within earshot. "What's wrong?"

She wasn't alone. Tom waved them toward the church. Others emerged onto their porches, some of the older folks and children. The news could spread only so quickly; the spirit of panic and confusion had already overtaken the village.

Thaddeus emerged from his house, mopping his brow with his kerchief and looking lost. Someone moved behind one of his windows, and that could have only been Holly.

Tom waved to him and limped over.

"Jeremiah's been killed. It was *not* an accident," he added before the older man could even think of pushing back. "Everyone needs to go to the church."

Thaddeus didn't even hear that, though. It was as though the news had been witchcraft itself, something to turn him into stone. Thaddeus wasn't anything like stone, though. He was soft—soft in his midsection, soft in his sensibilities, and, Tom was beginning to suspect, soft in the head. He grabbed the older man's sleeve, steered him toward the church, and gave him a push.

"To the church," he repeated, gesturing.

On Sundays the townspeople flowed into the church like an impeccably dressed and groomed river, but now it was like herding squirrels. Worse, Tom's mind wasn't really there. It was still in the woods with Jeremiah's body. He didn't know if it was shock that the man was gone or shock at how profoundly he had been wrong. It all hurt.

Where was Friendly Field's newest widow, Mrs. White? Mary and a few other women were with her on her porch. Tom wasn't about to bother her. Phillip returned without Jeremiah's body. It seemed Tom's intention hadn't been clear—someone had dutifully gone out with the sheets, but they hadn't brought the body back; it was still lying in the woods.

Tom clarified that and dragged Phillip into the church and up to the front.

Workers from the far fields were still making their way in. Irksomely, there wasn't anything to stand on: no pulpit, nothing to put him up high enough to be seen and heard properly. The Quakers liked to walk around the church when they preached. Tom didn't feel like walking.

"Are you doing this or am I?" he asked bluntly.

"What?" Phillip asked.

"Do you want to address them or should I?"

"What do I say?" Phillip asked dazedly.

"Not a damn thing," Tom told him tiredly, letting go and raising his hands. "All right, everyone. All right."

They quieted miraculously quickly. He had to give them that: they were a well-mannered bunch.

"Um, peace be—," he began. "Screw it. Listen up, you all."

That got their attention. Now was his chance, but Tom didn't have the words. How was *he* supposed to know what to say? He wasn't a mayor or a preacher; he just couldn't stand chaos. And if nobody said anything, chaos was exactly what they'd all get.

"Is everyone here?" he demanded, scanning the faces.

There was Mary. And Asher. He didn't care much about anyone else, but everyone had to be accounted for. They had to know everyone was safe.

"Where is my mother?" Mary asked, looking around.

"She would not come out," Mrs. McHenry replied, frustrated. "She has been stubborn of late."

"Anyone else?" Tom called out. "Is anyone else missing?"

"Where is Jeremiah?" a woman asked. Clearly word hadn't reached her.

Tom couldn't put it off any longer.

"Jeremiah's dead," he announced, and it was like he'd told them God was a cow. "Shut them up," he muttered to Phillip, who looked at him as though he'd sprouted horns. "Do it," Tom ordered.

"Uh," Phillip said, making some calming gestures. And the Quakers were so polite that it more or less worked. He'd managed to live this long without raising his voice, and he planned to go on the same way.

"Listen," Tom said as loudly as he'd ever said anything. "You all need to listen. We got a problem, but we have to be calm. Stay in those pews and listen to what I'm telling you. Thaddeus, come up here. Yes. You," Tom added, pointing at him. "You're a leader in this village, and you'd better have something to say when I've said my piece."

Thaddeus was at the back of the sanctuary, dripping sweat. He mopped his face and hurried forward, visibly panicked.

Tom cleared his throat.

"I'm *not* your leader," he said. "But I'm doing the talking because I don't see that anyone else can or will. Saul Matthews did not die in his sleep. Well, he did—but not because he was ill. Someone killed him." Tom tapped his chest. "Stabbed him in the heart."

He should've been relieved that wasn't greeted with a storm of noise and panic, but it was almost more alarming the way the Quakers looked: uncomprehending.

"That's nonsense," a man said, getting to his feet.

Tom was genuinely startled, but as far as these folks were concerned, it *was* unthinkable. Murder was like a fairy tale to them: something that happened to other people, or maybe not at all.

"It isn't," Tom replied. "Jeremiah lied about it. He didn't lie out of sin or evil or any of that. He did it because he didn't want you all to be afraid. But now someone's done the same to him. And we need to find out who's done it and why."

They weren't hearing him. They were still hung up, hung up on murder itself—no, not all of them.

A bearded man Tom didn't know well stood up.

"If anyone here has killed someone, it's you," he said bluntly. "I know about you, Tom Smith. You said yourself you're a cardplayer. You think our people are like the money you like to win. You want to be king of

Friendly Field. This trouble started when you came here. There is talk of your past, and now this."

The man hadn't done a good job of putting it into words, but the sentiment was exactly what Tom had feared. Well, "feared" wasn't the word. He wasn't afraid.

There was a murmur of agreement.

"Yeah," Tom replied, "I take your meaning. But I don't want to be your leader. It's a burden, not a privilege. I wouldn't take it if it was offered to me freely, let alone kill for it. You *have* leaders. They're right here." Tom pointed from Phillip to Thaddeus. "I'm not going to lead you. I'm going to say what needs saying, and they're going to lead you. Jeremiah tried to lead and got himself killed. Someone here is a murderer. It's not an outsider. I've been wrong about things, but I'm not wrong about that. It's someone in this church with us."

That got the people muttering and looking around, but Tom wasn't finished.

"And you need to know that. If there was someone like that around, I would want someone to tell me, so I am telling you. That is what I'm doing, sir." Tom wished he knew the man's name, but he couldn't remember everyone. "I'm telling you because Jeremiah tried to tell you and you didn't listen. You remember when he talked about watching for the devil? What he meant was to watch your backs, because he didn't know who had done for Saul."

The man didn't seem to have anything to say to that.

"Who saw Jeremiah last?" Tom demanded. "I saw him yesterday in the evening when it was dark but still early." He didn't want to call out to Mrs. White by name. He didn't mind being rough with these Quakers; they needed it—but she had just lost her husband. He turned to Phillip. "You were still with him when I left. How long did you stay?"

"Not long," Phillip replied, licking his lips. "And Mrs. White returned."

Jeremiah hadn't been alone, then.

"Did anyone else see him last night, then?" Tom addressed the others. There were some tears and some muffled sobs, but he pressed on. "After dark? He was killed in the night. I know that much. Anyone?"

Nothing.

Tom's temper stirred, or maybe it was his pride. They were all staring at him. Not at Phillip, not at Thaddeus.

"Thaddeus," he said, and the older man jumped as though someone had struck him. "You're Jeremiah's neighbor. Did you, or anyone in your household, see anything?"

"No," Thaddeus replied quickly, dropping his handkerchief. He stooped to pick it up. "No, of course not. No."

"Miss Adams?"

Holly got to her feet, pale but calm. She wasn't as fragile as these Quakers. "No," she replied shortly. "I saw nothing to remark on."

"All right. And Mr. and Mrs. Pilkin. Your house is the next nearest. You saw or heard nothing?"

Mr. Pilkin was shaking his head, his wife right next to him.

Tom pulled Phillip over. "Go and ask Mrs. White when she last saw her husband. Be as considerate as you can, but someone has to ask. And it shouldn't be me."

"All right." Phillip was too rattled to be bothered by Tom ordering him around.

Tom faced the congregation again, thinking fast. "I gather that no one here has a notion of why anyone might have wanted to see Jeremiah dead," he said finally. "But do any of you know of any grievances against him? Is there anyone who didn't like the man?"

Silence.

Tom sighed. "I thought so. At any rate—" He wasn't finished, but he was cut off.

"What about you?" That came from a man Tom knew: his name was Friedrich, and he did all the wood-working for Friendly Field. "I know Jeremiah was thinking of asking you to leave last night. *You* had a grievance with him, Tom Smith. What were your where-abouts?"

Tom twitched. He felt no fear or worry, but he didn't have time to consider the most practical reply or even to begin to craft a lie that would do the job. Mary didn't give it to him. She got to her feet.

"My house—," she said, and there was only the slight-est hint of coolness in her voice. The rest was all calm. It was almost a challenge. "—is where he was all through the night, and I can assure you that Jeremiah's name wasn't mentioned."

The church had already been quiet; the Quakers were too unnerved even to whisper. Now it was as though they'd all just died on the spot, though only for a moment. All eyes turned on Mary, who wasn't fazed. She stood with her hands clasped over her apron, that same vaguely regal look on her face. She didn't look at Tom.

Her eyes flitted over to Mrs. Heller. "Spare me,"

Mary said to her. "We're all equals here. If you can overlook one indiscretion, you can overlook another."

It was as though she'd smashed a barstool over the head of every Quaker in the sanctuary. And shot Thaddeus in the face; if he'd gotten any redder, he'd have burst.

"Oh, hell," Tom muttered.

CHAPTER TWENTY-SEVEN

TOM WAS NO stranger to a full day's work—not anymore. And it did take the day, or very nearly all of it, to get the work done. To keep the Quakers in line, even when they grew tired and restless from waiting in the sanctuary. When they were hungry and afraid.

Mrs. White had nothing to add. She had gone to bed while her husband had brooded downstairs, no doubt over what to do about Tom. She said it first to Phillip, then to Tom himself, and with no particular ill will. She wasn't angry; she was just lost. Her husband hadn't been a young man, but he'd been strong and spry, so there had been no expectation from anyone that his time was coming soon. The loss was such a shock to her that the detail that it had been murder—she hadn't gotten around to giving that much thought yet.

Or at least she said there was no one she had reason to suspect. She couldn't suspect Tom; she'd sat next to him in the sewing room these weeks. She knew he

wasn't afraid in the slightest of being thrown out of
Friendly Field.

After a full day spent asking questions in the sti-
flingly hot church, there were only a handful of people
who hadn't been accounted for the night before. Everyone had a family; there was nowhere for any of them
to go.

Friedrich had been in his shop until late into the
evening, working by lamplight. There was only his
word for that, but he'd had no reason to hurt Saul or
Jeremiah, and he wasn't a woman.

An old man who still believed in God despite out-
living all five of his children had likewise been isolated
enough that no one could vouch for him. He walked
with a stick, and potatoes grew faster than he could
move. He barely had the strength to lift his eyelids,
much less a knife. He wasn't capable of committing the
murders or of getting up into the hills and the woods
to make that thing with the feathers.

Mrs. Washburn was the same; she'd been shut up
alone ever since leaving Mary's house, and though she
was bad-tempered enough to kill, Tom couldn't picture
it. It was *possible*.

Once Jeremiah's body was brought back, Tom discovered that he'd been stabbed in the back as well.
That wound had probably been inflicted first and sent
him to the ground. Then the murderer had said whatever she wanted to say to him before inflicting the
wounds that had killed Jeremiah.

An older woman might accomplish that if she could
take her victims by surprise, and that was probably
what had happened. Saul had been killed in his bed.
Jeremiah had first been struck from behind.

But Mrs. McHenry, who was hosting Mrs. Washburn,

said that Mary's mother was weaker than ever, and Mary seconded that. Further, it was clear that Mrs. Washburn had scarcely left the house.

There had been more to the job of killing Jeremiah White than just sticking a knife in him. His killer had lured him out of his house and done it without alerting Jeremiah's wife. Mrs. Washburn—she had the brains for it, but Tom just couldn't see how she'd have carried it all out without being seen.

Still, she was the one who stuck in his mind. He knew now why she had left Mary's house, and it wasn't just to allow Tom to spend the night, though he was convinced that was part of it. Like her daughter, Mrs. Washburn chafed at some of Friendly Field's hypocrisy. Holly's arrival had upset quite a few people. It was one thing to know of a secret vice, and another for it to be flaunted in everyone's faces. Thaddeus' decision to simply have Holly in his house was fairly brazen, at least to Tom's sensibilities. But the old man wasn't trying to make trouble or offend people; he was just old and not especially bright. The effects of his actions on other people were lost on him. If he'd had any sense, he'd have just ridden out to Des Crozet and seen the women there, then come back.

But he didn't have any sense, and he was probably lazy and didn't want to make the trip.

Holly and Thaddeus and all of it—they irked Mary and Mrs. Washburn. But a lot of things irked people, and they generally didn't reach for knives every time they were irritated. And why go after Saul and Jeremiah? Why not kill *Thaddeus* if that was what this was about?

Among the meager handful of people who *might* have been free to commit the crime, Tom couldn't find even one with a half-decent reason to do it.

Evening was coming on when he had Phillip let them all out of the church. They'd lost a whole day's work, but he didn't care about that.

"What if there was more than one?" Asher asked as they stood in the waning sunlight, watching the Quakers disperse. Some were going to see to essential chores, and others just returned to their homes.

A few were openly grateful to Tom for trying to sort things out. Others were angry or suspicious, and they were all afraid. Mary had gone to her mother, but there was no reason for her to hide. The scorn and whatever else she might have expected wasn't coming, at least not today. It wouldn't matter once Tom married her, which he fully intended to do if she'd have him, but he couldn't very well get on with that with this mess unsettled.

It shouldn't have been his business; it should've been the business of the town's leaders. But now there were only two of them: one useless and one too new to the job to be any good at it.

Phillip had pulled himself together, though. He joined Tom and Asher, pausing to massage his temples. It had been a long day, and his head had to hurt just as much as Tom's did.

"I thought of that," Tom murmured to the boy. He had, when they'd discovered the wound on Jeremiah's back. "I stewed on it for a while. And I don't think so." He yawned. "It would explain a lot, if it was more than one murderer, and they could lie for each other and so on, but I don't think so. There is"—he gestured vaguely—"a secret, a reason, for those two men to die. And if folks knew what it was, they'd be acting . . . different. People like this—if they were knowingly hiding something, we would be able to tell."

"A conspiracy," the boy supplied helpfully.

"If that's what it is, I like to think I'd be able to see it. See the ones who aren't acting right. The only one acting suspicious is Mary's mother, and she's not killing anyone. And the rest? They wouldn't make good criminals."

"Could it be one of your outlaws?" Asher asked.

"If one of them had survived and found us, he'd be after *me*. And Saul died before the Porter gang even knew me," Tom pointed out. "There's a woman here in Friendly Field, and she's no witch. She's just mad as hell."

"You sound so sure," Phillip said.

"I am, because I know exactly how she feels." He rubbed his face. "I was on a boat on the Missouri, and a man I beat in cards accused me of being a cheat. Then he tried to accuse me of attacking a woman. None of it was true. And then *another* man said he trusted the man who did all that. I was mad enough to kill. This woman feels like I did that night."

Asher was staring at him.

"What?" Tom asked.

"You sound as though you are on her side," the boy remarked.

Tom sighed. "No. No, we'll have to stop her."

"And then she'll hang." That came from Phillip, and Tom wasn't sure he'd heard the man correctly.

"Do you mean it?"

The big man scowled. "I don't know," he admitted after a moment. "I'm angry as well."

"You all have been through enough." Tom watched the Quakers jerkily try to get back to their day, as though that were possible. Things had changed. The murders. Mary's words. Thaddeus.

For a long time, Saul, Thaddeus, and Jeremiah had

looked after these folks and done a good job. They had kept things the same. They worked their long days, but they lived in peace and comfort. It was as much as anyone could have asked for. It had to change, though. Those three men hadn't been getting any younger, and sooner or later, something would've come along. If it hadn't been Tom and Asher, it would've been the Porter gang.

Or someone else.

Tom didn't know which would be worse: having to hang another of their own, or keeping the murderer prisoner and waiting for some lawman to come and deal with it. It would be a nightmare either way, and he didn't want Mary to have to go through it.

The door of Thaddeus' house opened, but no one appeared. After a moment, a bag tumbled out into the open, falling down the steps and into the grass, then another. Holly appeared, carrying her other things.

"What in the world?" Tom said, frowning.

"She appears to be in a hurry," Asher noted, and what was that? Amusement in his voice?

Tom wasn't listening. He limped out across the grass toward her as several of the Quakers looked on.

Holly couldn't possibly have all her things, but it was still enough that she couldn't conveniently carry it all. Tom saved her from dropping them, and she glared at him.

"What's happening?" he asked, bewildered. "Is he throwing you out?"

Her mouth dropped open. "Throwing *me* out? *No*," she hissed.

"You're leaving?"

Of course she was. This wasn't what she had come here for. Two people had been stabbed, and they still didn't know why or by whom. All Holly knew was that she wasn't very popular in Friendly Field. She didn't feel safe, and Tom couldn't very well blame her. For all she knew, she'd be the next one to wake up with a knife in her. Tom was fairly certain that wouldn't be the case, but her comings and goings were her own business.

"He got his money's worth," she told him, and it sounded as though that was all the justification she planned to offer for leaving before whatever time agreed upon.

"You can't walk to Des Crozet," Tom told her flatly.

"I will not wait."

"Hey, Finn!" Tom called out to a man carrying a sack of apples toward the church.

"Yes?"

"Thaddeus has offered Miss Adams a horse," Tom lied. "Any one she likes. Can you go get her fixed up? She wants to leave right away."

Whatever irritation the Quakers might have felt at giving Holly a horse would be easily overshadowed by their relief at seeing her leave. They couldn't help but see her as being far more of a problem than the fool who'd summoned her. Given enough time, they would twist the memory into one in which the wicked temptress had led the virtuous man astray instead of the amorous old fool spending money that wasn't his on the very things he preached against.

That, Tom could live with. He didn't care for it, but the sun would keep rising.

These killings, though—he couldn't look at them quite the same way.

"I'm not a damn lawman," he muttered as he walked away.

"Your pardon, Mr. Calvert?"

"It's nothing, kid."

He wouldn't ever see Holly again, though he hadn't realized he wanted to until she had turned up here. She was pretty and good at what she did, but it was her decency and sense that Tom had always liked. Now what he liked about her was familiarity. Everything was so strange here and only getting stranger—so there was comfort in having someone he had a feel for around. Someone who knew *him*. Not just who he was or who he was trying to be, but who he had been.

"Make some dinner, will you?" Tom prodded the kid's arm. "I'm starved."

"All right. Where are you going?"

"I'm going to call on Mrs. Washburn. And make inquiries about her health. Find Phillip and have Thaddeus come over to eat with you and me. Don't take no for an answer. If Holly's leaving, there's no one to cook for him."

"Why with us?" the boy asked, taken aback. "I do not mind," he clarified quickly, "but there cannot be any shortage of families keen to host him."

"He'll feel safest with us," Tom replied honestly.

"But we are strangers."

"Yeah. I'm also the only thing in this place that scares him more than this murderer." Tom took his hat off to fan himself, and in the light of the sunset, he could see the look on Asher's face. "What?"

"You believe him to be in danger?"

"I don't expect him to last the week. If our witch doesn't kill him, his heart'll likely give out. There're two people in this village hiding something, and he's one of them. I don't know why he'd be good at keeping a secret. He isn't good at anything else."

* * *

M RS. MCHENRY WAS in her parlor with Mary. They both rose to their feet at Tom's arrival, and he took off his hat. Mrs. McHenry couldn't have been glad to see him, but at least there was no hostility on her face or in her voice. The sleeves of her gingham dress were stretched where she'd been clutching at them.

"Peace be with thee."

"Also with you," he replied, taking in the raw vegetables on the table and the cold stove visible in the kitchen through the door. "We're having supper shortly. Could I bring you something?"

"No, I will get started presently."

"Mrs. Black, may I have a word?"

"Of course."

He took Mary into the hall but kept his distance. "I apologize," he told her.

"For what?"

"All of it."

"I chose for myself to say it." She couldn't have possibly felt as carefree as she made the words sound. "And I did so on the one day it might *not* be the biggest scandal in Friendly Field."

There was a smile with those words, and Tom had to admit she was right. A clever way to ease her conscience while also easing the consequences. He doubted she felt any genuine guilt about what she had done, but she didn't like dishonesty. She had *wanted* to tell. And she had to be far more troubled by the murder than by the scandal in any case.

"Would it cause great offense if I waited until things settle down before I propose?"

She gave him a look. "Why broach the subject if not to do it?"

"I guess to assure you it was my intent," he replied, a bit sheepish.

"I never thought otherwise," she murmured, then snorted. "If it *wasn't* your intent, there would have been another murder in Friendly Field."

Tom was surprised to hear a joke like that, today of all days. Maybe today was when they needed it. Trying not to laugh, he twisted his hat between his hands.

"No need for threats, ma'am. There's nothing I want more. I'd like to do it right," he went on. "I'll even get down on one knee."

She frowned and eyed his leg. "Can you?"

"It'll hurt."

"Do it standing, then."

"Well, fine, I will."

"Very well, then."

"Very well. Is your mother in?"

Mary sobered at once and nodded. "She is upstairs."

"Is she well?"

"She's out of sorts." That was what Mary said, but she was worried.

"May I see her?"

She frowned and glanced past him, but Mrs. McHenry was busy in the kitchen.

"For what purpose? She is not inclined to callers."

Tom believed that, but that wasn't all he believed.

He sighed and looked her in the eyes. "She knows something."

The frown deepened. "Of . . . ," she began but halted, brows rising. "Do you mean to say she knows something of Saul and Jeremiah? That's nonsense, Tom. How could she?"

"She's a sharp lady. If it's nonsense, I'd like to hear it from her."

Mary was at a loss. Seeing that he was serious, she licked her lips and straightened up. "All right," she said, looking dazed.

"Thank you." Tom ducked his head and went upstairs. The Quakers built sturdy homes, and the fresh pine hardly creaked at all.

He knocked.

"Is that Tom?" Mrs. Washburn asked wearily.

"It is, ma'am." He let himself in to find her in the chair by the window. She made no obvious show of displeasure as he closed the door behind him. In fact, she wasn't even looking at him.

"There's weather coming," she predicted, gazing out as the last light of evening faded.

"Seems calm enough."

She shook her head. "It's too still."

"It's never too still for me." Tom set his hat on the dresser.

"You haven't lived to see as many storms as I have," she replied. Mrs. Washburn looked well enough; she wasn't weak or sickly.

"You suspect one's coming?"

"I don't have to suspect. It's clear as day," she told him before going back to looking outside. "The sky's the wrong color, and the air doesn't feel right. Are you here to ask for my blessing?"

"No, but I might as well. Do I have it?"

"Of course not. She has known you less than a month, and you're nothing but trouble." Mrs. Washburn gave him a flat look, not exactly challenging, just tired.

"Sorry you feel that way, ma'am."

"She knows all that," she added, as though it affronted her that he might not have been aware of it. "But if she wants to overlook it, what am I going to do about it? She's too old to scold, and I'm too old to do it."

"You worried about her soul?"

Her poker face held, and she didn't say a word.

"What about yours?" he pressed.

Tom didn't have a prayer of staring her down; she was more than a match for him there. He went over and perched on the bed, facing her directly.

"Maybe you aren't as superstitious as the rest, but you won't tell me a lie in front of God. You know who she is," he said, "the one who's doing this."

Seconds passed.

"You want to protect a murderer?" he pressed.

"Do I look as though I can protect anyone or anything?" she asked. She wasn't afraid; she might have been the only person in Friendly Field who wasn't. Her hands were shaking, but it wasn't fear. It was rage.

"Did you want Saul dead?"

"No," she replied at once.

"And I know you had nothing against Jeremiah." He was wrong about that, though. He'd played cards with her, and he knew the corner of her mouth would give a twitch when she was squirming inside. "Or maybe you did," he said, and she scowled at him.

"I don't wish murder on anyone."

"But you don't mind standing aside," Tom said quietly. "You know who it is and why she's doing it. And maybe you don't wish it on them, but you're not putting a stop to her. You don't blame her."

Mrs. Washburn's mouth had become a tight line, but she didn't do anything as obvious as grip her apron.

"You know why," Tom said simply. He was right about that much. "What did Saul and Jeremiah do that they brought this on themselves?"

She looked vaguely contemptuous, though only for a moment.

"It's not them. It's all of us. Sin might seem to be left in the past . . ." She stopped there for a moment, turning to look out the window. "It's always there, though. Just behind us. You as well, Mr. *Smith*. And me."

Mrs. Washburn didn't see this woman as a murderer; she saw her as the hand of God. She just didn't have the stomach to watch up close as it unfolded. That was why, after Saul's death, when she'd realized what was happening, she'd come here and shut herself up in this room.

And she hadn't come out when Jeremiah was killed. That meant Tom was right: it wasn't over.

"I'll give her a chance to hang it up peaceably if you tell me her name."

She hesitated. "I don't know her name."

Tom wasn't sure what to make of that. It couldn't have been an outright lie—she wouldn't do that. It was still a deception, though. The lie was that she didn't want these men dead. If she didn't, she'd tell Tom what he needed to know instead of trying to leave him in the dark.

"What did they do that they needed to be punished for?"

"Nothing," she replied, smiling bitterly. "They did nothing."

He wasn't going to break through, and he couldn't very well beat the truth out of her. Besides, he had a

feeling he'd be on her side when it came down to it—
but there'd been enough killing, justified or otherwise.
Tom was the last man to open his mouth about pulling
the trigger, but someone had to.

"Tom," she said.

"Yeah?"

"I like you. I don't like you for a son-in-law. You're
too arrogant. But my daughter likes you, so . . ." She
trailed off, waving a hand, then sighed. "Go home and
mind your own affairs."

"I liked to think Jeremiah and I were friends," Tom
pointed out, "or something like friends. Doesn't that
make it my business?"

"You are blind and you are a fool. Go to bed, Tom.
Go and stay there. It will cost you if you do otherwise."

CHAPTER TWENTY-EIGHT

ᵔ

H OW COULD MRS. Washburn have it figured and no
one else did?

It had to go back to that witch they'd hanged, but
Mary's mother wasn't the only person who remem-
bered that. It had been less than twenty years ago.
Mary remembered it; most everyone did.

Yet everyone else was baffled. True, Mrs. Washburn
was smarter than most, but that alone didn't explain it.

Tom stepped down from the porch and looked back
at Mary in the doorway of the McHenry house. She
was worried, but no amount of reassurance from him
could change that. She needed to be with her mother,
and at the end of a day like this, romance was the last
thing on her mind. Tom's as well.

It still would have been nice to eat with her, but that
wasn't in the cards.

Mrs. Washburn was right about the uncanny stillness that had fallen over Friendly Field. It wasn't just

quiet because of what had happened, though that added to it. The Quakers were never boisterous, but they weren't entirely without humor. It was almost fully dark now, and no one was laughing in Friendly Field as Tom limped home.

The windows glowed in the house. The kid was good at looking after a home, and he was ten times the cook that Tom would ever be. It would've been nice to eat with Mary, as planned, but this was more important.

Thaddeus was at the table with a cup of tea, and Asher nearly had the meal ready.

"Need help, kid?" Tom asked, hanging up his hat.

"No. I will serve presently."

He didn't say it for Thaddeus' benefit; he was as bad as Tom when it came to asking for help. Tom took his place at the table.

"Peace be with thee," he said to Thaddeus, a touch ironically. The older man was not at peace, though he looked a good deal better than he had in the church.

"Thank you for having me over, Tom."

"Of course. I hope you aren't too upset about what was said today."

Thaddeus shook his head. "No, no," he replied, "not at all."

He must not have even heard what Mary said, and Tom wasn't surprised. Thaddeus was struggling. Of course, even if he'd heard, Tom hoped Thaddeus would be the last man to give anyone any grief about fornication. He might do it in his sermons, but even he wasn't so far gone that he'd do it face-to-face.

Not to Tom's face, at any rate.

"Someone has to take charge," the older man went on. "It was always for Saul and Jeremiah to give voice to God's will. I don't know what to do. But to pray," he added.

"Praying's all well and good," Tom told him frankly, "but it doesn't bring in the harvest. We have to roll up our sleeves and do that ourselves."

Thaddeus grimaced and nodded. "Yes."

Asher brought out the meal, a stew with chicken and corn bread.

"Did Mrs. Heller give this to us?" Tom asked.

"I baked it," Asher replied. "There was a sack of cornmeal in the larder. I expect no one to miss a little."

"Who taught you to make it?" Tom asked in wonder. There was nothing the kid couldn't do.

"My aunt."

"You've done a nice job."

"Yes," Thaddeus agreed.

"Thank you," Asher said. "I am glad you like it."

Tom cleared his throat. "Thaddeus, do you know why anyone would want to kill Saul and Jeremiah?"

The older man choked briefly, then peered at Tom with watery eyes. "I believe it is the last thing any one of us would ever wish for." He appeared to mean what he said.

Tom chose his words carefully. "It's been suggested that this is balancing the scales for what happened before, years ago. The hanging."

Thaddeus' brows rose, as though such a thing hadn't even occurred to him. And just as Tom predicted, Thaddeus took him at his word. No one had suggested that, not really—no one but Tom. Thaddeus looked thoughtful.

Asher stayed quiet.

"To balance the scales," the old Quaker mused

sadly, eyes distant. "It feels like a long time ago. A life-time."

"That's fair to say," Tom replied encouragingly. He felt the boy's gaze on him, and he ignored it. The kid should've known they weren't hosting Thaddeus out of the goodness of their hearts. On the other hand, there was a lot of goodness in the boy. Maybe he *had* believed this was a simple act of charity. "Was it that bad, what happened?"

Thaddeus groaned tiredly, still staring into the past. The night was so still that every creak and rustle hung in the air.

"The devil came here," he said with a small nod. "He was in Friendly Field, to be sure. I suppose that was when I learned that none of us is safe from him. No one," he repeated.

"Would you do it again?" Tom asked. "Hang a witch?"

Thaddeus grimaced. It was clear the memory brought him enormous pain; he appeared to shrink inward just at the mention of it.

"It was a horrible thing to do," he admitted at last, "to one of our own. And for what?" Tom had the sense that Thaddeus wasn't really talking to him anymore, but to himself. "For the iniquity of weakness?"

"We all have them," Tom pointed out.

"Not all weaknesses will take a life, though. An innocent." Thaddeus' face was gray now. "A mother," he added, looking surprised at himself.

Tom almost dropped his spoon. "What?"

Thaddeus blinked and looked up. "Hmm?"

"The woman who was hanged had a child? A daughter?"

Thaddeus grimaced, and it took him a moment to answer.

"Yes," he replied finally. "She concealed that she was with child from nearly everyone."

"How old was the girl when you hanged her mother?" Tom demanded, and the old Quaker flinched.

His mouth moved as he floundered. "But an infant."

"Jesus," Tom said, forgetting himself. "Where is she now? What's her name?"

Thaddeus was clearly taken aback by Tom's sudden intensity.

"I don't know," he replied, a touch of defensiveness in his voice. "Gone from here. Taken."

"By whom?"

"There— Mr. Smith, there were those among us who could not abide what was done," Thaddeus said, pained. "It was they who took the child and left Friendly Field. They are long gone."

Of course. Of *course*, there had been some Quakers who couldn't stomach a hanging.

"So if that girl came here, you wouldn't recognize her," Tom said.

Thaddeus just stared at him.

"I guess not," he said. "But why would she come here?"

CHAPTER TWENTY-NINE

W<small>HAT DO YOU</small> think, kid?"

They stood together by the window, watching Thaddeus carry his lamp into the dark, heading back to his house.

"You'd want to get back at the people who hanged your mother, wouldn't you?" Tom asked.

The boy licked his lips. "I would," he replied.

Tom watched Thaddeus vanish into the night. "Me too."

Mrs. Washburn knew about the baby. She must've noticed something that tipped her off that the child had returned. As for how the child got on this path, the Quakers who'd taken her must've told her what had happened to her mother. And the girl hadn't adopted a very Christian view of it clearly. Tom didn't blame her, but he still had to do something.

"Why do you think they'd do it?" Tom asked, straightening up. "Hang someone like that. Wickedness? Or stupidity?"

"Wickedness," Asher replied without hesitation. "To kill without cause."

Tom was surprised; usually the boy was the charitable one. Now the tables were turned. "See, I like to think they believed they were doing what was right."

"That would give very little comfort to the dead," the kid pointed out, "or those left behind."

Tom hesitated, struck by the words. "True enough."

He was fairly sure there was only stupidity to blame for what had happened—or was there? No one had mentioned the hanged woman having a husband, only a child she'd borne in secret. He remembered—Mary had mentioned the witch lying down with the devil. Well, if the Quakers thought the devil was the father, they were as wrong about that as they were about everything else.

"Kid, you still got my old derringer?"

"Of course." The boy held it out.

"Thanks." Tom tucked it into his pocket. "Whatever the reason might've been, they're paying for it now."

Asher nodded. "So they should," he said.

Tom leaned against the wall and folded his arms. "All of them?"

"They act as one," Asher pointed out.

"Some objected."

"Those who remain did not." The boy shrugged.

"I reckon that's what Mrs. Washburn meant. She wouldn't say what Saul and Jeremiah had done to deserve this. I got a notion they didn't do a damn thing. They were more or less in charge back then. They could've stopped it, but they didn't. That's the grudge that got them killed."

Asher didn't have anything to say to that. Tom put his hands out toward the window, but the air out there wasn't moving.

"I guess it would get to me too," he conceded. "But that's where I am now, isn't it? If I get out of the way, I'm just like them. But that's what Mrs. Washburn wants me to do."

"Does she really?"

"Yes." Tom ran his hand through his hair.

"What about your scandalous behavior with her daughter?" Asher asked mildly. "How does she feel about that?"

"She's got enough sense to know God doesn't give a damn about things like that."

"Quite the theologian you've become in your time among the Quakers, Mr. Calvert," Asher said as he went over to sprawl on the bench, fanning himself with a hand. The night just wasn't cooling off any.

Tom snorted. At least the kid was in a good humor. "You aren't reading tonight?"

The boy was just lying there. "Not tonight."

Maybe it was the weather that was making him uneasy; it bothered Tom as well. He'd never felt stillness like this. The kid had made a good point; if the townspeople had *really* objected, there would have been no hanging. Well, they were just starting to pay for it. The loss of Jeremiah hadn't truly been felt yet, and it wouldn't be until his leadership was needed.

Thaddeus was kind and even sensible during calm times, but when things got bad, he was useless. Phillip didn't have Jeremiah's brains. In fact, the only person who came to mind who had what it would take to lead these people was Mrs. Washburn.

But the Quakers would talk until they were blue in the face about how they were all equals, and then they'd likely balk in the same breath at the notion of a woman making decisions.

So Phillip would lurch from one hardship to the next, doing the best he could, and Tom would let him unless he asked for help. The one thing he wanted even less than to watch the Quakers flail around as the world closed in on them was to be responsible for them.

He wanted to spend his days in the fields and his nights with Mary. And to spend a little time with the boy; now that Asher had a little confidence, he actually made for pretty good company.

"Don't wait for me, kid." Tom took his hat and went to the door.

"Don't you worry that I will look down on you for being of low character?" Asher asked idly. He didn't even open his eyes.

Tom paused. The kid thought he was going to call on Mary. "Well," he said finally, "if you were going to look down on me for something, I guess I'd hope it would be for killing folks. Not for this."

"I told you before, some folks need killing," Asher pointed out. "Those outlaws, for example."

"Maybe so."

Tom went out, and the thick, warm air draped itself over him like a blanket. The quiet pressed in, an invisible fog. It was so quiet that he should've been able to hear, but there was only the gentle pressure on his ears.

The windows of the house glowed in the dark. Friendly Field wasn't his to look after; he was just being a busybody one last time.

Then he could hang it up for good.

CHAPTER THIRTY

HOLLY WAS GOOD at fooling people. She had to be; it was part of her business. Tom had been vain to think that because he read people for a living he couldn't be deceived.

Of course he had.

And Holly? She must have had plenty of practice pretending that her head was empty and that she actually enjoyed the company of men and not just their money. Tom liked to think she had enjoyed *his* company, at least as much as he'd enjoyed hers—but he had a feeling that a lot of fellows thought that way. They were probably wrong, and he was no different.

He'd never had the slightest inkling that something like this lurked in her, but that wasn't what troubled him. He'd judged her age as not *so* much lower than his own. Was she really not even twenty? Well, she just had people fooled in all sorts of ways.

Seducing Thaddeus to make her way into Friendly

Field couldn't have been difficult. Thaddeus' hiring of her *was* a little much—it seemed as though everyone had known of his vice, yet Holly's arrival had been an escalation. Tom sensed it wasn't something that Thaddeus had done entirely on his own; perhaps Holly had put the notion in his head. He wasn't a difficult man to persuade, and Tom had his suspicions about just how persuasive Holly could be.

Once she had been installed in Friendly Field, committing a murder without being caught would have been almost too easy—indeed, the theatrics with the feathers likely hadn't even been necessary, though they'd had the desired effect of confusing and frightening people. Frightened people never thought clearly; that was why that woman had been hanged in the first place. Fear. For a bunch of people who said they could trust God to protect them from anything, they certainly seemed to spook easy. If they actually believed that nonsense or had a shred of faith, they'd have been a bit more easygoing.

Saul had been the easiest target imaginable. His wife was gone, and the young woman in his house really had been there to cook and clean. All Holly had to do was make sure she wasn't seen, and that was simple enough to do in the night.

Then why had she waited to strike at the next man? Likely to see how the people would react and where their suspicion would fall. Holly was smart and worldly, but she wasn't like Tom. Compared to him, she had no blood on her hands at all. She was angry, but it seemed she could also be cautious. She was taking her time and thinking ahead, just as Tom liked to do.

In fact, it was as though she were doing it all just the way he'd have taught her.

Well, no. Tom would've told her to just shoot them dead, but Tom wasn't living with the anger that had brought her here. The one time he *had* tasted that anger, back on the Missouri—well, he'd taken care of that problem right away. He could only imagine what it would have been like to live with that rage and resentment, letting it fester.

To carry it through the years.

He was fairly sure that, in Holly's shoes, he'd have been ready to pick up a knife as well and use it.

For just a moment, the wind had risen up outside, strong enough to make the entire house creak, but then it had gone. The stillness came back, even thicker now.

There wasn't a sound, and in the dark Tom waited.

He would always be waiting; he knew that now. He had waited until he was good enough at cards to sit with the real players. He had waited for his leg to heal, or waited to die. He'd waited for the troubles of Friendly Field to be over so he could propose to Mary. If he didn't do something about it, he'd just go on waiting instead of living. His eye was always turned forward, and only now was he beginning to see how it was wearing him down. It was his hurry to get there that made him impatient, and his impatience made him seek the most efficient solution.

At the end of the day, he suspected that was why he was always reaching for his gun.

Why had Holly gone after Saul and Jeremiah? They were the two who had run the place. It was that simple. She couldn't very well kill every Quaker in Friendly Field, so she would kill the ones who'd been in charge when the deed was done.

Maybe they'd been the ones to propose hanging that woman who'd been taken by the devil. Or maybe they'd just stepped out of the way when someone else wanted to do it. Either decision was more than enough to buy them tickets down, at least in Tom's reckoning. That was what made it difficult to be the one who had to end it. If someone had tried to stop him from killing Jeff Shafer that night on the Missouri, Tom wouldn't have taken kindly to it.

At least not at the time. Now—*now*, as he thought about it, maybe it wouldn't have been so bad. There were ways he might have sorted that business out without bullets. Probably. Tom couldn't be certain, because that particular gambler had had a powerful man for an ally. Would a courtroom have gone against a rich man? That didn't happen often. Maybe killing Shafer *had* been the only way.

And maybe Holly thought the same. Maybe she thought there was no other justice, and there was a good chance she was right. Would the Quakers take the word of a prostitute over their own revered leaders? Even knowing their vices? Could they have ever been convinced that they had made a mistake?

Tom still didn't know much about Quakers, but he knew people. It wasn't easy to make them understand that they were wrong, let alone to get them to admit it. Holly couldn't have ridden into Friendly Field with a story about injustice from years ago. What would that have gotten her?

There was some business you just had to handle yourself. Holly understood that, just as Tom knew that every time he took things into his own hands, there was a good chance that not everyone would take kindly to it. Did Holly know that? Of course she did; one woman had already been hanged.

She was risking her neck anyway.

The creak was ever so slight. In the dark, Holly was just a shadow.

She'd barely made a sound when she crept into Thaddeus' house. Friendly Field had three leaders, after all—or it had, back when they'd hanged Holly's mother, the supposed witch.

One was still alive, so the job wasn't done.

Of course, Thaddeus should have been the easiest of the three for Holly to get to, but he couldn't very well be murdered in his bed if everyone knew *she* was also in that bed. That would bring suspicion on her right away.

Luckily, the whole community had seen her flee. Now, when Thaddeus turned up dead, no one would think *she* had had anything to do with it.

Holly had planned all this out and planned it well. Would she bother with the feathers? Tom still wasn't sure what their purpose was. Had they been intended to confuse the Quakers? Scare them? Or make a point? Had Holly used them to draw the Quakers' attention to that witch they'd hanged so they would know why they were being punished?

Of course, that thing that Tom and the kid had found in the woods—they'd found that before Holly had arrived in town. How had Holly swung that? Had she scouted Friendly Field in advance? How had she known someone would find it?

She was almost to the stairs and just a pace away from Tom's chair in the corner. Thaddeus was up there, fast asleep. He didn't even realize Tom was in his house, so he certainly wasn't expecting Holly.

Tom had been holding his breath ever since he heard the doorknob turn. Now he let it out.

"Don't move an inch," he said.

Holly didn't listen. A blade glinted, and Tom fired both bullets from the derringer. He liked Holly, and he hadn't wanted her dead—but he liked Mary more. He couldn't get married with a knife in him, so this was how it had to be.

The knife clattered to the floor.

A light step and a stumble—then Holly thudded to the floorboards. There were a few ragged breaths, then nothing.

A crash came from overhead as the noise of the shots sent Thaddeus tumbling out of his bed.

"Stay where you are, Thaddeus," Tom called out to him, and he hoped the old Quaker would listen better than Holly had.

For a moment misery took shape, racking his throat with pain. This wasn't what Tom had wanted. He'd entertained visions of convincing her to stop and spiriting her out of Friendly Field.

Would anyone have been able to convince *him* to stop when he'd been after Jeff Shafer? One of his friends had tried, and Tom had hit him so hard, it was a wonder he could still use his right hand.

But he could still use it, and he had. After a moment, he set the empty pistol aside.

"Mr. Smith?" Thaddeus asked uncertainly from the top of the stairs.

"I told you to stay," Tom replied, and that shut the old man up.

Maybe it had been wrong to stop her. Maybe Thaddeus had had this coming.

No—Mary would never have been able to accept that. She wouldn't even have been able to look at him if he knowingly let Thaddeus be murdered. The truth was it didn't matter what Tom did. He'd always feel like it had been the wrong move afterward. He'd never stop second-guessing.

Mary wouldn't care for him shooting a woman, either.

Tom rubbed his face, then struck a match. He leaned over and lit the lamp, then got tiredly to his feet and picked it up. He limped over, letting the glow illuminate Holly's body.

For a moment, there was nothing; he looked without seeing.

But he did see, and despite all evidence to the contrary, his mind still worked.

The lamp shattered on the floor, but Tom didn't notice. He hadn't noticed it slip from his fingers, and he didn't notice the oil and flames spreading across the floor.

CHAPTER THIRTY-ONE

I T WASN'T HOLLY dead at his feet.

It was Asher.

The knife lay beside the boy's hand, and the feathers were there, protruding from his pocket. His eyes were open, and he wore a look of genuine surprise.

Tom had a sense of someone there—and someone grabbing him. He didn't taste the smoke that he choked on as he was dragged out of the house by Phillip. There was Thaddeus, gleaming with sweat in his nightshirt, looking disbelieving.

"He saved me," Thaddeus was saying as some of the men futilely tried to throw water on the fire. The pillar of smoke, gray and sooty, stood out against the green and black of the sky. Without any wind, the embers didn't know what to do, just like Tom.

He took a step toward the house, then a step back. It was fully aflame now.

Mary appeared at his side, but he couldn't hear her over the roaring fire.

He'd been wrong so many times, but never like this.

She gripped his hand, wanting to know what was happening, but Tom just pulled free and backed away. All the Quakers were here; the shots had gotten them out of their beds, and the flames had brought them out of their houses.

They were confused, but they didn't know what confusion was.

Tom's brain raced. It went anywhere it could to push Asher's shocked face out. Thoughts punched through his skull. *How* could he have suspected Holly? For her to be the one, she would have been going to bed with one of the very men she meant to kill. How had that escaped him? And that object in the woods—Holly hadn't arrived yet.

He tried to swallow, but his mouth was dry.

Shaking Mary off a second time, he turned away from the inferno, stumbling across the dry grass in the dark.

Mrs. McHenry's door stood open. Mary had rushed out and left it this way.

Tom climbed onto the porch and went straight in. Mrs. McHenry was there, clearly not as quick to dress as Mary, but intending to come out. She opened her mouth, saw Tom's face, and got out of the way.

There'd been a time when Tom hadn't much cared for stairs on account of his leg, but he didn't notice them now.

Mrs. Washburn was in her chair by the window, a blanket covering her lap. Thaddeus' burning house was clearly visible, but she didn't appear to be watch-

ing it, just gazing at the book of prayers in her hands.
Her thumb absently rubbed the leather cover.

Tom closed the door behind him. "Thaddeus is still
alive," he said, and the words seemed to come out in
someone else's voice.

She nodded; she must have seen him from the window.

"Did you really not know the name?" he asked.
"The real name?"

The old woman sighed. She still didn't meet his eyes,
and when she spoke, she sounded even worse than
Tom. "She always talked about naming a daughter
Ashlyn."

Tom saw the kid's delicate hands holding a needle
and sprinkling spices over the camp stove.

He remembered how the kid had refused to bathe
around other people on the trail.

Now he knew why. That was who Scarf and Ben Garner had seen in the woods. The kid doing as she'd done
all along, bathing in private so no one would find out.

To think how many times Tom hadn't been able to
fathom why the kid wouldn't want to kiss a pretty girl.

A part of him wanted to laugh, but he was holding
that part back with everything he had. Instead, he put
his hand on the dresser and squeezed until his knuckles were white.

"When did you know?" he asked.

"She's the picture of her mother."

Of course. Mrs. Washburn wasn't the only one
who'd known the kid's mother, but she was the only
one who'd sat with her at a table and looked, really
looked, night after night as they'd eaten dinner and
played cards together.

She had known, and how could she not? Now that
he knew the truth, Tom could only look back and see

how poor the kid's impersonation of a boy had really been. The kid hadn't been a scrawny fourteen-year-old boy; she'd been a perfectly ordinary seventeen- or eighteen-year-old girl. Maybe even older. Why? Because she had known she had a journey ahead of her and that it would be safer to travel alone as a boy? Or because if she was a boy when she walked into Friendly Field, that would make absolutely certain that no one expected the retribution she was bringing, that no one saw it coming?

The trouble had arrived with Tom; it just hadn't *been* Tom, for once.

The kid had started it all herself, methodically laying the groundwork for what she had to do. Why had she demanded that Tom teach her to kill when they'd been a part of the Fulton wagon train? Because she'd been planning to kill some people, and Tom hadn't seen it. Friendly Field. From the beginning, this was what the kid had wanted. She had used Tom to get her here, used him to give her the skills and the knowledge she would need to bring her vengeance to these people. If he'd gotten the impression the killer was doing things his way, it was because she *had* done things his way, just as he'd taught her to.

They hadn't found that thing with the feathers by chance. The girl had planted it up there in the hills, then let Tom witness her supposedly finding it, throwing him off the scent before she even made her opening move. It was just a harmless object, ugly to look at, and perfect for stoking fear. Where had the girl learned to make it? Maybe she'd just thought it up; she'd had an active imagination, after all. Now no one would ever know.

"She's dead," Tom said, and though her face didn't change, some of the light went out of Mrs. Washburn's eyes. "I shot her in the dark, thinking she was someone else." His eyes strayed to the window and the fire.

Horrified, the old woman turned and looked, and she seemed to crumple in her chair.

She had wanted the kid to see it through. Tom had come up here to get the truth, but he already had it. The devil *had* been in Friendly Field, and he had a name. It hadn't been mere ignorance or foolishness that had hanged the kid's mother.

Someone had gotten her pregnant, and Tom wagered it was Thaddeus. These pious people hadn't hanged the kid's mother to hang the devil; they'd done it to protect him. They'd done it to shut her up and discredit anything she might say about one of their community's leaders. There had never been any witchcraft; that had just been their excuse to silence her and insurance that no one would believe anything she might have said. What had they done? Waved some feathers around and called it evidence? From what Tom had seen of these Quakers, just the word of the elders probably would've been enough.

The people who took the kid away knew it had all been a farce; that was why they hadn't been able to stomach Friendly Field any longer. They'd told the kid when she was old enough, and the kid had run away to set things right.

That was when she met Tom.

All three of them had to have been a part of it: Saul, Jeremiah, and Thaddeus. Only one of them had been the father, but all three had had a hand in the hanging. If even *one* of them had stood up for what was right, the kid would have still had a mother. And her life.

Tom looked at Mrs. Washburn. Men like Thaddeus— there was never just one victim. It probably hadn't begun with the kid's mother, and it certainly hadn't ended with her. There were others. Tom saw now that Mrs. Washburn was probably one of them, and Mary—Thaddeus had even reached out to her when her husband died.

No wonder Mrs. Washburn hadn't wanted the kid stopped. The kid had been doing God's work.

Mrs. Washburn wasn't going to say anything else; she couldn't. Tom couldn't forgive her. He couldn't blame her, either.

Why hadn't the kid brought him in on it? Because she hadn't trusted him. And why would she? All she'd ever seen him do was lie to people and shoot them.

Because it seemed like that was all he ever did. The Quakers had welcomed him to Friendly Field because of his candor, but even that hadn't been the whole truth. He couldn't tell the whole truth because it was ugly, and it was ugly because it was full of bullet holes.

Right up to the end.

He could've overpowered the kid so easily, or any woman. Taken the knife away, even in the dark. Tom put his face in his hands.

Mrs. Washburn had been right: he was blind *and* he was a fool. The kid was gone, and he couldn't change it. He'd chased the truth as though it mattered, but now that he had it, what good did it do him?

He had admired Jeremiah's willingness to do what he had to in order to keep things running smoothly in Friendly Field. Apparently that had included murder, and yet had that really been for Friendly Field? No. That had been for them, those three. Their convenience, their ease of clinging to the very positions of authority that they wanted to claim didn't exist. They'd done it for themselves and managed to convince their flock it was the right thing.

The kid had come a long way to pay them back, and she'd gotten two bullets for her trouble.

Tom staggered out of the McHenry house to find Thaddeus' house blazing, and everyone gathered around it to watch. There was no putting it out.

Voices filled the air, but Tom didn't hear them. Mary was here; she must've been afraid to go in after him. That was for the best.

"Is it true?" she asked from ten paces away.

"What?" Tom called back absently.

"That Asher was going to kill Thaddeus?" she asked, appalled. Tom nodded, and she stepped back, covering her mouth with both hands.

The shapes of the Quakers blurred together against the burning house, and their voices were momentarily covered by a rumble from the sky. Tom felt a prickle and looked down to see the hairs on his arms standing up. His throat was still full of rocks, and there was a curious emptiness where his stomach was supposed to be. He felt light on his feet in a way that he didn't fully understand.

The Quakers had quieted at the distant thunder, and for a moment there was just the crackling of the blaze.

Tom walked past Mary, beginning to push his way through the crowd.

These people could probably have put out the fire out if they really wanted to. Just like they could've stopped that hanging. Just like Tom could've done something other than pull that trigger.

Phillip and others were there with Thaddeus, who stared at the flames in horror. Horror at his brush with death? Or horror at the loss of his home? Horror at what had happened? Horror because there was probably a lot of money in that house, now going up in smoke?

Thaddeus had seen the kid, dead on his floor. He'd told his people what had happened.

They had questions for Tom, but Tom wasn't inclined to answer.

"Tom," Phillip said, hurrying toward him.

"Find me some rope," Tom replied, still pushing forward.

Phillip's dazed look grew only more puzzled. "What for?"

"A hanging."

CHAPTER THIRTY-TWO

THUNDER CRASHED IN the dry, heavy air, shutting out whatever Phillip had intended to say. Tom pushed him aside and went to Thaddeus, taking a handful of his shirt and pulling him close.

The old man tried to form words, but Tom didn't let him. He didn't have to. Thaddeus was nothing if not predictable.

"Why? Why did the kid want to kill you?" Tom said, raising his voice enough that everyone could hear. "Why would anyone want to kill their own father?"

Thaddeus just spluttered, uncomprehending.

"You didn't see the resemblance?" Tom demanded, pointing at the burning house. "Because Mrs. Washburn did. What was her name? The woman you hanged?"

"Tom," the old Quaker began, and Tom rammed his knee into Thaddeus' groin.

Thaddeus crumpled to the ground with a hoarse gasp, and a cry of alarm went up from the Quakers.

"I didn't ask what *my* name was," Tom said, standing over the old man. "I asked about her. Hell, do you even remember?"

Thaddeus hadn't shot the kid. Tom had done that.

"Tom!" Phillip was there, but Tom halted him in his tracks with a look. The big man hesitated, swallowing.

"What was her name?"

Thaddeus groaned on the ground as the Quakers looked on in horror. They were beginning to edge backward, away from the two of them.

Only Phillip stayed where he was.

"Do you know?" Tom asked him calmly.

"For heaven's sake, Tom!" Phillip cast about, mortified, but he stood alone. The other Quakers just looked on.

"It was Vera! Vera Holmes," a woman shouted, horrified.

"Holmes," Tom repeated.

The body of Ashlyn Holmes was probably nothing but a charred skeleton now. He could see her lying in the back of the wagon they'd shared, with her nose in that book.

"But, Tom . . . ," Phillip said desperately, taking a step closer.

"What?" Tom snarled, turning his gaze on the Quakers, who shrank back. "She had the devil in her?" His fingers closed into fists. "I don't think so."

Thaddeus was trying to inch away, but Tom hadn't forgotten him.

"What did you do when you found out she'd given birth to your child?" he asked. "Offer her some money? Try to send her away? She wouldn't take it, would she?"

The faces of the Quakers gave it all away. They were

shocked and appalled, yes—but the women, at least, they weren't nearly shocked enough. This wasn't some revelation to them. The only surprise was in hearing it spoken aloud.

"What?" Tom pressed, staring down at the man on the ground. "What stopped her? Did she decide it was time to end it? She wanted to be the last one. You were in charge, and you could take advantage of anyone you wanted. She wanted it to stop, because even if she kept her mouth shut and went away, it would be someone else next. She wanted to talk, and you couldn't let her."

Mary was there, standing like a statue, clutching her sleeves with a look of simple terror on her face.

Thaddeus tried to protest, but Tom wasn't having it.

"So you called her a witch so no man would believe what she said. If there were any men too blind to see, but I suppose I can believe that. I was blind too. And then you hanged her so any other girl would know just what would happen if *she* tried to speak up. You people don't hate outlaws, but you hate witches. The problem is that outlaws are *real*."

A greater silence had fallen over Friendly Field.

Thaddeus lay there. He didn't try to deny it; the light of the fire showed Tom's face clearly. The old man was a fool, but he wasn't blind. The truth was finally out, and nothing could put it away again.

"Saul and Jeremiah let you do it. They didn't like it, but they didn't stop it. Maybe because you had the purse strings for the whole village, maybe because they couldn't be bothered. Or maybe you weren't quite so soft back then."

"Tom . . . ," Phillip said, and there was a hint of something like a warning in his voice, but what was he going to do? He had no gun. None of them did.

"The only thing I can't figure," Tom went on, "is why no one put a knife in you sooner. Your own daughter wanted to kill you, and I don't blame her. And when it comes to killing, I'm a lot better at it than she was. So if you want to admit what you did, now's as good a time as any. If you want to get that burden off your soul."

But the old man just stared at him, face white but dripping sweat. He wasn't speaking because he couldn't. He'd probably managed to fool himself, the way so many people did, that he wasn't really in the wrong.

There were children watching, but Tom Calvert wasn't superstitious. Or sentimental.

He put his boot on Thaddeus' throat and pressed down.

"Tom, stop!"

Phillip grabbed him, and Tom shoved him off. The other man hit him from behind, tackling him to the grass. Tom wasn't so much startled as he was disinterested. It shouldn't have surprised him that the Quakers might object, but that simply wasn't where his mind had been.

Now it was.

What did Phillip want? To save Thaddeus?

That wasn't going to happen.

Phillip didn't know what to do. What *could* he do? Arrest Tom? Give him a beating?

A sermon?

Tom pushed him off and rolled onto his back, but Phillip was right there at once, holding him down. He was a big man and strong. He was also afraid.

"Tom, this isn't right," he said.

The sky flashed in the distance.

Tom tasted copper; he'd bitten his tongue. He politely turned to spit out the blood, then looked up at Phillip.

"No shit," he snarled, and struck inside Phillip's elbow, weakening his grip. He planted his good foot on Phillip's chest and kicked him off, sending the other man staggering back, arms flailing. Phillip stumbled into the grass, and Tom rose, wiping his mouth.

Phillip picked himself up, a strange combination of conviction and uncertainty on his face. He didn't know what he was going to do, only what he *wasn't*, and that was to let Tom murder Friendly Field's last elder.

Tom advanced on him, and the larger man initially started to shrink back—then he appeared to remember he was a head taller than Tom and easily twice as strong. And when he saw that, there was a look of surprise, as though it didn't make sense that a weak, battered cripple would do such a thing.

But Tom didn't really think of himself as a cripple anymore. His limp slowed him down, sure enough, but he'd always been patient in cards, if not in other things. The night was young.

"You want to protect him?" he asked.

"We can't have murder here," Phillip replied, for lack of anything better.

Tom glanced at the burning house. "Too late. Even if you didn't know, you know now. And you want protect *him*. Not the women he's hurt. Him."

Phillip would've replied to that, but Tom had reached him, and he wasn't interested in discourse. The big man tried to protect his face, but Tom drove his fist into his belly, doubling him over. He struck him in the temple, sending him reeling. Phillip had the presence of mind to lunge forward, but Tom wasn't about to be tackled again. He planted his foot and caught Phillip trying to hit him low. Tom used his knee again, this time on Phillip's face and this time without holding anything back.

The Quaker reeled back, a fountain of blood erupting from his shattered nose. Eyes out of focus, he fell to his knees, blood streaming down his face to soak into his white shirt.

Tom caught him by the collar and raised his fist, but his eyes fell on Phillip's wife.

She had the kids with her.

He hesitated, teeth grinding.

"They shouldn't be out of bed," he said finally, and in the perfect stillness the words carried.

Mrs. Lester's mouth moved, but no sound came out.

Tom put his palm on Phillip's face and pushed the big man over, turning away.

Thaddeus, with his age and his belly, was no faster than Tom and his limp, but he'd made good time. He was quite a ways off, just a pitiful, shuffling figure in the night, heading for the stables.

"Go home," Tom said to the Quakers. "Hide under the covers. Pretend you don't see or hear anything. That's what you're good at."

He limped past them, after Thaddeus.

The stirrings in the clouds were more frequent, and a breeze had risen, just enough to make the air swirl with embers from the house.

Tom spat blood and didn't look back, his eyes locked on the figure ahead. He wouldn't leave the kid's work half-finished.

He'd wondered, back on the trail, what it had been when she would get that look on her face and stare into space. He'd always figured it was the past she was looking at; after all, someone so young wouldn't be making their own way if everything behind them was all perfect. It wasn't what she'd come from, though—that wasn't what she'd seen.

This was what she'd seen.

She'd pressed him to teach her to fight and nearly gotten herself killed in her eagerness to test her skills. She hadn't been a fool, just young.

Tom didn't have that excuse.

He stopped and looked back at Mary; she was a few paces behind him, a good distance from the crowd of gawking Quakers. Like Phillip, she didn't know what to say or what to do.

So she stood there and looked at him in the dark. Lightning crackled in the sky, and nobody cared. No one could worry about a gathering storm when there was already one in their midst.

Tom wiped his eyes, and it took everything he had to unclench his jaw and form words.

"The kid only wanted one thing," he bit out.

It was too dark; he couldn't see her face. In the distance, Thaddeus hauled open the stable doors and vanished inside.

Mary didn't follow Tom. The wind was blowing harder now, stirring up dust from the fields. It stung Tom's eyes, but he didn't stop.

He limped to the doors, and he heard the hoofbeats inside.

Thaddeus burst into the open on the back of a brown mare, and Tom caught him by the belt and dragged him out of the saddle. The old man crashed to the ground, and Tom was thrown from his feet. He didn't feel his landing, and the darkness that flooded his eyes wasn't the Idaho night. There was lightning crackling above, and stars swam in front of him.

He tried to sit up, but the burning imprint of where the horse had kicked him put him back on the grass. The mare was already gone, and Thaddeus was there beside him, groaning.

Tom started to laugh, but the pain was too much, and he just wheezed.

This had to be more moving around than Thaddeus had done in years. His arm was broken, and probably some ribs as well, but the old man wanted to live. He was trying to get up.

Caught between a laugh and something else, Tom rolled onto his front. He couldn't remember everything from the trail with the kid, thanks to the fever. But he remembered the night Asher had faced down the Fulton brothers at the card table. When it went bad, Tom had intervened. He'd climbed out of the wagon and fallen to the snow, very much a cripple at the time.

But he'd picked himself up and killed four men to keep the kid safe.

He never would have believed there could be anything worse than that bottomless black rage that had moved him to pull that trigger, but there was. There was one thing: that same rage, but instead of directed at a man who'd done him wrong, now he had it pointed at himself. Thaddeus dragged himself into the stable, and Tom staggered after him.

The old Quaker looked back, still trying to crawl away.

A coil of rope hung on the wall, and Tom looked from it to Thaddeus.

"Did you think you'd never have to settle up?" he asked.

It was a foolish question, though. Of course Thaddeus had. The man could delude himself into anything. He could tell himself that he wasn't doing anything wrong, and then he would *believe* it. *He* wasn't to blame; the devil was.

Tom hadn't sensed the guilt in him because there was none. It had always been someone else's fault.

Not Tom, though. Tom's mistakes were his own, and he was learning to keep them close, because if he didn't, he had a tendency to forget.

"Forgiveness," the old man choked out desperately. "We are taught to forgive in the face of repentance."

"You can twist that book to suit anything," Tom told him tiredly. "Something tells me repentance wouldn't stick."

"Freedom is only found in forgiveness," Thaddeus said desperately.

"Oh, I forgive you," Tom wheezed, lifting the rope from its hook. "Seems like the kid couldn't, though. It's her business I'm here on, not mine."

He prepared to cast the rope over one of the beams, but something on Thaddeus' face made him look over his shoulder.

For the second time that night, there was a blade coming toward him and no time to get out of the way. Tom didn't have his derringer this time.

He raised his hands to protect himself, and hot blood dotted his face. He fell back against the wall, his eyes taking in Phillip and the sickle, its point buried in the wood. Blood dripped from it.

Severed pieces of rope fell, and blood streamed freely from his right hand.

A moment ago, Phillip had been committed to action. He'd swung that sickle at Tom's back like he meant it.

Maybe it was the sight of the blood, or what was left of Tom's hand, but something had changed.

Tom leaned against the wall, feeling the warmth from the blood spread along his arm, trying to breathe with his injured ribs, watching the other man just stand there. It was a sad sight: Phillip with his muscles and his bloody face looking so lost.

Without breath, with his hand like this—Tom didn't know that there was anything he could've done, but Phillip didn't make a move.

Maybe that was what made them different. Tom could draw blood without batting an eyelid. Phillip couldn't.

A wave of dizziness came over Tom, and that just made him angry. He straightened up, keeping his eyes locked on Phillip's.

"You just want things to stay the same," he said.

The big man swallowed, still in a daze. "We—," he began.

"They *can't*," Tom snarled, and that woke Phillip up. Tom didn't care how hurt he was, or how strong Phillip was, or what any of these Quakers wanted.

"Tom—," the other man tried to say as Tom looked down at the sad remains of his hand.

"Phillip," Tom interrupted, surprised at how calm his voice sounded, "I'm going to count. If you're still here when I get to three, your kids are going to grow up without their father."

There it was, just for a second, as though he'd forgotten the beating he'd gotten a minute ago. A look of skepticism on Phillip's face, but that didn't linger when Tom looked up. He didn't have to count; Phillip glanced past him at Thaddeus, hesitated for the space of a heartbeat, and then turned his back.

Tom watched him go, and he heard the door bounce from the jamb behind him. Thaddeus had gone out the rear door.

Tom had told himself that it was his trigger finger that had gotten him into trouble. Now that finger and a couple more were lying on the floor of a stable in Idaho.

His rope was all cut up and bloody; it wouldn't be hanging anyone, and he couldn't tie a noose with one hand.

Tom snorted and looked toward the back door, still swinging.

The old man could run. They would see who tired out first.

Tom reached up to grip the handle of the sickle with his left hand and wrenched it free of the wood.

The dust and the wind surrounded him as he emerged into the night. Thaddeus was ahead, stumbling into the fields, tripping and staggering among the potatoes.

He kept trying; no one could deny that. But Tom knew better than most that there were things that couldn't be escaped, and tonight he was one of them.

He walked among the plants, and Thaddeus fell, but kept scrambling until he couldn't anymore. He turned to look back, trying to find the breath to speak up over the howling wind.

"Stop," he called out. "Stop!"

Tom stood over him. They were a long way from the village, deep in the fields, and no one would interfere now.

"Anyone ever say that to you?" he asked, and Thaddeus swallowed but didn't answer. "Did it do them any good?"

The old man licked his lips. "Vengeance," he said.
Tom nodded. That was the word.

"'Vengeance is mine; I will repay, saith the Lord,'"
Thaddeus went on. "In the book of Romans, it is written that vengeance is His alone!"

The noise was like thunder, only louder. It shook the ground, and Tom staggered from the shock and the pressure, his ears seeming to burst. The sudden wind nearly bowled him over, kicking up such a wave of dirt that he was blinded.

Ears ringing, buffeted by the wind, he turned away, peering back into the dark, where that fearsome crash had come from. The noise became a deafening roar.

Two shattering bursts of lightning arced across the sky, lighting the world up blue, and he saw it there, standing against the light: a towering, twisting storm descending on Friendly Field. The buildings and houses crumpled like old paper, but going up instead of down, being drawn up in spirals into the heart of the storm, all distant and tiny. All their hard work, their crops and their sturdy buildings, just fine dust in the gale.

Tom looked down at Thaddeus at his feet, and his fingers tightened on the sickle.

"The hell it is," he said.